Anne

Quarry Hall: Book Two

Michelle L. Levigne

M Zion Ridge Press
Books Off the Beaten Path

www.MtZionRidgePress.com

Mt Zion Ridge Press LLC
295 Gum Springs Rd, NW
Georgetown, TN 37366

https://www.mtzionridgepress.com

Copyright © 2013 by Michelle L. Levigne
ISBN 13: 978-1-962862-27-1

Published in the United States of America
Publication Date: May 15, 2024

Editor-In-Chief: Michelle Levigne
Executive Editor: Tamera Lynn Kraft

Cover Art Copyright by Mt Zion Ridge Press LLC © 2024

Chapter One

The great thing about working for the Arc Foundation... well, there were so many great things to list, it would take forever. Right now, however, Anne appreciated and enjoyed the chance to learn new skills. Specifically, installing micro-miniaturized security equipment and feeling like a super-spy while doing so.

She paused and glanced over her shoulder. She had gotten used to working while wearing night-vision goggles, but her eyes still caught phantom movement in the green-lit darkness. She depended on Argus, her bodyguard and nursemaid, to watch behind her while she worked.

No, she hadn't heard anyone creeping up behind her through the public rooms of the battered women's shelter. However, she had *felt* something. Not quite a breath of air, not quite that creeping sense that someone watched her. She trusted her sense of trouble, even though that sense had come too late to save her great pain in her childhood.

Argus whined like a fretful puppy instead of a full-grown German Shepherd, and walked across the big room full of folding tables where the women and children ate and socialized and worked on crafts. He stopped and looked out into the hallway that led to the kitchen on the right, and the bathrooms and sleeping rooms on the left. Anne waited, until his tail switched back and forth three times and he turned his head to look at her. She smiled, shook her head, and turned to finish her task. Four rooms with cameras and microphones installed, two more to go. Equipment, courtesy of Ma-Car Tech. When Joan Archer came to Quarry Hall, she had done more than answer her father's prayers. She had brought powerful friends and new allies: Sophie Atreides, as their Internet genius, and all the technology wizardry of Ma-Car Tech that Matt Cameron could offer.

In several ways, Joan was the reason Anne was here, sneaking around at 2am, upping the shelter's security systems. Granted, without their knowledge. As the Arc Foundation grew, gaining allies and partners, investigating worthy causes to determine if they were indeed worthy, the information network it belonged to grew as well. A disturbing pattern of accusations against women's shelters had emerged over the last year, only recognizable as a pattern to the practiced eyes of people who learned to see them everywhere for the sake of survival: Joan and Sophie.

Five times in the last year, a woman with two daughters and one son came to a shelter, seeking protection from a man — father, brother-in-law, another male with authority over them—who hunted them. This man abused the mother, one daughter, both daughters, the son—the story changed each time. After a stay of only a few days, not even enough time to settle in, a worker in the shelter would be accused of a horrific crime against the children or the mother. Threats, physical abuse, or theft. Government regulations and the way the media always handled such accusations meant the shelter workers were essentially considered guilty until proven innocent. The accusers were always assumed to be the victims until proven otherwise. Then the mother or some new friend at the shelter threatened to take the story to the media, destroy the shelter, shut it down, and humiliate whatever organization sponsored the shelter, unless they paid large sums of money. Money always seemed to be the cure-all. That should have been the first sign to the shelters that something more was amiss, but they were too frantic to protect their reputations and keep their workers out of jail to think clearly. As soon as the money turned to cash in their hands, the alleged victims and their new friend vanished.

The shelters appeared on a map in a zigzag pattern, crossing state lines, curving as if it would eventually return to where it started, in a large circle. Joan, Sophie, and Harrison Carter believed the scam artists masquerading as a destitute, terrified family had a home base where they stayed between their money-making forays. They were smart enough not to move in a straight line or use the same story and accusation twice. Hopefully they were arrogant and confident enough not to realize they had established a pattern. The goal was to catch these people before they added one more shelter to their list of victims or moved on to another hunting territory. Anne, Kathryn, Joan, Jennifer, and Brenda had each gone to a women's shelter in the theorized target area, equipped with the best of Ma-Car Tech, to set up extra eyes and ears and hopefully catch the accusers in their lies before any more damage was done.

The money paid to the accusers was enough in three cases to shut down the shelters. The women and children who had found refuge under those roofs had to go out onto the street again, putting them within reach of the people they had been fleeing in the first place.

Anne knew intimately what it was like to be cast adrift, thinking no one cared or even believed her when she was the victim. Knowing gave her reason to walk into a place like this that reeked of despair and fear and pain, despite the pretty decorations and comfortable beds and the shutters that wouldn't let people see in. Knowing she offered help to those who were where she had once been made her feel stronger. She imagined herself a knight errant, hiding her mortal wounds under her armor, earning another drop of healing salve for every soul she defended.

"Yeah," she muttered as she walked away from the last microphone-and-camera setup tucked inside the valance for the curtains. "I know I see everything as a faerie tale. Tell me something I don't know."

Argus nudged her thigh with his head and whined. It wasn't his "someone is coming, you have to hide" whine, but the one she thought of as his nursemaid whine. Essentially, he urged her to stop playing secret agent and go to bed.

"Just a little bit more, fur-ball," she whispered, and stroked from between his eyes, across the top of his head and down his neck to the thicker ruff of fur by his shoulders. Argus closed his eyes and swished his tail like a windshield wiper in a driving rain.

Muffling a chuckle, she slid her night-vision goggles up onto her forehead and stepped into the hallway. The small nightlights installed there, ten feet apart, played havoc with the goggles. Moving down the hallway to the first security door, she only heard her own breathing and the soft clicking of Argus's claws on the tile floor. Anne made a mental note to get him to a veterinarian soon and get those claws filed down. Just a little. The Arc Foundation's dogs depended on their weight and menacing postures to ward off danger. Usually they could stop attackers by barreling into them and knocking them down, even breaking ribs if necessary, but claws sometimes came in handy too.

"Either the pedicure or take you home and let you run wild and dig to your heart's content," she whispered, her voice barely louder than her breath. "Would you like that? Can you hold on for that?"

Argus didn't respond with even a tail wag. He knew when they were in a fragile situation. Until Anne tapped out the security code at that locked door, they were in danger of being caught. Not that she would get in trouble for moving around when everyone was supposed to be in their beds, but questions were so awkward at the start of an investigation.

The keypad on the security door didn't even ping, but the lock made several audible clicks and a softly buzzing hum as it opened. Anne knew the comparative quiet of the night made those noises seem so loud. She slipped through into the next room, what the staff referred to as the "air lock," a buffer zone between the front reception room and the living quarters. It cut down the chances of someone who bullied or lied their way into the shelter getting a look at the fugitives who might be his — or her — target.

Anne shivered, remembering that evening by the fire in the Great Hall at Quarry Hall, when Joan had told the story of how she obtained her only childhood friend, a now-threadbare teddy bear she had called Fuppy.

Her mother had been on the hunt for the fugitive girlfriend of one of her associates. As a favor to him, and ensure he owed her help in the future, she tracked down the woman by pretending to be an abused, destitute mother. Three-year-old Joan, big-eyed, hollow-cheeked, and unusually quiet, had opened the doors of the shelter. A social worker there gave her Fuppy Bear. Her mother's target had died only a few days later, either a suicide or murdered and made to look like a suicide.

After hearing that story, the daughters of Quarry Hall understood a little bit better why Joan had a passion for helping shelters enhance their security and their ability to screen the people who came to them.

Newcomers to this shelter stayed in the "airlock" area for a day or two, while a search was made for arrest warrants, missing people reports, and information from local, state, and federal law enforcement. If nothing showed up to indicate guilt, they were assumed to be victims, even without evidence to prove their stories, and allowed into the secured part of the building.

Anne moved around the two public rooms of the airlock and the bathroom facility, installing more camera-microphone packs. All four bedrooms were occupied tonight. She couldn't go inside those bedrooms until the women and children passed on to the inner rooms.

That task finished, she keyed in the code for the door that led into the reception area, placed two more equipment packs, and went out the side door to the parking lot. A grin spread wide enough to make her cheeks ache, as she thumbed the control of her truck's augmented key fob and got no response from the dark green extended cab pickup sitting in a sheltered corner inside the high fence of the parking lot. Sophie and Joan were geniuses in their own right. One little button made it possible for Anne to know if someone had tried to tamper with her truck while her back was turned. Installing a homing signal or slitting a tire wouldn't set off the regular alarms built into her truck, but the sensors added to all the vehicles belonging to the Arc Foundation—again courtesy of Ma-Car Tech—indicated if something had changed on the truck. No tiny blue pin lights flashed on the bumper or fender or the frame of the rearview mirror, meaning no tampering.

"Sometimes, this job is way too much fun," she told Argus as they reached her truck and she opened the door to let him climb in first.

The passenger seat flipped up, revealing the hiding place for her notebook computer, along with the controls for the camera-microphone packs installed throughout the shelter. They provided the energy needed to run the equipment, and enough storage to collect two weeks' worth of images from all the cameras. The pattern so far had the false charges levied within the first week, before anyone could learn enough about the invaders to help track them down after they left the shelter.

Once she verified the signals were coming in clear and the recording equipment functioned as intended, Anne pulled out her cell phone and dialed Quarry Hall. Sophie would be on duty in the communications center until all the field agents had reported in, verifying the installation was complete. Brenda had done her installation two days ago. Her assignment had been easy, because it had been at a shelter run by the Arc Foundation. She didn't need to sneak around at night, worrying about offending someone who thought they were being investigated as a possible recipient of Arc funding. Jennifer also had a slightly easier assignment, sent to a shelter she had actually worked at for a year when she was gaining her degree in childhood education and psychology. Still, she hadn't been able to openly install the equipment, but she had instant access. Joan, Kathryn and Anne all had to pass inspection and have their credentials verified before they were given security codes and access to the whole shelter. Which was proper procedure.

"Hey, sister," Sophie greeted her, opening the connection. "I was wondering when you would call in. Joan ran into a snag, so she called to ask how everyone else was doing."

"What kind of snag?" Anne's heart skipped a beat, wondering what could happen to make Joan admit to a "snag" in her assignment. In the year since Harrison Carter's daughter had joined the family at Quarry Hall, she had come to think of the older girl as a big sister, their natural leader. She admired Joan's strength, even as she recognized the pain and scars that made her so strong and determined.

"Some bozo followed his girlfriend — only she's not his girlfriend, he just won't take no for an answer — and came back with some of his caveman buddies to break her out, hopped up on something nasty and claiming she'd been kidnapped by a cult, can you believe it?

"Joan and Ulysses had to shift into superhero mode, and now there's a little too much attention from the local police. All of it good, fortunately, but it's a little hard to sneak around a shelter and put spy eyes in place when everybody's asking for your autograph."

Anne laughed, which was what she knew Sophie wanted. Somewhere amid all the hyperbole was a story that shared the same basic outline. Essentially, Joan had used the hand-to-hand combat skills Vincent drilled into all the daughters of Quarry Hall before they were allowed out onto the road. She had taken down intruders, keeping them from getting to their intended target until the police could show up.

Once she finished reporting in and exchanged messages to and from the residents of Quarry Hall, Anne said a silent prayer of thanks that it had been Joan who faced that unpleasant situation and not her. Now she felt the effects of her very long day and the alert tension that had kept her going during her task. While it was tempting to curl up in the back of the cab and sleep, which she had done often and comfortably enough, Anne knew she had to get back inside the shelter. Everyone who had seen her go to bed that night needed to see her leaving that staff bedroom in the morning, or there would be questions. And the chance that the wrong people would get suspicious and wonder what she was doing, wandering around the shelter, even going outside, so late at night.

Argus stayed by her side, and she relied on his senses, his guidance to walk where the floors didn't creak, to sense if anyone was awake and listening or watching, as she made her way through one security door after another. In the staff bedroom, where her roommate had very graciously offered to let her have the bottom bunk, all was silent and dark, except for an occasional snuffle and snort from the top bunk. Anne smiled into the darkness as she slipped out of her jeans, loosened her bra, and curled up under the light sheet. She let her arm drape over the side of the bed, so her hand rested on Argus's back. All was well. No one had stirred the entire time she was at work. Argus would have told her otherwise.

Silently, she said her bedtime prayers, asking for safety for her sisters on their assignments, for safety, comfort, and healing for the people in this shelter. A thin flicker of anger cut through her weariness that made her own voice sound fuzzy in her head, as she prayed the false accusers hadn't targeted this shelter. In just the three days she had been here, Anne had grown to love the workers and the children and their bruised, fearful, hurting mothers.

She knew what they were feeling.

~~~~~

Argus didn't like the new family that had arrived after dinner last night. His ears pressed flat against his skull and he stared up at the mother, older daughter, and the son as they came down the short hallway from the airlock bedrooms. His tail wagged three times for the youngest child, a little girl who looked maybe four years old, with tangled hair and a smear of something dark across her cheek. Anne hoped that was residue from a chocolate chip cookie, given as a treat before bed. The alternatives didn't agree with her stomach, which was always sensitive when she didn't get much sleep.

Anne worked the airlock breakfast line today, and she planned to be assigned to that part of the shelter until the family attacking shelters like this one had been caught. Everyone living in the inner rooms had already been cleared by Sophie and the Arc Foundation's far superior background check process. No one matched the patterns established by the previous lawsuits or false claims.

She suspected this family because Argus didn't like them. Whenever a guardian dog's reaction contradicted what people said, what the circumstances appeared to be, the daughters of Quarry Hall had learned to always listen to their dogs. As Su-Ma so eloquently and mischievously phrased it, their dogs were programmed by the angels to be living, breathing, growling Creep-o-Meters.

"Good morning," Anne said, smiling but not trying to be too cheerful, as the stocky, sullen-faced boy approached the table. "Hope you're

6

hungry. What would you like? Some of everything?"

"We can't have some of everything," he mumbled. "There's never enough."

"There's more than enough here. Go ahead." She picked up two pancakes with the plastic tongs and held them out, ready to drop on his plate. "Sausage and bacon? Eggs? Oatmeal?"

The boy visibly thawed out before her eyes. Anne made a mental note to see if someone could get closer to him, and find out if his belief that there wasn't enough came from his home situation, or perhaps one of the previous shelters he had been in. Some places operated on a shoestring budget, rationing every bite of food.

Please, Lord, I can't possibly be certain it's them, she prayed, and offered a wink to the boy as he headed off to a table with a loaded plate. *It's too soon. I will not jump to conclusions.*

Anne muffled a snort of laughter as she remembered a bitter comment from a friend in college, who refused to attend any of the local churches. Jesse maintained church people only got exercise by jumping to conclusions, and the skinnier the preacher, the nastier the congregation.

Charlotte, working on the other end of the table, had already taken care of the older girl and was filling a plate for the littlest one. That left the mother for Anne.

"Welcome. Did you get a good night's sleep?" Anne held out two pancakes in her tongs.

The mother wasn't any more talkative than her three children. She took coffee with no cream or sugar, oatmeal, and dry toast, then took six containers of jelly. Anne wondered what an analysis of food choices would tell her about the family.

Only three more people were staying in the airlock — a runaway teen girl with dozens of empty piercing holes marking her ears and upper lip and nose; an emaciated, balding woman who smelled like she had slept the last week in a wet dumpster; and a sweet-faced, white-haired little black woman who wouldn't talk above a whisper. Anne and Charlotte finished serving, walked around offering seconds, then cleaned up.

"Anybody interesting out there?" a woman resident of the inner rooms asked when Anne carried the trays of food back to the kitchen.

"I'm not the one in charge of answering questions," Anne responded with a chuckle.

"You'll find out soon enough," Charlotte said, cutting her off before Anne could ask the woman her name.

Charlotte nudged Anne in the small of her back to keep moving.

"What's wrong?" Anne asked in a whisper, when they stepped into the kitchen. A shiver of warning raced up her back when she glanced over Charlotte's head and saw the woman watching them. The moment their gazes met the woman ducked into the public room where the residents were having their breakfast.

"Don't like that one. There's the paranoid kind of nosey — they can't relax until they know everything about the place. There are the fun nosey ones, they just love learning everything and meeting everyone. There are the ones who want power, and in their situation, there isn't much power to be had. But knowledge is power." Charlotte set the carafe of coffee down on the long tray of the industrial-strength dishwasher. "But Maryanne there, I can't figure out. And that makes me suspicious. She's been here a week, and she wants to know every day if someone new has showed up. I find it hard to believe she's run out of people to talk to already."

"Some people are just picky about who they socialize with, I guess," Anne offered. That earned a grin and a shake of the head from Charlotte.

Less than an hour later, Anne wandered into the main room with Argus close on her heels, hoping to find something interesting to take to the airlock and offer to the children as a bridge to get them talking. A game, a book, drawing paper and crayons. They were a very reticent bunch. Anne was used to the watchful, wounded quiet of abused children, or the confused ones who had been bundled out of their beds in the middle of the night and weren't sure of anything except that "Mommy cries a lot," and another adult had been yelling far too much. Or started throwing things. Or throwing their mother around the house. Anne and Argus were experts at getting through to the children, earning their trust. She was convinced that children in disrupted situations had a radar that came alive and sensed when they were with people who had felt the same pain and confusion and wordless certainty that maybe they were to blame. That led the children to trust her.

These three children were different. She couldn't put her finger on it. Not yet anyway. Some time talking and laughing with them would help. If she could only find something to catch their interest. What did the inner rooms have that hadn't been supplied to the airlock?

Chapter Two

"Interesting." Maryanne stood on the other side of the table as Anne looked over a stack of puzzles. "Your ring."

"Petoskey stone," she said, and curled her left hand into a fist to better display the oval of silver-gray stone with the fossilized flower in the middle. Her father had given that ring to her mother during a trip to Michigan. He had bought the stone and took it to a local jeweler, who cut it down to better display the fossil.

Her parents had often done small, personal things like that for each other, and for her. The extra effort, the personalizing, made little things special and valuable beyond any monetary reckoning. The ring was one of the few things Anne had kept from her life before the Ogre had destroyed everything. She had been wearing the ring in the mental hospital against hospital policy, as if the nurses had been struck blind, when the man she only knew as the Black Prince rescued her and carried her away to Quarry Hall, to healing and sanity. The ring hadn't left her finger in years.

"Must have cost a pretty penny."

"I don't know. It's an heirloom." Anne glanced down at Argus, who lay on the floor next to her, his muzzle resting on the top of her sneaker. He raised his head and looked up, as if he could see through the table. His ears lay flat on his skull for the second time that morning.

"Heirloom?" The woman cracked a grin. "I thought you people gave up everything, took a vow of poverty before you could work here. How'd you manage to hold onto something like that? Must be expensive."

"Like I said, it's an heirloom. Some things are worth more than money. And I seriously doubt the people running this place are required to give up *everything*."

"Oooh, touchy." She grinned. "Maybe this place is better off than it looks from outside."

A warning shiver prickled Anne's scalp. She felt the rumble in Argus's chest, threatening to become audible, vibrating in her legs. He didn't like Maryanne. Something had triggered his protective instincts. When Argus and other dogs from Quarry Hall went into "silent running mode," the situation was about to turn sticky, at the very least.

The odd thing was, Anne remembered Maryanne sitting across from her just four days ago during a Bible study, and Argus hadn't reacted to her at all. He had been quiet, sitting against the wall behind Anne's chair at the table. Something had changed about this woman since then. Something Argus read in her attitude, her tone of voice, her posture. But what could it be?

"This place runs on donations, always on the edge of having to cut back. That's why it relies on volunteers. Like me." She gathered up the books she had barely glanced through. Just enough to determine there was a variety to offer the three children in the "airlock."

"Why do people like you volunteer, anyway?" Maryanne followed her, stepping around the table. "I mean, don't you have work to do? A job you need to hold onto?"

"A lot of people volunteer their vacation time or come for internships for their college majors." A shiver of certainty told her trouble waited to pounce. This woman seemed to be fishing for information. Finances in general? How well-funded the shelter was? Or just how rich the volunteers were? "At the end of my vacation, I'll be gone." She offered a smile that she doubted had much sincerity. "Let's hope you're on your feet and you don't need help by the time I come back here."

"Well, yeah, that's what this place exists for." The woman shrugged and nodded.

Was she oblivious, or just so tied up in her own deceptions she didn't realize Anne had been just a little snarky?

"You know, you got a point," she continued when Anne reached the security door. "Volunteers. And what have I got but time? It'd be nice if I gave back, you think?"

"Oh, definitely." Anne pressed the green button that opened the door. During the daylight hours the security measures for going out were turned off. Only at night were the security codes necessary. She wasn't sure what she would have done if Maryanne had tried to read a security code over her shoulder.

The boy in the family of four was Joe. His little sister, Tess. The two children pounced on the books, delighted with the sewing boards and pop-up books and dinosaurs.

Their older teen sister, who still refused to give her name, stayed seated with her mother while the younger children settled at a plastic kiddie table in the corner. Maryanne sauntered over, coming up from behind Anne. The teen glared at one of them.

"Hey there, the name's Maryanne. You know, we don't use last names here, so don't worry, I won't ask yours," she said, holding out her hand to the mother. "Anything you want to know about this place, to make it easier, just ask." She glanced up at Anne, who stayed standing, her hands braced on the table. "That's okay, isn't it? Answer some questions?"

"Sure." Anne glanced down as Argus pressed against her leg,

vibrating in silence.

She didn't need to be hit over the head with the implications. Anne made sure the mother and daughter didn't need anything, then she excused herself.

After helping distribute lunch, Anne stepped outside with Argus and sat in her truck, harvesting images from the cameras recording in the airlock rooms. She emailed Sophie photos of the new family of four and Maryanne, to be sent to the directors of the victimized shelters, to see if they recognized anyone among the five. Then she emailed Sophie to do a search for the patterns of the woman who showed up as a friend to the complaining family: how long did she arrive before the family came to the shelter? What did she look like? How long before she struck up a friendship? And most important, how much time elapsed between that meeting and the first complaints and false accusations?

Her cell phone rang before she had crossed the parking lot to go back into the shelter.

"So your puppy doesn't even like the kids?" Sophie said by way of greeting.

"Yeah, and how often does that happen?" Anne turned to put her back to the wall next to the security door, opposite the keypad. "But get this—he was okay with Maryanne a few days ago, but now he's ready to vibrate his fur off with silent growling."

"My condolences, little sister. Want us to send reinforcements?"

"You found a pattern already?"

"I've been making charts, comparing every little detail since you all jumped in your trucks and headed out. Yeah, she fits the pattern. Maryanne, or whatever her real name is, is their weak link. If she's the same woman at each shelter—nothing but vague descriptions to go on, at this point—she's there exactly a week before the family shows up. And here's something else I caught. None of the shelters had any security cameras. Want to bet part of her job is to scout the territory, find the best place for the fake assaults to take place, where they're least likely to be caught or heard or stopped?"

"I don't gamble. Especially when you're right." Anne sighed and slid down against the side of the building, stretching her thighs and pressing her back hard against the bricks. "Any pattern to predict which of the kids gets to be the victim this time around?"

"Yep. If they stick to the pattern, it'll be the boy this time. Do you have any male counselors?"

"Two guys working on their degrees. They get course credit for volunteering."

"Get them to skip a few days. Or tell them to stay away from the boy."

"Oh, yuck." Anne thought about the procedures for handling new refugees. How long could she keep these people isolated before they started asking questions? Would they leave, or would they break pattern and make their accusations while they were still in the airlock? Quickly, she explained the background checking process and asked Sophie to factor that into her assessment.

"I'm guessing this shelter has run into this kind of trouble before. They won't *refuse* to help someone, but they never immediately trust anyone who comes running with a sob story. Okay, let me make some calls, confer with the other sisters out there. Joan is closest. Want me to send her over to give you backup?"

"Someone else coming in this soon after me could make them suspicious. Besides, what if I'm wrong? What if it's all physical stuff that makes Argus so touchy? Maryanne could have gotten hold of some drugs, and the smell in her sweat makes him dislike her now. If you pull anybody from their assignment, the real troublemakers could waltz in and do it again while our backs are turned."

"Dang, I hate it when you kids are so smart." Sophie's temporary accent dripped with cornpone and molasses.

"But if those photos I sent you get a positive identification, I want the Marines and the Air Force for backup."

"You got it. And triple the prayers for all of you."

~~~~~

Anne's phone buzzed against her hip, tucked into the pocket of her sleeping shorts, yanking her out of a sound sleep. She sat up, fumbling through the controls before she got her eyes open enough to see by the bright light of the screen. The camera system shunted images to her, showing a dark figure hunched over the keypad outside the kitchen door. She couldn't see much detail, other than a flickering of light in a cylinder attached to the keypad with a thin black cable.

"Creepazoid is using computers to break in," she muttered to Argus.

Anne pulled on a t-shirt over her pajama top and slipped out of the bedroom in her bare feet. She sent a text to the desk sergeant at the local police department, who had been established as a contact before the Arc Foundation moved in with its investigation. Because of Harrison Carter's shadowy past in the information underground, one major rule was to be aboveboard, always open and cooperative with local law enforcement. That meant notifying someone in authority and creating a contact before going in to investigate a situation that might turn dangerous. It helped that Sgt. Willis had worked with a daughter of Quarry Hall less than five months ago, so he understood how they worked.

Almost immediately, the response came back on her phone screen, acknowledging the message, the situation, and promising backup. Anne next texted Jocelyn, the shelter manager. She hated waking the woman, but Jocelyn had insisted everyone be able to contact her, day or night.

That task was accomplished before she reached the hallway leading to the kitchen. Still no sounds from outside. Anne sent up a prayer that the intruder would run into technical difficulties.

Argus pushed past her and went to the heavy metal fire door of the kitchen. Anne wondered for the umpteenth time about the pros and cons of having such heavy, secure doors for outside entrances that opened into shadowy areas hidden from view by high brick walls. Would it be more secure to allow people to look out through a window, to assess the situation before stepping outside? Or was it safer to keep intruders from being able to see in?

"Moot point," she breathed, as a loud *click-buzz* signaled whoever was outside was very good with technology that decoded security keypads.

The pneumatics on the door sighed and groaned as the heavy panel swung inward. Argus stepped sideways into the shadows, as the stream of warm yellow light beyond the back door area spilled down, through the door. Anne ducked down behind the worktable. She grinned as she came eye-to-eye with all the heavy aluminum pots and pans, big enough to cook for dozens at a time. The Arc Foundation didn't believe in using guns, although there had been discussions lately on arming its representatives with tazers and pepper spray. Thanks to Vincent, all the daughters of Quarry Hall could handle themselves in hand-to-hand combat. He trained them to be able to walk into a room and come up with impromptu weapons. It didn't take much imagination to figure out what to do, defensively, with these pots and pans.

A single footstep. Argus growled, the sound low and rumbling, vibrating in some of the stainless steel utensils and bowls hanging from the equipment rack over the table. No more footsteps. Anne thought she smelled the sudden rancid perfume stink of fear-sweat, blowing in on the cool evening breeze. She held her breath, listening.

A smartphone pinged. Not her phone. She checked it in her hip pocket, just in case. She caught whispers of movement, the tiny clicks of even tinier keys, perhaps? On her hands and knees, she looked around the side of the table, and saw a lean shape, dressed all in black, with a hood making the head bullet-shaped. Light gleamed from inside its cupped hands. What was this hopeful robber doing responding to a text?

Unless this wasn't simple robbery, but an attempt to get at one of the women taking refuge here? Was someone inside helping him? Joan's story about her mother came fresh to Anne's mind. The worst thing about abusers was that they considered themselves justified in the harm they caused, and they considered themselves victims when people helped their targets escape to safety and freedom. If she attacked, the intruder could claim he was only coming to check on his girlfriend, that he was worried

13

about her, that he wanted to make amends. Anne couldn't strike until he did something first to endanger the residents.

Sometimes, Anne hated being one of the good guys. They had all the rules to abide by, while the bad guys basically lived by the motto: *Whatever works.*

She ducked back into the darker shadows of the table and waited until the intruder finished his text message. Argus wouldn't attack until she gave the signal or he thought she was in danger. That one growl had been fair warning, giving the intruder the chance to realize he had been discovered, and to retreat before he went too far. Anne slid backward on the clean tile floor a few more feet. For her purposes, the intruder needed to be caught in the act.

The smartphone pinged again. Anne muffled a sigh and froze when the intruder turned to face her as he pulled out his cell phone. The light reflected from the screen revealed his face. He looked very young. Young enough to have the fuzz of a first beard and be so proud of it, he left it on his face no matter how patchy it looked. He scowled and pursed his lips, tucked his flashlight back in his pocket, and texted a response.

What kind of a break-in was this?

With a sigh, the intruder jammed his smartphone back into his pocket and turned to walk over to the big wooden kitchen table, on the other side of the kitchen, by the back door, without raising his head. He never saw Anne. Shouldn't someone with nasty intent be a little more alert? The intruder sat down heavily, sighing even more loudly, and slouched like a pouty teenager. Which Anne decided he was. She took a chance and whispered for Argus. No response from the young man at the table.

Argus crept around the back side of the table and settled down next to Anne. Just in time. She had barely rested her hand on his neck when the kitchen door swung open and a girl scrambled across the tile floor, barefoot, wrapped in one of the new neon green thermal blankets Anne had brought to the shelter. She dropped the blanket as she leaped into her boyfriend's arms and settled on his lap.

"You didn't tell anyone where she was hiding, did you?" Anne called as she stood and reached for the bank of light switches by the swinging kitchen door.

The girl shrieked as her terrified boyfriend stood up, dumping her to the floor. At the same moment, flashlights pierced the darkness outside and two officers darted through the door, each with a light in one hand and a gun in the other.

~~~~~

"Thank goodness it was only two hormone-driven teenagers," Jocelyn murmured that afternoon, once things had settled down.

Kurt, Brittany's boyfriend, hated her bully father with a passion. The

14

teen wouldn't tell the man where to find his runaway wife and daughter if he pulled out his toenails with red-hot pliers. Or at least, that was what Kurt vowed a dozen times over the last thirteen hours, when various authority figures confronted him.

Unfortunately, Brittany had violated several rules of the shelter, starting with lying about having a phone and then using it without permission. Secrecy was the most important ingredient in creating a safe haven for abused and fugitive women and children. Brittany compounded her transgression by not only revealing her location, but telling how to get in. Despite the evidence of hormones scrambling their brains, both teens were in the gifted-and-talented program at their school, and they had created the electronic lock-picking gizmo Kurt used to get inside. A disturbance that brought the police to the shelter also threatened its anonymity. Neighbors would notice the activity, and someone would remark on it, and the more incidents there were, the more people would talk. Eventually, the wrong person would find out and the shelter wouldn't be safe any longer.

"They make a good team," Anne offered.

"And it looks like he's had good examples of how to treat the women in his life. Brittany is safe with him. Once they survive high school." Jocelyn slouched a little in the battered wooden swivel chair behind her overflowing desk.

"The police were impressed with how he got in. My contact in the department has offered to hook them both up with the FBI. Get them scholarships and training."

"Hmm, yes. Your contact with the department." She tipped her head slightly to one side and looked Anne over.

The moment had come. Anne had managed to stay on the periphery of the excitement, moving back and forth between her duties in the shelter, keeping the other residents from finding out what had happened – panic was another threat to the security of the shelter – and monitoring the interrogation of Kurt and Brittany. She had expected Jocelyn would save her for last. The shelter's director hadn't reacted beyond a long, quizzical stare and a deep frown when Anne confessed to the existence of the security camera by the door that alerted her when Kurt broke in. The time had come to admit her visit wasn't just to evaluate the shelter for assistance from the Arc Foundation.

"We have very strict guidelines for how we maneuver out in the field. In very broad terms, we try to avoid any situation where our integrity can be compromised or called into question. When we're investigating a possibly dangerous situation, we let local law enforcement know. When we deal with children, we never do it alone – always with witnesses. And we're never alone in a hotel room or similar situation with a man who isn't a proven co-worker or a relative. Every encounter must be as public as possible. And once someone has been proven above suspicion, we don't keep secrets from them."

"I was under suspicion, then?" Jocelyn sounded almost relieved, making Anne wonder what threats the shelter had faced in the past.

"We're still picking up patterns, but I've weeded out some possibilities, so it definitely isn't an inside job."

Slowly, Anne laid out the information as it had been presented to the team when Harrison and Elizabeth Carter decided the Arc Foundation needed to do something about the problem. The statistics for the threatened shelters. The characteristics that paralleled Jocelyn's shelter. She related what Sophie had passed on to her the other night, and what the other four Arc girls were doing at the other possible targets.

"I'm still waiting for a response from the shelters that were already targeted, to see if they can identify the five people I suspect," Anne said.

"So you think those people are here, getting ready to accuse my people of harming their children." Jocelyn shook her head, looking over the diagram again. "I'm grateful, and I understand why you had to be so secretive. If I didn't have so much else on my mind, I might even be furious that these people are so callous, so greedy, they're profiting from hurting the very people who are trying to help people just like them."

"That's the thing — until we get background data on these people, how can we be sure they really are in need of assistance?"

Chapter Three

"For all we know," Anne continued, "the husband is involved, maybe directing everything from outside. A man does show up, claiming to be a lawyer. The woman who arrives a week before the family —"

"Maryanne, if you're right."

"When the accused workers resist long enough, she always claims to know a lawyer. At the second shelter, he did show up. It's too bad none of these other places had security cameras. We could harvest those images, get Sophie to perform her magic, find out his identity."

"So what's the pattern? How soon can I expect them to claim that one of my workers was indecent with one of the girls?"

"If they follow the pattern Sophie picked up, it'll be the boy. I already asked the two male social workers to stay away from the family," Anne hurried to say, when Jocelyn opened her mouth to respond. From her widened eyes and the flush of color, that was anger more than fear. Or maybe horror. "I don't know what kind of a kink the vetting process here will throw in their timeline. It could buy us some time, help us gather more evidence."

"Or it could make them break their pattern," Jocelyn said, nodding. "I watch enough cop and profiler dramas, I can guess the possibilities." For a long moment, they just met each other's gazes, wordless.

Anne willed the woman to put all her trust in her, in the Arc Foundation. The slightest bit of doubt, of distrust, of refusing to accept that someone would be so selfish and greedy that they would destroy what existed to help others, might interfere in the cooperation needed to stop these people here and now. Yet at the same time, Anne prayed she was wrong. That she was attributing suspicious motives and actions to these people, and they were innocent of everything except being unable to trust. And what if Jocelyn decided to confront these people, instead of waiting for them to hang themselves? If Anne had matched up the patterns and evidence incorrectly, the shelter could be hit with a lawsuit for defamation and false accusations.

The only thing to do in such situations, besides hire the most incredible, imaginative lawyers in the world, was to pray. And in such situations, prayers for safety, resolution, and justice, should come first.

"Tell me more about these guidelines to avoid compromising situations," Jocelyn finally said. "I think we need to upgrade our policies."

"The easiest one for your people to learn is to avoid all skin-to-skin contact. If a child's clothes get dirty, instead of peeling them out of those dirty or wet clothes right away, put another layer over them, to protect their surroundings and preserve the evidence."

"Evidence?"

"If that child is injured, or there was sexual assault, you want someone with training to examine them first. Someone with authority. And have medical personnel or social workers nearby when the clothes are removed for the first time. Even if it's something as simple as a child falling down, injuring a knee, they can't walk or refuse to move themselves — wrap a blanket around that child before picking them up. That extra layer between you and them makes it harder to make accusations of improper touching while in close quarters."

"All the training we had, we never..." Jocelyn sighed. "It's amazing how... how oblivious you can be, when you're operating from good intentions. How naïve, never expecting people to be looking for foul motives behind every good thing you do." She nodded once, sharply. "Tell me more. Or maybe I should call in my team leaders, have you tell them at the same time, and start that training today."

"Whatever you want to do. We have manuals ready for download, guidelines to help you. That's what the Arc Foundation is here for."

~~~~~

The new family, Anne learned by bedtime that night, were the D'Agostinos; Sharon, Lacy, Joe, and Tess. She gave their information to Sophie, to verify if their sketchy backgrounds were valid. If they were smart, there really was a D'Agostino family living in the general area Sharon said they were from. Anne shuddered when it occurred to her, as she returned to her bed, that these people might be so careful to cover their tracks that the real Sharon D'Agostino and her children were missing from their home. She prayed hard that these were the real D'Agostino family.

But she doubted it. Maryanne had spent a large amount of time whispering with Sharon and Lacy during the day — too much time for a new acquaintance. The excuse of simply offering to show the ropes to the newcomers, offering a helping hand to someone in a worse situation, didn't wash with her. Not when staff workers reported that until Sharon and her children showed up, Maryanne refused to socialize. There was no reason for the sudden turnaround, from wallflower to cruise director.

Another strike against innocence was Sharon's complaint to Jocelyn before bedtime and lights out. She was upset that the two male social workers ignored her son. She wanted Joe to have some male bonding, a male role model to look up to during this transition time — her words, not Jocelyn's. Anne bit back a remark that it sounded like Sharon had been nibbling at psychology and counseling textbooks. Travis and Al spent their service hours inside the shelter with children they already knew, and until the D'Agostino family passed their background check, they wouldn't be allowed past the "airlock."

"How long can you keep them there?" Anne asked, when she had conferred with Jocelyn.

"One more day. Then we have to either eject them or let them inside. I'm a little worried that they haven't complained about the wait. Most of the time, when we've had people come to us who have been at other shelters, they do complain. They don't like our precautions. They think we don't trust them." Jocelyn's expression turned bleaker, weariness darkening her eyes. "The ones who understand, who appreciate our precautions, are the ones who have had experiences with careless shelters. The people they're hiding from were able to get inside and make them move on."

Anne wondered if the lack of complaint about the delay was another warning sign. These people were too intent on getting inside where they could find their prey, make their false accusations, so they avoided making waves. She wished Sophie could have given her some data on Maryanne, at the very least, but there was some trouble getting hold of the people who had encountered the accusers at the other shelters. Either the shelters had closed down, or the accused workers had been fired because the managers were terrified at the slightest accusation, and afraid to investigate. Sophie had promised one more day before they could have someone look at the pictures. Anne didn't like the idea of having to let the D'Agostinos inside. She had known they were trouble the moment Argus reacted so badly to them.

But no court in the land would accept the testimony of a German Shepherd.

An hour into the next morning, Anne knew time had run out.

Sharon D'Agostino didn't come to breakfast. Maryanne huddled with Lacy and Joe, glaring at everyone who approached. She didn't let the two children go to the line to get their breakfast, but fetched it for them. Argus growled from his resting place under the serving table whenever she approached. Anne barely noticed, her mind racing through the possibilities of what had happened and what would happen. Every few minutes, her mind seemed to jolt back to one question: Where was Tess, and what had happened to her?

Anne was in Jocelyn's office, updating her on what she had observed in the airlock during the breakfast period, when Sharon knocked on the office door and walked in. Her eyes were red and swollen from weeping, with dark smears under them, her hair lank and tangled. She twitched regularly, glancing over her shoulder, refusing to meet Jocelyn's eyes.

Anne wondered how long the woman had studied body language.

Did she have a degree in psychology? Had she studied acting? Were the physical signs of distress the result of makeup or drugs, or had she genuinely spent a restless night, revising her scam and false allegations, since the male counselors wouldn't come anywhere near Joe?

Sharon wouldn't talk with Anne in the office. She looked like she might burst into tears at any moment and spoke almost in a whisper, huddled in her chair in front of Jocelyn's desk in visible misery.

Anne wondered if the ringleader was Sharon's husband, who played the false lawyer. Maybe she lived in fear of him? Maybe she really was a battered wife but was too securely under his control to make a break for it. He played a sick mental game of sending his family into shelters specifically to damage the places that would have helped Sharon escape him.

Such speculations made Anne's head hurt. She told Jan, in the craft room, that she was going outside for some fresh air, and hurried out to her truck with Argus on her heels. There was no need to listen to her gut instinct, the chill-up-the-spine sense of impending doom. She called Sophie and updated her, asking for prayers to protect Jocelyn and the shelter. Then she called Sgt. Willis and warned him that the "explosion" she feared might happen soon.

"If you blocked the scam they were most likely to use this time around," he said, after she explained what Sophie had predicted, "yeah, it's a good bet. They might not realize that they're under suspicion, but any change in the pattern, the game plan, makes them dangerous. My sister-in-law is our liaison with the children and family services department. Want me to give her a heads up?"

"They usually don't contact any authorities. The other places they've hit cave in and hand over the money, either with the first threat or when the fake lawyer shows up, or..." Anne stopped, breathless with the understanding that seemed to turn up the sunshine about fifty watts brighter. "Or Maryanne makes her call to the local children and family authorities and gets them scrambling to pay up and hush them up before they're shut down. She always calls and rescinds the accusation, but what if she never really *placed* the call in the first place? Yes, please, warn them to be ready. Then we have more evidence against them."

"If you dare let it play out to the bitter end," Willis cautioned her. "You're talking about a place that does a lot of good, and the reputations of a lot of good people. Don't go playing any games with them."

"We have evidence that will stand up in court. And if these people are as smart and slick as I think they are, it'll never get to court." She sighed. "But if they're who I'm looking for, your sister-in-law might have to act fast, to take these kids away from their mother. She's definitely not a safe guardian or a good role model."

"Tell me about it."

When Anne returned to the shelter, she took a detour through the "airlock," and found the door closed on the D'Agostino family's room. None of the other temporary residents were in sight. There was an eeriness to the quiet that made the hairs stand up on Anne's bare arms. She watched Argus as they walked around the few public rooms, checking for anything unusual her big guardian might find. In more than one place where she had been involved in disproving false allegations, the guilty party had planted evidence, trying to stack the odds in their favor. Packets of drugs. Child pornography. Bloody handkerchiefs or ropes. All depending on the allegations. Anne wasn't going to let the D'Agostinos stack the deck against Jocelyn and her shelter.

She prayed hard as she walked through the rooms, letting Argus lead the way.

To her relief, her companion found nothing.

When she went into the main rooms of the shelter, she discovered Maryanne was nowhere to be found. No one had seen her since breakfast. Anne thought she knew where Maryanne was. She settled in a corner of the kitchen where she could see all the activity around her – but Argus was not allowed to accompany her – and used her smartphone to access the memory of the recorder controls in her truck. She grinned a moment, appreciating yet again the technical wizardry Joan and Sophie brought to the Arc Foundation and its various endeavors. It took only a few moments to access the right cameras to follow Maryanne as she moved around the "airlock," attending to the D'Agostino children. Tess was still nowhere to be seen. Anne fought down a fear that the little girl had been smuggled out of the building during the night, and Sharon was right now demanding that a search be made for her daughter, that she had been kidnapped. That wasn't a money-making proposition for people like her, mostly because an accusation of kidnapping would bring in outside authorities. Her trump card in shaking down the shelters depended heavily on their desire to protect their reputation and hush scandal.

The odds were good that Tess was still in the bedroom where she had spent the night, now closely guarded by her sister, brother, and Maryanne. They were probably coaching her on what to say if anyone asked her questions. A child as young as Tess would be easy to terrify into silence, either threatening her with punishment or simply convincing her that the people who would talk to her were bad people, that they wanted to hurt her or her mother. The Ogre had destroyed Anne's childhood using that tactic, terrifying her into keeping silent about the vile things he did to her in the quiet of the night.

Anne wanted to rain destruction down on anyone who would destroy the innocence of any child for their own profit.

Once she had verified Maryanne's location, Anne went back into the main rooms and took up her duties for the day. Jocelyn sent for her less than half an hour later.

"According to Sharon, Travis gave candy to Joe and Tess last night. Drugged candy," Jocelyn said, when Anne had settled into her office with the door closed. "While they were asleep, Travis came into their room and molested Joe, but Tess hadn't eaten the candy, so she woke up. He threatened to kill her mother and sister if she didn't keep quiet."

"How much money will buy their silence?"

"Oh, she hasn't gotten to that part yet. She's very good at playing outraged, but she knows her lines too well." The shelter's director shuddered and visibly forced herself back in her chair, fighting the tension that bowed her back. "She refused to let the children be examined by a doctor before I finished making the suggestion."

"She knew what your first response would be."

"I think she's had some kind of training in situations like this."

"Where do things stand with her? Is she going to let you talk to the children?"

"She says they're both too upset. I think she has to do more preparation, that this is outside of the patterns you mentioned."

"Definitely outside. Tess is the weak link. She'll probably change her story several times, and any good lawyer or child psychologist will tell you she's adapting to give the adults around her what they want, that she's learning from their questions, maybe even taking her responses from what she's overheard. There are far too many ways to throw out the testimony of children who are too young to understand the crimes being committed against them."

"Even in this day and age, with all the filth on television and in the movies that they're exposed to," Jocelyn said, nodding slowly. "What do we do?"

"I've already passed the word along, to Arc and to my contact here. We'll push them, recording everything they do, everything they say to you, and wait to see how far they'll go. We won't," Anne held up a hand to stop the protest she could predict Jocelyn would make, "let it go so far that the reputation of this shelter will be destroyed. We just want to gather up enough evidence to hang these people once and for all."

~~~~~

By lunchtime, Maryanne had gone to speak to Jocelyn, expressing her alleged outrage over what had happened to her new friend. She stormed through the shelter, glaring at Travis and Al, snarling at them—always in front of witnesses—that if she had her way, they'd never be allowed near children ever again. Jocelyn and Anne agreed not to let the two men know the accusations made against Travis, just to preserve the sense of reality.

The hard part in all this was letting the whispers circulate. Anne didn't look forward to the damage control Jocelyn and her staff would need to do, once this was over. But on the bright side, it would only be hurt feelings, and nothing worse.

The D'Agostino family stayed in their room, and Maryanne stayed with them, except when she made two more ventures in search of snacks and toys for the children. She always went into the inner rooms of the shelter, coming close to other residents and workers, muttering under her breath, her words understandable, caught on camera and microphone.

Anne received a call from Sgt. Willis, letting her know that no calls had been made to child and family services, despite Maryanne's threats to do so if something wasn't done immediately about the situation. Following instructions emailed to her from Sophie, Anne linked her smartphone program to a smartphone of a detective in the police department. Now Lt. Rachel Houston could also monitor the recording equipment in her truck, and watch everything that happened at the shelter. If anyone showed up in response to Maryanne's bogus phone calls, she would get to the shelter in less than twenty minutes, with an entirely different response.

When a lawyer showed up at the door of the shelter at 4:37 that afternoon, Anne felt as if a silent starter gun had gone off. She kept the children busy in the playroom and stationed herself in the doorway to watch the hallway he would take to Jocelyn's office. The tension coiling in her gut tightened when Maryanne appeared in the doorway leading from the airlock, her face bright with eagerness—until she saw Anne watching her. Eagerness turned into an agonized expression of bereavement.

Then the lawyer in his dark brown trousers and matching vest, his suit coat caught up in one arm, strode down the hall, following Carla, who had door duty that afternoon. Maryanne stared at him, her mouth falling open, looking like she had been swatted between the eyes with a baseball bat.

She doesn't know who he is. But she was expecting a lawyer, Anne mused. She glanced up as the man strode past her doorway. He winked at her. Two seconds later, he turned the corner and she heard Carla rap on Jocelyn's door. Anne's smartphone buzzed against her hip.

"Raphael Hernandez should be inside the shelter by now," Sophie announced, cutting off Anne's greeting. "He's a lawyer and an investigator for the state, working on these shelter cases. The big boss decided it was smart to get the Feds on our side."

"He knows what I look like?" Anne guessed.

"Definitely. We don't want our own taken out in a fire fight, know what I mean?"

"Too well." She flinched as doors slammed open. "Okay, this is going to be interesting. Call you back later," she hurried to say, and cut the connection as Sharon and Maryanne darted past her, heading for Jocelyn's office. Her phone rang again before she got four steps down the hall to follow. This time it was Lieutenant Houston, letting Anne know she was on her way, that she had seen the man approach the door and announce himself as a lawyer.

By the time Anne explained that the lawyer was on their side and not the ringleader of the gang, the first tearful tirade duet from Sharon and Maryanne had already reached its ebb. She missed most of it, only aware of shouting voices in the background as she and the detective came to an agreement. She heard Sharon, her voice strained with tears, accusing Jocelyn of being a hypocrite, thinking only about herself, by bringing in a lawyer to bully the innocent victims of a horrendous crime into silence. Anne tapped on the door and stepped into the office before Jocelyn could answer.

"Miss Hachworth," Hernandez said, rising from his chair. He extended a hand to shake hers. He didn't muffle his smug smile when Sharon and Maryanne's mouths dropped open, stunned into silence. "Excellent job with the surveillance video."

"Arc passed all that along to you, I'm guessing." Anne hesitated to shut the door. Jocelyn's office was a little too crowded. Five people in an office that started out as a supply closet, jammed with filing cabinets, a desk, and two chairs threatened to overwhelm her with claustrophobia. Argus, the traitor, stayed out in the hall.

That just confirmed what a smart dog he was.

"Surveillance video?" Maryanne said with a weak voice, half an octave lower than her usual speaking tones. Anne guessed she thought higher pitch would make her sound more righteously angry.

Chapter Four

"We have surveillance equipment, audio as well as visual, all around the shelter," Jocelyn said. "We can prove that none of our male staff had any contact with your children. They didn't come into the restricted area, and your children didn't leave the restricted area."

"Tess was mistaken," Sharon hurried to say. "She only thought it was a man who came into our room."

"No one has gone into or out of your rooms except your family and Maryanne," Anne said. "Unless you're accusing her of molesting your children?"

"I'd like to have that doctor's examination, now," Jocelyn said.

"Those video cameras don't go into the bedrooms," Hernandez said. "I wouldn't put it past them to have manufactured evidence on the children's bodies by this time."

"How dare you?" Maryanne shrieked, staggering backward. Anne was in a position to see her reach back with one hand, aiming for the doorknob. "How can you accuse a mother of being so cruel, she'd harm her own children that way?"

Anne spat three words in Greek. In the time it took Maryanne to pull the door open and turn around, Argus had reared up on his hind legs, one paw braced against the doorframe, putting his head on a level with the woman's face. He bared his teeth and growled, loud and deep. Maryanne shrieked and stumbled backward, knocking Sharon to the floor, and taking a small avalanche of folders down from Jocelyn's desk on top of them.

"Very slick move," Hernandez said. "I've heard about your dogs, but..." His grin widened as he shook his head.

Anne's phone buzzed. Lieutenant Houston was outside the shelter and had just placed a man under arrest who claimed he was the lawyer for Sharon D'Agostino. However, the real Sharon D'Agostino was currently on an overseas assignment, with her husband and infant son, at the London office of her pharmaceutical company.

"Ah, the wonders of the Internet," Hernandez said, when Anne passed along the information. "If you know where to look and who to ask, you can find out anything. Too bad criminals like these depend on people being too afraid to ask the right questions."

Sharon burst into tears, until Maryanne swore and slapped her.

Argus took two steps into the room, teeth bared, no need to growl. She huddled in on herself with her arms curled protectively over her head.

~~~~~

Anne stayed three more days at the shelter, to encourage Jocelyn and her staff, who feared the fallout from the attempt would prompt their many sponsors to withdraw funding. She taught the senior members of the staff how to maintain the security system she had installed — after Sophie's background checks came in and cleared all of them — and gave lessons on the principles and practices the Arc Foundation had established to avoid any accusation of wrongdoing or inappropriate behavior.

What tore at her heart the most were the reactions of the children living in the shelter. Despite the best efforts of the workers and their mothers, they sensed something had threatened their safety. Whether they overheard their mothers and the staff talking, or they simply picked up on the tension, it didn't matter — the children reacted. Some became aggressive, striking out at others, as if they had to prove they were strong and didn't have to be afraid. Others grew clingy or withdrew, and most of the children had nightmares at least once. Anne stayed because Argus gave the children comfort, and he could sense when nightmares were about to start. She took to sleeping on the couch in the main room where it wasn't so long a walk down the halls to the bedrooms, when Argus woke her. She was able to get into a bedroom and wake the mother or an older sibling before the nightmare grew bad enough for tears. Waking in the arms of someone they loved and trusted seemed to be the best cure for the nightmares and drove them away.

During the day, Anne gathered the children around to tell them stories of good wizards and wise women and warriors. They traveled the world disguised as ordinary people, seeking thieves and liars, and people who pretended to be good and kind and helpless, so they could enter the hidden places where orphans and widows went for shelter. When they found those liars and thieves, the warriors, wizards, and wise women took the evil people away and punished them.

Anne finished every story by telling the children that every time these good people helped widows and orphans, they made one of them a warrior or wizard or wise woman, to help in the battle against evil. By the third day, several children came to her after the stories to ask how they could join the secret army. Jocelyn took over at that point, and assured Anne she had several people on staff who could keep telling the stories, to encourage the children to be brave and understand that they could be warriors, too.

"How did you get into the habit of explaining things as faerie tales?" Jocelyn asked her, over late night mugs of herbal tea, as they assessed the children's healing.

"I... know what they've been through. The children. Making it a story about princesses and evil wizards and monsters puts all the... well, the pain at a distance." Anne shrugged, swirling the cooling dregs of her tea around in the mug, unable to meet Jocelyn's eyes. She hated that flash of pity and understanding.

Argus whined and got up from his sprawl on the floor under the table, to put both forepaws on her lap. Anne sputtered and put the mug down to hug him. When she looked at Jocelyn again, the older woman had a glimmer of tears in her eyes, but she smiled.

"Like the warriors, you have to leave once your job is done, don't you? And go out finding more liars and thieves and attackers of the innocent," she murmured.

"It's what we do." Anne could smile now, as that thread of tension in her gut snapped and weariness washed over her.

~~~~~

The false Sharon and Maryanne turned out to be cousins, and the fake lawyer was Maryanne's husband. The children belonged to Sharon's sister, Karen, who was in prison. Through her lawyer, she sent thanks to Jocelyn and Anne for their part in stopping the two women, because she hadn't seen or heard from her children for nearly two years. The three children would be wards of the state and taken for regular visits with their mother until she was released in three months.

Karen wrote:

They won't tell me anything about you, because of the security issues with the shelter, but I want you to know you are angels from God. I'm getting my life back on track, and that includes reading my Bible and praying, and I promise all the gals in the Bible study in our cell block will be praying for you. Thank you, from the bottom of my heart.

"This makes it somehow all worthwhile," Jocelyn said, after she and Anne both read the letter.

"Yeah, but that doesn't mean I want to go through something like this again. What's the ancient Chinese curse about living through interesting times?" Anne stood, and muffled a chuckle when Argus seemed to leap straight from a sitting position at her side to standing outside Jocelyn's office door. He was just as eager to get going, to head home to Quarry Hall, as she was.

"But isn't that what you people at the foundation do all the time? You go around, solving problems, investigating, helping people."

"Yeah, and most of the time it's pretty routine. We do background checks, then we send people to live in the area, work at the shelter or school or whatever to soak up the atmosphere, do a litmus test, I guess you'd call it. Most of the time, thank the Lord, the people we're investigating are exactly what they appear on the outside." She hefted her backpack into place over her shoulder. "It's when we run into a place that's wearing a mask, or when people have secrets they're willing to fight to keep hidden, we have trouble. I'd prefer to stay away from the hypocrites, thanks very much."

"Don't we all?" Jocelyn said with a chuckle. "Oh, no you don't. You're not getting out of here without a hug," she added, rising from her desk as Anne took a step toward the door.

Other members of the staff wouldn't let Anne leave without a hug, or in the case of the cook, a bag of sandwiches and cookies and rawhide chips for Argus. She had hoped to leave once the morning rush hour traffic was gone, but it was nearly noon by the time her truck turned onto a main road out of town. And her phone rang. Sighing, Anne glanced at the display, with her phone sitting in the cup holder on the console of her truck. The caller was Elizabeth Carter. She glanced down the street and saw the parking lot for a defunct car dealership. Putting her turn signal on, she snatched the phone up and opened the connection on the fourth ring. Driving while on the phone was forbidden, both by Quarry Hall rules and state law, and Anne's inner law demanded that neither Harrison nor Elizabeth Carter ever be made to leave a message.

"How are you feeling?" Elizabeth asked. "Were you able to rest during the wrap-up?"

Anne grinned at Argus, whose ears had perked up at the sound of Elizabeth's voice coming from the phone. The last few times someone had called from Quarry Hall while she was supposed to be on her way home, they would have asked to make sure she had stopped somewhere before answering the phone. Either Elizabeth was preoccupied, or she had decided Anne didn't need reminding anymore. It was a good feeling.

"It wasn't that stressful an assignment. It's not like I had anyone coming after me with a gun. The worst part was the children." Anne sighed. "The children used in the scam, even more than the ones thinking they were going to lose their home."

"It's always the innocents who suffer. I can almost guarantee you this next assignment won't be very stressful. Strictly observation and assessment." Elizabeth chuckled. "Although you might feel some stress, imagining Joan breathing down your neck."

"Why Joan?"

"You know her friend, Xander Finley, the lawyer?"

"I know about him, but I was never at home when he came down for the meetings."

"Oh, that's right. Well, we're thinking about expanding his support. It's time for Xander to add some staff, make some of them full-time, and we're considering offering help to other new lawyers through Common

Grounds. He was already cleared when we first set up the sponsorship, back when Joan joined us, but it's *because* he's a good friend of hers that we need to be scrupulous and conduct another investigation before increasing our support."

"Unfortunately, that makes too much sense." Anne closed her eyes and slouched in the seat. Suddenly, the bright sunshine was too harsh and made her eyes feel tired.

The Arc Foundation was engaged in an ongoing battle with former associates, of one kind or another, who refused to give up the power and authority they wrongly believed they held. Then there were the occasional attacks from outside organizations, self-proclaimed mouthpieces for God, who swooped in and demanded Arc throw vast sums of money at them, or blindly support their organization. The worst of these encounters involved people who were very sincere, legitimate, well-meaning, and honestly dedicated to God's service. However, too often the standard investigation revealed that at some point they were so sure of the rightness of their position and their goals, they stopped praying and checking regularly with God. By contrast, the hypocrites and scam artists, who thought wearing choir robes and quoting huge chunks of scripture would convince the "religious idiots" to fork over money, were a refreshing change. Exposing their lies was always gratifying, energizing, and sometimes even fun.

As a result of the constant pressure from self-appointed watchdogs in the religious community, with constant criticism and accusations of wasting funds, the Arc Foundation had to move with more caution than ever. Even when increasing funding to an outreach that had already proven it was worthy, did good for the community at large, and operated with total transparency. Such as Common Grounds Legal Clinic.

"You're a very good judge of character, Anne."

"I just don't know anything about lawyers. Outside of some bad experiences of my own," she hurried to add, before Elizabeth had time to say anything.

"We want a layman's viewpoint of the whole conduct of a legal office. We want you to meet the part-timers. Get a good sense of the atmosphere of the office, the people who come to the clinic for help, the type of people Xander and his associates attract. Watch him at work, watch him interacting with opponents, with officials in the legal system. You might see something that Xander doesn't realize he's doing, or that he's lacking. You'll spend a lot of time sitting on the sidelines, watching and making notes. Unfortunately, there will be situations where you can't take Argus."

"Not without pretending to be blind and dressing him up as my Seeing Eye dog."

"That's why we've arranged for an apartment for you near some of

Joan's friends in Tabor. They can look after Argus, let him relax, while you're busy elsewhere. If you agree to take the assignment, of course. You've earned a rest at home, and we won't push you to go on to this new assignment unless you're willing."

"I've always wanted to check out Tabor. From what Joan has said, it's nice." She opened her eyes and turned to look at the traffic streaming past on the road just a dozen feet away. "It's funny, I've been living in Ohio five, six years now, and I've never been farther north than the shopping plazas along Market Street, heading into Brunswick."

"Then it's high time you expanded your horizons."

"Will I have time for exploring? Sounds like I'll be busy with Xander. Will I have any jobs to do at the clinic, to help out while I'm there?"

"It should be mostly observation. Although, from comments Joan has made, despite the efforts of the incredible Hannah Blake, he might need help with his filing and such." Her voice turned rich with repressed laughter. "His reports are always at least a month late and have the strangest stains sometimes. Coffee. Mustard. Other assorted substances we don't think we want to analyze."

"Oh, so you're siccing me on him as a kindred spirit, to teach him the error of his ways?"

"Hardly!" Elizabeth's laughter made the sun even brighter, and Anne grinned for quite a long time after the call ended.

Heading across Indiana toward the Ohio border, Anne tried to remember everything Joan had told her about the town where she had lived for four years, before moving to Quarry Hall and joining the Arc Foundation. It sounded incredible, the perfect mix of city life, with a well-established, private university that sprawled across the town, access to major highways, buses and trains for transportation nearly everywhere, and yet a small town feel, with a major branch of the Cleveland Metroparks running through the middle of town. Joan recommended Tabor Christian Church, though she hadn't attended very often. Xander was a member, along with Matt Cameron and his cousins, Rocky and Tris. Joan had gone to their pastor, Glenn Carson, for counseling when she first started getting her life put back together. Her recommendation was enough for Anne to decide she would attend Tabor Christian while she was living in town.

The apartment waiting for her was with Joan's former landlord, Mandy Gordon, who had promised to look after Anne. It was also situated across the street from Dr. Holwood, Joan's former advisor at Butler-Williams University. Dr. Holwood and his wife, Doria, were also the foster-parents for Joan's half-sister, Nikki, who had run away from home more than a year ago. Doria had assured Joan that she and her current crop of foster-children would be delighted to have Argus while Anne was busy in places where he wasn't welcome.

A fierce storm came rolling west toward Anne when she reached the Indiana/Ohio border. The blackness of the sky and the rapid-fire flashes of lightning chilled her, so at the first possible opportunity, she got off the highway. She found a truck stop and was able to park up against the building, putting it between her truck and the storm for a little bit of wind break. After ten minutes of feeling the wind and rain pounding on the windows and roof, she decided to risk being drenched for the sake of more secure shelter and dashed with Argus for the truck stop.

Thankfully, the truck stop was a homey sort of place that looked like it hadn't been renovated and hadn't needed renovations in twenty years. The lights were dim, oil lanterns wired for electric lighting, one hanging over each booth. The furnishings were all wood, rubbed to a warm, dark shine through years and use. Anne's stomach growled at the first sniff of the air, a heavenly combination of chili, chicken soup, fresh bread, and apple pie. Her plan to just get coffee evaporated, along with the lunch that she had eaten an hour ago. The waiter, who later revealed he was the owner, and uncle of the cook, met her with a grin that seemed bigger than his face. Argus wagged his tail hard enough to hit the sides of the booths and the man greeted him without hesitating.

The storm lasted through the afternoon, and Anne dashed outside to her truck to retrieve her computer from the compartment under the seat, to get some work done while she waited. Argus curled up on the thick-cushioned bench opposite her and never even flicked an ear when thunder crashed around them. She finished up her reports on the assignment at the shelter, checked out the web site for Common Grounds, and looked through all the information Sophie had sent to her once she accepted the assignment. At four o'clock, the storm was still raging, so she called Mandy Gordon and the Holwoods to let them know she wouldn't be arriving at the time they had planned. Mandy laughed and said it was a sunny, bright, warm day in Tabor. She said she would just go over to the old house that had been turned into apartments and hide a key, so Anne could let herself in whenever she did get there.

A few trucks stopped and their drivers came in, dripping and laughing, to take shelter. They were all regulars, some of them as old and wrinkled and cheerful as Seymour, the owner. Anne let their friendly chatter and slightly coarse jokes wash over her, background music half-muffled by the rattle and drone of the rain. Seymour stopped at her table from time to time to refill her coffee, ask about the work she was doing, comment about possible washouts of roads and bridges and make suggestions for different routes, once she left. If she ever left. He always had a kind word for Argus, but was smart enough not to try to touch him. He offered a bowl and water and later meat scraps for the dog, without

Anne having to ask. And he laughed when she asked if he was a dog person.

"Got allergies something fierce. Thank God for modern medicine. See, my wife, she was a vet before I met her. Couldn't ask her to give up her critters for me, could I? And wouldn't you know it, our daughter followed in her footsteps. So I love the critters, all God's critters, but I just can't have them in the house. Oh, no, here is fine. No problem," he hurried to say, when Anne apologized for bringing Argus into the truck stop. "Like I said, wonders of modern medicine. And it'd be a hard, cold heart that'd make any creature stay outside when God's shaking the sky like that." He pretended to shudder, then cracked a grin at her and left with a wink and a chuckle when one of the men sitting at the counter asked for a refill on his chili.

The storm slowed down enough that Anne could pack up and get back on the road just a little after six in the evening. She ordered a chicken sandwich and onion rings to go, and chatted a bit through the pass-through with Sylvia, Seymour's niece, while the onion rings were frying.

Approaching the town of Stoughton, a little more than half an hour from her apartment, according to the GPS, Anne saw signs for a shopping center just off the highway. One of those signs included a grocery store. She decided it would be smart to stop now and get provisions for her first few days in Tabor, rather than arriving in the darkness and trying to navigate through unfamiliar territory. Besides, she needed to stretch her legs. And even if she didn't, Argus did.

The grocery store was set back from the street across a long expanse of parking lot. It glistened under the sporadic lights, thanks to the rain that still tried to fall in spurts and gusts. Anne parked as close to one of the few working lights as she could, but all the shoppers who had gotten there before her had the same idea. For a few seconds, she considered turning around, leaving, getting back on the highway, and taking her chances once she got to Tabor.

Chapter Five

Argus whined and rested a paw on the latch for the door on his side of the cab. He definitely needed to get out. Sitting curled up on the floor of the cab for hours at a time was not good for him. Sighing, Anne decided she was just tired. The store looked far more desolate than it really was.

She stepped down out of the truck, right into a puddle of water. The parking lot was full of potholes and ruts. The landlord either didn't have the time or the funds to maintain it, or else he didn't care. No wonder there didn't seem to be enough lights — he wasn't replacing bulbs as they burned out. On the plus side, the pools of shadows meant she could let Argus run around, splashing in puddles, working off some of his restlessness for a good fifteen minutes before she put him back in the truck, and no one would see.

Once Anne got inside, the grocery store was well-lit and clean and well-stocked and had more customers than could be accounted for by the number of cars outside. Halfway around the store, she realized why that was — there was a second entrance on the other side of the building. She glanced out through the doors and saw a parking lot with plenty of cars and all the lights lit. Of course, she had chosen the back entrance. And of course, the cash registers were on the other side of the store. And she was so tired, she had brought her backpack into the store with her, instead of just putting her wallet and phone and keys in her pocket.

The long day made itself felt, by the time she came outside twenty minutes later with just the barest necessities to get through the next day or two. Bagels, two bananas, two apples, a box of salad from the salad bar, a quart of orange juice, a quart of milk, and four cans of dog food.

She started across the parking lot, sending up a silent prayer of gratitude that the rain had stopped. A prickle traveled up and down her neck as she looked around and saw most of the cars were gone now. Her truck was just a dark shadow beyond the closest lights. The clouds were still thick and black, blocking the moon and churning across the sky.

Chicken, she scolded herself, and picked up her pace for a few steps before she regained control and slowed to a normal pace. The surest way to attract attention was to act afraid, to act as if she expected trouble. She wished she had left Argus sitting outside, in the shadows by the back doorway. No one would have seen him, and he was too well-trained to run away, even if tempted by a cat or someone with convenient dog biscuits.

Anne heard a footstep on the wet pavement and almost stopped. The lights of the grocery store seemed to withdraw, from fifty feet away to five miles in a split second. She took a deep breath and kept going, her steps brisk as she analyzed what she had at hand, if she couldn't get to her truck in time.

In time for what, exactly? It could just be someone crossing the parking lot, totally innocent. Maybe even afraid she would attack him, instead of planning to attack her. Whoever it was would make a run for it as soon as she opened her truck door and the interior light came on, showing the big dog inside, ready to leap to her defense.

Dog food in the right-hand bag, with her bagels and the plastic carton of tossed salad on top of them. Fruit, juice, and milk in the left-hand bag. Mass versus weight. Bruise her fruit versus losing her salad across the parking lot.

Anne could almost hear Vincent scolding her, laughter making his voice rich, for always getting off track at the worst possible moment.

"So, I'm warped," she breathed, as a tight smile touched her lips. That was her weakness and her gift, thinking slightly askew from the expected and the norm.

Another footstep splashed in a puddle. Whoever followed her wasn't as careful as he should have been about staying quiet. A sign that he didn't mean her any harm?

A soft, metallic click almost made her stop. Anne knew that click. The daughters of Quarry Hall didn't carry guns, but that didn't mean they didn't know how to use them, or identify them, or defend themselves. The person behind her in the wet darkness had just cocked a gun.

Sophie had been paralyzed from the waist down by a bullet. Vincent had been shot just a month ago during a preliminary investigation of a building that a missions organization wanted to turn into a community center in a truly wretched part of their city. Being gunned down by an idiot or a madman was high in everyone's thoughts lately. When God called for someone to stand in the gap, Elizabeth and Brooklyn both reminded the daughters of Quarry Hall, He never promised that person, man or woman, would not be hurt. Or even killed.

Keep moving. Don't let him know you know.

Anne grinned into the darkness. Why did she think the person with the gun had to be male? There were a lot of angry, stupid, selfish women out there, too, who thought a weapon entitled them to take anything they wanted. Evil wasn't the sole province of men.

Her dark green pickup rocked a little. She heard the muffled barking of Argus, and imagined him bouncing on the seat, then leaping into the back compartment, trying to get out that window, then back to the side window.

Whoever was in charge of collecting abandoned carts hadn't been doing his job. She had to detour around a cluster of carts, huddled like frozen moths in the puddle of uncertain light. Maybe they were frightened of the dark.

Stop wandering. No doubt the image of grocery store carts afraid of the darkness would appear in one of her silly stories someday soon. She always told stories to explain things she couldn't quite understand herself. That was another weakness of hers, always trying to play with people's minds instead of giving a straight answer.

Gravel crunched under the feet following her. Anne adjusted her grip on the lefthand bag and prepared to swing. Would he give warning? Or would she hear suddenly running footsteps, barely giving her time to turn?

Six more steps to the truck. It gave an extra deep bounce as Argus leaped from the passenger side to the driver's side. She heard him growling, muffled through the glass and the rising moan of the wind.

"Gimme the keys." Two quick steps and the cold muzzle of the gun jabbed into the back of her neck.

"My dog—"

"I can handle dogs. They like me." Definitely a man. A young voice. Maybe a few notes higher in tension or fear?

"Not this time," Anne whispered, and bent to put the bags down.

"Don't move!" The gun pressed harder into her neck.

"How am I going to get the keys out of my backpack if I don't empty my hands?" She adjusted her stance and wrapped the plastic handle of the grocery bag once more around her hand with a simple twist of her wrist. Muscles tensed, preparing to swing.

Silence. She ground her teeth—how long did this guy have to think about it?

He yanked her backpack down her back, effectively binding her arms. Anne made a mental note to use a hip pack from now on.

This is totally humiliating. She heard the zipper scream as the would-be thief yanked hard on it. The movement threw her off balance. She stumbled backward, her shoulder nudging the man until he stepped aside. She caught a glimpse of a dark blue jacket, a pale face, and rain-slicked, dark hair. He shoved her away. Anne used the motion to turn and swing. The bag of groceries hit him hard, low in the ribs. He grunted and stumbled sideways. Argus barked rapid-fire and made the truck rock, throwing himself against the window and door, trying to get out to her. He was going to break the glass any moment now. He had done it before.

Anne kept a grip on the second bag—ludicrously worried about her salad—and stumbled to the truck. She opened the door, intending to jump in and slam it shut again. The door was never locked. Why lock it, with Argus keeping guard? Besides, the keys were in her jeans pocket, not her backpack. A backpack could be stolen, after all.

Argus leaped over her head. His hind feet slammed into her shoulders, knocking her off her feet. Anne stumbled, still off balance and went down with a squawk, right into a puddle. Her salad went flying.

The would-be carjacker yelped. Water splashed as he stumbled backward. Anne turned, struggling to get to her knees, getting more water on her clothes.

"No, boy! Down, boy! Go away!" he squeaked. Argus advanced on him slowly, one step forward for every step the boy took backward. He growled. Anne imagined his eyes glowed red in the dim lighting.

"Argus, behave yourself. He can't help it if he's stupid," Anne said, as she struggled to her feet. "Give me the gun."

"What?" He stared at her and actually lowered his arm, taking the aim off Argus.

"Give me the gun and come with me to turn yourself over to the manager. It's really the only smart thing to do." She held out her hand.

"Give you my gun? Do you know how much it cost me?" Big brown eyes grew wider. He acted like she had just asked for his first-born child.

"You mean you actually earned money to pay for it? You didn't steal it?"

Anne heard echoes from the future, laughter from Elizabeth and Harrison and whoever else was at home at Quarry Hall, when she would tell this story. Only she would think of such a thing, confronted by a nervous, wet kid — he couldn't be more than nineteen — in a rainy wet, dark parking lot.

"Hey, I'm no..." A blush crossed his face for a moment.

"I'm your first hold-up, huh?"

He nodded. Anne held out her hand again. He looked at her hand, looked back over his shoulder at the grocery store, looked at Argus. The big dog was quiet now, still standing on alert, teeth still bared, advertising his willingness to bite the minute the young gunman did anything wrong. Just because Vincent trained all the Quarry Hall dogs to never bite, that didn't mean they couldn't or wouldn't *threaten* to bite. It was amazing, Anne reflected, what the power of suggestion could do in a tense situation.

"Look, couldn't you just... like forget I was here?"

"I'm soaking wet. Tomorrow's lunch is in a puddle. I'm going to have one doozy of a bruise in the morning. Getting held up after a day of driving in the rain is not going to be easy to forget!" She managed a grin, though the shakes were working their way up from her guts.

Please, Lord, don't let me get stupid, now. My guardian angel has already been working overtime lately.

"No, you have to let me go."

"You need help. Nobody decides just to take somebody else's total worldly goods without some kind of reason." Anne reached into her pocket.

"What're you—"

"Just let me give you my card. It has a number you can call for help. That's what we do. We help people. Even dumb ones." She grinned and pulled out her wallet. The keys came with it, falling to the ground with a jangle-splash sound.

"How about you give me all your money and I let you keep the truck and we call it quits?" he said, his voice shaking a little. The gun lowered a tiny bit more. Still not low enough to suit Anne. She had a mental image of the gun going off, the bullet bouncing off the pavement and hitting her somewhere totally embarrassing.

The grocery store door squeaked open, distracting them both. He turned a little, raising his gun. Argus growled.

"Argus—"

"Hey, what's going on over there?" a man shouted. He stepped out into the parking lot lights, revealing himself as tall, balding, dressed in dark slacks, white shirt, and the long red apron the store workers wore.

"Don't tell them anything!" the gunman demanded, his hand shaking now. He took a step backward and pointed the gun at Anne.

Argus leaped, aiming for the gunman's chest, to knock him to the ground as trained.

"No! Down!" she screamed.

The man in the doorway shouted something.

The gun went off. Rapid-fire shots, as if the gunman couldn't figure out how to stop.

Argus yelped and twisted aside.

Anne flung herself on the gunman, getting a fist into his chin, a knee into his gut, kicking hard at his hand as he fell. The gun went off again as it went flying. She heard shouts and screams and running feet. The gun hit the pavement and skidded away. Then something else cut through her fury and fear mixed.

Stupid! Stupid! Stupid! Get some priorities!

"Argus?" She leaped off the downed man and stumbled across the soaked asphalt.

The big dog lay crumpled in a puddle of blood and rain. The blood caught the parking lot lights and seemed to glow like lava. His sides heaved as he panted for breath. A whimper escaped him and his eyes half-closed as Anne flung herself to her knees next to him.

She heard shouts and running footsteps. From the corner of her eye, she saw the gunman scramble across the pavement for a few yards on his hands and knees. Then he leaped to his feet and raced to her truck. She curled herself around Argus, tears filling her eyes.

"Please, Lord, don't let him die?"

The engine turned over and the truck peeled rubber as it raced out of the parking lot.

~~~~~

"Are you sure you're okay?" the Stoughton officer asked. The brass plate on his shirt read, "Peterson."

Anne opened her mouth to scream at him—yes, for the fiftieth time, she was all right. Then she really looked at herself for the first time since a police van took her and Argus to a local vet, lights flashing and siren blaring. She had made sure the big dog was in good hands, and the vet understood he had to save him, no matter how bad he looked, before she let the police officer take her to the station to make her statement. Her jeans were smeared with mud and dark, crusty streaks of Argus's blood. More blood streaked her blue sweatshirt. True, it was old and faded and the iron-on of the unicorn was crumbly and peeling away, but it was her favorite.

"I'm not hurt. Just shook up." She shuddered. "That scumbag took my truck!"

"Yeah, well, at least he didn't shoot you. Lots of carjackers think they have to hurt the people they robbed, just to keep them quiet."

He looked like the officer who appeared just before the commercial breaks on *America's Dumbest Criminals.* The one hiding behind dark glasses and a stiffly pressed uniform, who looked like an advertisement for the Marine Corps. But at least he smiled. His gray eyes were bloodshot this late at night, sweat stains at his armpits, his sandy hair mussed from the rain and wind.

When he leaned across the table and turned on the tape recorder and asked for her statement, Anne didn't have as much trouble as she expected relating the sequence of events. She refrained from repeating some of the more off-beat thoughts that had gone through her head. He had taken statements from the other people at the grocery store already, giving Anne time to get Argus settled at the vet and ride over to the station. She appreciated it, and the time to settle down mentally and emotionally. When she finished, Officer Peterson nodded and looked down at the table for a few moments after turning off the recorder.

"You know, when you realized he was there, if you had just turned around and gone back into the store—" he began.

"The carjacker would have hit on someone else. Or he might have given up and gone away. Probably. I thought about that." Anne nodded and toyed with the straps of her backpack to keep from looking him in the eye. She bit her lip to keep from adding: *But he was scared enough, he might have shot the next person he went after.* What was her truck, all her clothes and books and notebook computer, compared to another person's life? Even the loss of Argus.

It was very hard to remember that, very hard to keep the anger from taking over. Anne had a hard time with anger when it came to someone getting hurt. The sense of helplessness that came with it almost made her nauseous.

"Well, what are you going to do now?" Peterson asked, after a few seconds of silence. "I can probably scrounge up some clothes, to replace what you've got on."

"That would be great. I think I should call home."

"Phone's over — " He stopped, frowning, as she lifted her backpack to her lap and pulled out her cell phone.

"Funny. Usually I leave my backpack in the truck, but tonight I had it over my shoulder and didn't realize it until I was down the first aisle. All my really important, irreplaceable stuff is in it." Anne tried to smile. "Like my credit cards. My allergy warning cards. Insurance card. My emergency chocolate." She stopped short when she realized her hands shook again.

"Let me get you those clothes. I bet you could use a shower, too?" He hooked a thumb over his shoulder toward one of the hallways into the recesses of the station house. "Plenty of hot water in the locker room this late at night."

"Yeah. That'd be great, thanks." She put the phone away. She would call when she was clean and maybe alone. After she had composed her thoughts some more.

~~~~~

"You could have gone back into the store," Sophie said with a sigh, after Anne related the events of the last three hours.

"Yeah, I know." She closed her eyes and leaned back against the wall in the women's locker room. She had it all to herself; no women on duty at the start of the third duty shift.

Officer Peterson had found her soap and towels, along with a wide assortment of clothes from the lost-and-found bin at the back of the station. She passed up an extra-large Brunswick Blue Devils sweatshirt for a gray and green Stoughton Mustangs muscle shirt, a baggy, dark blue sweater and fleece drawstring pants in off-white. She had thought to describe her outfit when she called home to Quarry Hall, hoping to make a joke about her fashion sense improving. The joke stuck in her throat when she looked at the bloodstained clothes lying in a pile on the floor only a few feet away.

Anne's hair was wet, drying in little ringlets around her face. She sat cross-legged in the corner facing the shower stalls, glad for the privacy while she made her call.

Sophie had answered the phone after the first ring. Anne had been startled. She had been hoping to leave a message on the machine. It was past ten now.

"Not that I'm ungrateful for anything, but what—"

"Am I doing on the switchboard this late at night?" Sophie finished for her with a sighing chuckle.

"Well, considering how big Vincent is on plenty of rest and exercise and... Did somebody get a visitation or anything?"

"If Messenger has been talking to Joan, she isn't talking. And if any other heavenly messengers have been visiting our other sisters, nobody else is talking. We've all just had this feeling... everyone stayed in tonight, pretty quiet, reading and studying instead of making it a popcorn and movie night. I came in here to check things before I went to bed. Timing is everything, sister dear."

"Yeah," Anne whispered. "Timing." She swallowed down a comment that Stoughton wasn't so far from Akron, they probably heard the gunshots, and her shriek of fury when Argus got shot.

"So, what are you going to do? I can guarantee, with the feeling in the house right now, everybody is going to come waltzing in here in another five, ten minutes, starting with Vincent. You'd think that man has the whole house bugged. There'll probably be a fight over who drives over to pick you up."

"I probably should come home, instead of heading for my apartment in Tabor. I talked to Mrs. Gordon when I stopped for all that rain, and she said she'd put my key in a crack in the brickwork on the porch, so I could get in no matter how late I arrived."

"But?" Sophie prodded.

"You mean besides the fact I don't have my truck? They offered me a cot in the back room here at the station. Then somebody's taking me to the vet to check on Argus first thing in the morning. I'll need to make arrangements to have him sent home." Her breath caught. "Once he's stable enough to travel."

Chapter Six

"Hey," Sophie murmured. "Argus is tough. And we're all praying for the both of you. You still have a lot of work to do, and you need Argus to do it. The Lord won't let you be deprived of your partner this early in the game."

"I hope so." Anne flinched at a new thought, but managed not to sob, though the stifled sound was like a sharp-edged lump in her throat.

What if this attack on her and Argus was a preliminary attack from Satan, to distract her and weaken her, so she couldn't do something very important in the weeks ahead? After all these years of healing and struggling and serving the Arc Foundation, Anne knew better than to dismiss that speculation as just a product of overwrought nerves.

"Well, I need to come home to restock. See what clothes I have left in my room, replace my computer. Good thing I sent in my last report from the road, huh?"

"Good thing you finally listened to me and made it a habit to back up everything over the Web. There's not a single thing on your hard drive you can't replace," Sophie added, her voice taking on that pedantic, lecturing tone she used to tease her "adopted" sisters when they resisted her directives for computer use and care. If Anne was standing in front of her right now, Sophie would finish with a nod and then stick her tongue out at her and add, "So there."

Anne fought a bubble of weary laughter. When she was tired and had been stressed out, she knew laughter could easily turn to tears. She refused to break down crying in the chilly locker room of a police station, no matter how cold, wet, bruising, and frightening a day she had endured. Better to wait until she was home at Quarry Hall in her own room, when she knew someone would sense her crying, even if they couldn't hear her with her face buried in her pillow, and come hold her.

Or maybe not. Some of the unassigned dogs at Quarry Hall, especially the half-grown pups, would find her room and gather around her. She didn't need Argus's absence to be emphasized by the presence of other warm, furry, loving bodies comforting her.

Her plans just a short time ago had been simple. Get to Tabor, find her apartment, get herself and Argus settled, go to bed, and sleep until noon. Or whenever Argus made her get out of bed. She would spend the day wandering Tabor, getting the feel of the place, and then find the old furniture store on Pearl Road that Xander Finley had made into Common Grounds Legal Clinic. She would spend the next few weeks observing Xander and his part-time associates in action, go to court with them, read through their case files, talk with court officials who dealt with them, and pray hard and often over what she had learned. Anne wasn't trained to understand the practice of law, but the leadership of the Arc Foundation was confident she would do a good job analyzing what Common Grounds needed to do, and how Arc should help in the growth of Xander's dream.

"Tabor is closer to Stoughton than Akron is. If the vet says Argus can't be moved... Well, maybe the best thing for me is to just get to work and stay close to him if he needs me. I'll need a rental to get around — "

"Uh huh. And just let those cars George has rebuilt sit and get dusty in the garage? Did that mugger hit you on the head? Or are you trying to get George riled enough he comes out of his secret sanctum and scolds you for how you treat his babies?"

"Sophie..." More laughter threatened in her throat, but it didn't hurt quite so badly to stifle the sound. Right now, she decided if she never met the mysterious George, a friend from Vincent's equally mysterious past, she would be perfectly happy. "Okay, I'll wait here until someone comes for me with a replacement. Seems like a waste of time, having two people do all that driving."

"What we do for family is never a waste of time. You're definitely worn out, because I know you have better sense than this."

"Yes, Mother..."

That startled chuckles out of Sophie, and Anne swore she could hear the chiming of the crystal beads in her multitude of braids. The sound relaxed her, helped soothe some of the aches that were more in her soul than her body.

"I'll wait until morning, because if anyone contacts George tonight, he'll fret. It's two hours to his place, and then back to you in Stoughton," Sophie said. "I'll get things started tonight, though. Okay if I call you about eight tomorrow? Let you get a good night's sleep."

Anne doubted she would do more than doze through the night, but she didn't tell Sophie that. Why give her reason to worry? Besides, someone would lecture if she confessed now that the nightmares had been creeping up on her, trying to drag her back into memories of the Ogre and the evil wizards who had hurt the innocent, trusting child she had been. Anne knew some people thought her a little odd, putting faerie tale labels on the traumatic events of her childhood. The tactic let her cope, let her deal with and examine the memories on her terms, in her territory, and her time. As long as she kept memories of the Black Prince close, ready to leap out and defend her, just like the mysterious man had done twice in her life, she could deal with it. And someday put the pain entirely behind her once and for all.

For almost half an hour after Sophie prayed with her and said goodbye, Anne huddled on the bench with her back against the chilly tile wall and let her thoughts roam where they would. She could barely follow them, ideas disintegrating before they were fully formed, flickering images from her past rising up from the darkness, confusing her, threatening to cast off the costumes she wrapped around them to make them bearable.

"Stupid," she scolded herself. What did she expect to feel and think, sitting there in the chill, with bloodstained clothes in front of her and the echoing silence of the showers to make her feel like a scene from a teen horror film?

The next room had that promised cot. It also had her backpack and her Bible. If she couldn't sleep, she could pray and read and try to put everything back into God's hands.

Maybe someday she would finally learn not to yank her troubles and pains *out* of God's hands, to try to deal with on her own. Life would be so much simpler then.

~~~~

Anne regarded the fast food restaurant sausage biscuit and hash brown cake and wished she had asked for a donut, instead. Didn't the police department believe in donuts, or were they too conscious of avoiding stereotypes? Then again, overdosing on sugar at 7:30am wasn't much of an alternative to grease and salt. She found swallowing hard, with her head still aching the way it was, but knew the food wouldn't get any easier to eat when it was cold. She said a silent prayer of thanks for a dry, safe place to sleep and warm food—especially coffee with double sugar and double cream—and the safety net of her family at Quarry Hall less than an hour away.

Soon she was licking the grease off the tips of the fingers of one hand while bending over to pick up her backpack and retrieve her Bible for some devotions.

"Anne?" Rhonda, the morning dispatcher, stepped away from the front desk and leaned over the side counter, gesturing to get Anne's attention in the little alcove where she had settled for the morning. On the other side of the room, with her back to the front doors, a petite black woman watched Anne with a smile. "Your ride is here."

She winced as she guessed all the phone calls that had been made, and how early the arranging and conferring had started, to make it possible for this woman who had to be Doria Holwood to get here from Tabor before Sophie called at the promised time. Anne got up, gathering up her trash with one hand and scooping up her backpack and the plastic grocery bags with her damp clothes and the remains of her groceries with the other. She hadn't been able to wash the bloodstains out completely, but she had been grateful to at least rinse them.

Her phone rang, of course. Doria laughed and stopped walking around the counter to meet her, giving her a semblance of privacy. Sophie. Anne was relieved to talk to her again, rather than Elizabeth or Vincent. That would make the situation too serious. If the leaders of Arc weren't worried about her, or even preparing to change her assignment, that meant everything would be fine.

"Mrs. Holwood is on her way —"

"Already here. Is something going wrong with getting a replacement?" Anne had yet to meet the mysterious George who worked miracles with Arc's motor pool. She only knew he had suffered some sort of brain damage that affected his personality, so he preferred to be alone and deal only with machines. He was a friend of Vincent's, and that was enough to recommend the man to her and stop her from worrying about any peculiarities.

"George decided to upgrade it to equal what you lost last night," Sophie said with a sigh. "His cars are his babies. Anyway, Mrs. H insisted on bringing you home, and arranging with Xander for transportation until your new truck is ready. She called this morning after getting the prayer list. It all works out. Be nice."

"What do you mean? I'm always nice." She waved with three free fingers at Doria and pointed at her phone, hoping the woman got the message that they were talking about her.

"Don't twist their brains into pretzels, okay?" Sophie laughed. "Their latest batch of foster kids are eager to meet you. Plan on being pestered, and Argus getting spoiled when you bring him up to join you. I'll call later to see how you're doing. Xander has your phone number, and he knows to contact you at the Holwoods', probably this afternoon. Vincent wants to know if you got an update on how Argus is doing, and if you at least broke the guy's face for shooting him."

"I think I broke a few ribs. Argus is going to be all right. He just can't walk for a while." Anne shivered, just thinking about those awful moments at the veterinarian, when the big dog's condition had finally been analyzed. She had never been so frightened, and so angry, in years.

The vet had actually started to recommend Argus be put to sleep, rather than make the extraordinary effort necessary to save his leg and repair the damage to lung and shattered ribs. Anne had refused. She knew a miracle when she saw it — if that bullet hadn't been slowed by Argus's leg, it would have gone through his ribs and lungs and heart and out his back like a stick through wet paper. She had refused, to the point of insisting on taking the dog to another vet, no matter how far away. That had impressed the man, enough that he promised to do the best he could.

When she talked with the vet this morning, Anne learned it had taken an hour of surgery to make the repairs.

She said goodbye to Sophie and continued walking around the front desk. Doria watched her, still smiling, concern in her big, liquid eyes. Anne had seen pictures of the Holwoods, but she just hadn't expected Doria to be so delicate, especially after hearing how she raised dozens of foster children and took care of a huge house, gardened, taught Sunday school, and headed several committees at her church.

"Anne?" Doria glanced at the dispatcher on desk duty, then took a few steps around to meet her. "We just found out this morning what happened."

"Sophie said." She waved her cell phone and stowed it in the front pocket of her backpack. "I really appreciate this, Mrs. Holwood. More than you can imagine."

"We're glad to help out. Joan is dear to us, and she considers all the girls at Quarry Hall her sisters, so that makes you dear to us, too. As strange as that may sound, since we've just met." She chuckled as she said it, soothing the prickling of discomfort that started to race down Anne's back. Her words called up too many echoes of people who had seemed accepting and generous at first glance, but then turned into quagmires and death traps when it was almost too late to get away from them. "And you're to call me Doria, all right? Mrs. Holwood is my mother-in-law and her mother-in-law, and so on." She winked.

"All right, Doria." Anne glanced at the dispatcher. The woman gave them both a puzzled little grin and stepped up to the counter. "Is it okay if I leave now?"

"Hey, you're not the criminal. Does everybody know where to get hold of you?" Rhonda asked.

The police and the vet both had her cell number, but just to be safe, Anne and Doria made sure they had the Holwoods' phone number and the number of Common Grounds, and the main number for the Arc Foundation.

"Are you feeling all right?" Doria asked, as they walked outside.

"Hmm? Fine."

"Dearie, I've raised a whole school's worth of teenagers, so don't try to pull something over on me. You're walking a little stiff, so I'd say you didn't sleep very well, and you're feeling the effects of fighting off that carjacker. You could use a long soak in a big, hot tub, and a decent breakfast and some clothes of your own instead of those borrowed rags, am I right?" She gave Anne a look that warned her not to try any nonsense.

"Yes, ma'am." Anne gave her a snappy little salute, making her laugh. The sound bounced off the buildings surrounding the police station.

"You keep that in mind, and I think we're going to get along just fine.

I'm taking you home with me for that soak and breakfast, and Joan assured me they would be sending more of your clothes up, so you'll be ready to go in no time. Since your apartment is right across the street from our house, we want you to feel free to walk on in when you need some advice or to do laundry or you have a hankering for lots of company. But let me warn you right now. Don't let any of our scapegrace kids talk you into helping with the chores. Everybody has a job to do, and they don't put it on anyone else's shoulders unless they have one foot in the grave." She nodded for emphasis as they reached a pale green van with stickers all across the back windows and doors, naming the various athletic organizations, bands, school groups, and colleges supported by the Holwoods and their numerous foster-children.

"What were Nikki's chores?" popped out before Anne could think.

Nikki James, Joan's half-sister and the Holwoods' foster-daughter, was constantly in the thoughts of everyone at Quarry Hall. They prayed for her, that she would be safe and return home voluntarily and soon. Anyone who was out on the road in any capacity kept an eye open for the runaway teen, to try to talk her into coming home.

"She helped me keep the others in line." Doria's laughter muted, softened by fading pain. Anne regretted doing that to her, but it was too late now, and she suspected she would only make things worse if she apologized.

"Well, I can hardly keep myself in line. How about if I help with the cooking?"

"Are you any good?" She opened the driver's side door and hit the button for the locks throughout the van.

"Nobody complains, and people take seconds." Anne scurried around to the other side and opened the door.

"Be careful. You might not be allowed to leave."

They both laughed as Anne threw her backpack in behind the seat and climbed in.

~~~~~

A black, older model Mustang waited out front of the Holwoods' house when Anne and Doria drove up half an hour later. Anne almost felt disappointed. She had liked looking at all the huge, ancient oaks and elms along the streets of Tabor, the Century homes, the small town/college town atmosphere of the place. She didn't want to lose the relaxed, comfortable feeling, to take in the next event in her already full schedule. But the man in the car got out as soon as the van pulled into the driveway and followed them up to the house.

He wore a dark suit, no vest, no tie. Wide shoulders and a smooth stride and lack of potbelly spoke of someone who maybe played sports instead of watching them on TV all the time. He had a rough kind of face, which Joan had very charitably described as "unfinished." Thick nose, thick eyebrows just a shade darker than his short-cropped head of hair. Square chin, just a shade too wide; deep-set eyes. He could only charitably be called homely, but there was something charming about the homeliness. Anne sensed strength in him, kindness in the gentle curves of his thick lips and a sparkle of humor in his mud-colored eyes. She had been out on the road a lot in the last eight or nine months, so she hadn't had a chance to meet Xander Finley, only heard about him from the other daughters of Quarry Hall and saw pictures of Joan's friend.

He shoved his hands into his pockets as he strode up the driveway to meet them, pulling back his jacket and revealing his pager and cell phone clipped to his belt. That spoke of a very busy lifestyle, completely contradicted by the easy swing of his steps. Whatever had brought him here to the Holwoods' house, it didn't make him impatient. Maybe he even welcomed the break.

"How are you, this gorgeous morning, Doria?" His voice rumbled, just a threat of cracking, in between tenor and baritone. Anne smiled, imagining him caught forever in the adolescent shift of voice.

"Need you ask? Since you're here already, I assume you got the story from Joan and didn't listen to a word she said," Doria responded with another of her warm chuckles. "Anne, this is —"

"Xander. I've seen pictures." Anne held out her hand to shake.

"Just as long as you haven't heard the stories." He grinned.

"Depends on the stories. Sophie called you?"

"And briefed me. You had a rough intro to the area, didn't you?" Xander looked her over, as if expecting to see residue from her bad night.

For the first time in she didn't know how long, Anne felt embarrassed about how she looked. She wanted to tell him that she had much nicer clothes in the back compartment of her truck. She almost bit her tongue off to keep from asking Doria to take her shopping, so she could replace her wardrobe. It didn't matter that she had clothes in her room at Quarry Hall, and when Vincent inevitably came up to check on her, he would bring them. The problem was that she had left those clothes at home because they either didn't fit, or she didn't really like them. Anne didn't have that many clothes on purpose. She had gone through a gluttony phase when she entered college, breaking free of her guardians, and had bought enough clothes and accessories to fill three dorm rooms. Once she got her head on straight, she had made a point of living simply.

Which meant the man who stole her truck had taken almost everything she owned in the world.

"Rough enough. But ready to get to work."

"Well, you're not taking Anne anywhere until she gets settled in. I know you, Xander, and despite that lovely girl who takes care of your entire office and probably keeps your personal life untangled, you're still one of those workaholics who think they can get by on cold coffee and stale donuts until dinner time," Doria announced, putting just the right measures of scolding and teasing in her voice. Anne wished she could learn that trick.

"Guilty!" Xander held up his hands in surrender.

"Then the two of you come inside and I'll fix some breakfast. The kids are gone until lunchtime, and Rance will be home soon to hear what's going on."

Doria hurried up the sidewalk to the back door and gestured for them to follow.

Once inside the house, she insisted that Anne search Nikki's drawers and closet for any clothes that would suit her, to hold her until her replacements came from Quarry Hall. Anne wondered what to think about this evidence that despite Nikki being gone more than a year now, her foster-parents kept her room waiting for her. Nor had they made a shrine of it, since they were willing to share her clothes. In a household that changed as regularly as the Holwoods' did, with so many foster children coming in and out, the natural thing would be to expect every bit of space to be grabbed up as soon as it became available.

Then Anne followed her hostess up the second flight of stairs in the big old Century house to the attic and revised some of her opinions and mental images. This would have been the servants' quarters, high up under the rafters. There were plenty of rooms on the floor below for foster children to stay in. She had caught a glimpse of them as she followed Doria down the hall. Big rooms with bunk beds and lots of space for toys and desks and a place for everyone to claim as their own. Upstairs, tucked up just under the sky, Nikki's room turned out to be more than half the top floor, the ceiling slanting in where the eaves came down. Windows touched the floor, and furniture was tucked in wherever there was room for it to stand up. The walls were filled with bookshelves wherever boards could be crammed in, dotted with stuffed animals, pictures, trophies, and ribbons. Third place in the spelling bee in sixth grade. Honorable mention in a school district-wide creative writing contest. Second place in the foot races at the Sunday school picnic. It gave her a better picture of Nikki, whom Joan had described to everyone on the road for Arc, in case they ran into her runaway sister.

Chapter Seven

The room also gave Anne a sense of how the Holwoods thought and felt. They had faith their daughter would come home, and her place was ready and waiting. They knew how hurt Nikki would be if she came home and found her place changed, given to someone else, even if through common sense. They knew she would hurt because the empty spot she created hurt them, too.

Anne set her backpack on the desk chair, tucked her cell phone into the baggy pocket of her borrowed pants, slung her sweater over the back of the desk chair, and hurried back downstairs. She would save that long soak in the tub and looking through Nikki's wardrobe for after breakfast.

Xander was helping Doria set the table in the big kitchen that jutted out of the back of the house. The Holwoods had taken out the wall between the kitchen and the back porch, after enclosing it, making it one huge common room. Anne paused in the doorway, studying the massive wooden table, a baker's dozen of mismatched chairs, and the big sash windows overlooking the tree-lined back yard. She imagined a handful of foster children doing their homework in here, helping bake cookies, learning to sew, coming inside through that heavy, old-fashioned screen door with their assorted bumps and bruises, and excited discoveries.

The only thing missing was a dog or two. But a dog wouldn't be good in a household that changed so much. Dogs needed to bond with people, and dogs with any brains became very possessive and protective of their people. Argus would be positively schizoid if she forced him to stay in a household where the members changed from month to month. He wouldn't know who to protect, who to accept, who to drive away. If he latched onto someone in particular to love, he would be hurt when that person left, taken away by the vagaries of the child welfare system.

Besides, she didn't think she could take the presence of a dog right now, with Argus still teetering on the edge at the vet's office. If he weren't under sedation, to keep him from tearing stitches open, she would be with him. Argus had been there for her when she was lost and alone, and struggling out of darkness, so she would be there for him.

When he was awake, and when she didn't have a job to do. Sometimes being responsible positively reeked.

"I hope you like waffles," Doria said, turning around to see Anne in the doorway.

"Love 'em. Can I help with anything?"

"An empty hand would be wonderful." She beckoned and stepped over to the open refrigerator. In moments, Anne had her arms full, cradling containers of butter and applesauce, jelly, whipped cream, sliced ham, three kinds of cheese, and a little carton of chocolate flavored coffee cream. "What's that grin for, young lady?" She winked, taking the bite out of her scolding tone.

"This looks like the kind of feast we have at home. No wonder Joan just laughed the first time we raided the kitchen at one in the morning, after she moved in, and then told us to wait until we had met you."

"Uh huh. She's been to some of our infamous breakfast parties. Did she tell you what we do with waffles around here?"

"Waffles?" a deep, resonant voice like a Shakespearean actor's boomed from the back door. Dr. Holwood stood with his hand on the latch of the screen, looking in at them. "My dear, you are trying to either impress these poor people or frighten them away. No one in the world eats waffles like we do." He opened the door and stepped inside. He slid his briefcase into an open spot behind the coat rack next to the door and extended a massive hand to Xander. "Good to see you again. I see you're here to look after Anne — or is it to drag her off to work ASAP?"

"Guilty of both." Xander chuckled and shook hands with Dr. Holwood and turned as Doria cleared her throat.

"Give me a moment, my dear. I'm working my way through the room." He winked at Anne and held out a hand.

Yes, Anne decided, he did look a lot like James Earl Jones, just like Joan had said. But there was something a little less formal about the man, frosted more with silver and snow than the dignified actor. She had an image of Dr. Holwood very easily getting down on the floor with the smallest of his foster children and playing dolls with them, having tea parties, filling in for the horses of their imagination, even building play huts in the back yard with crates and boards and blankets.

"Anne, I'm very glad to meet you, and very sorry that it has to be under such circumstances." His hand was gentle, despite the bulk of it; firm, not flabby. He was a scholar, but Anne felt calluses from manual labor.

"I think I've finally found the rainbow in this particular storm cloud, sir." Anne grinned when her hosts chuckled at her words. "I can't tell you how grateful I am that you're looking after me like this. I mean, I do have a place waiting across the street, but — "

"After what you went through, you need to be with people," Doria said, putting an arm around Anne's shoulders. "Now, let's get this feast of ours put together before it's too late for breakfast and too early for lunch."

"I have the feeling I'm going to regret this." Xander put down the last fork he had been holding. "I have a pre-trial hearing downtown this afternoon, and if I eat too much, I might just fall asleep. Judge Anselm is friendly, but not that friendly."

"She was the one who heard that ridiculous case against you, am I right?" Dr. Holwood asked. "I remember the subject coming up in prayer meetings a few times." He stepped over to a closet and opened it, revealing shelves of pots and pans, mixing bowls, electrical appliances and big clear plastic containers of what looked like flour, sugar, tea bags and cereal.

"Too right. The Lord was really looking out for me that day. I was originally scheduled to go before Judge Hooper, and he thinks every case deserves to be heard no matter how stupid it is. He also hates charity lawyers—it takes money away from 'honest lawyers,' as he calls them."

"Excuse me," Anne said. She stepped over and took the waffle iron from Dr. Holwood when he drew it from the labyrinth of cords and handles and gleaming stainless steel. "What are you talking about?"

Xander explained while they worked together to fix their late breakfast. He had a policy of investigating every case before he agreed to take it. He adjusted his fees to meet the financial abilities of the people who came to Common Grounds for help. If the people could not afford legal representation, his costs and salary were paid by the Arc Foundation's funds. Also, if Xander felt cases were frivolous or prospective clients lied to him, he refused to represent them. After only three years of this practice, he had a reputation for thoroughness, fairness, and ethics. As a result, some cases had been thrown out of court after the presiding judge heard that Common Grounds had refused to help the plaintiff. Just over a year ago, Xander was sued by a man who claimed his case was damaged because Common Grounds refused to represent him. It didn't matter that everyone who investigated his claims believed his case was a nuisance suit, a claim for fame and nothing more. Nor did it matter that the judge first heard from the plaintiff's own lips that Xander had refused to take the case, because the man hoped to lodge a complaint against Common Grounds.

When the man filed his suit against Xander, he made as much fuss and noise as he could, trying to get the media on his side. The *Tabor Picayune* had led several other media sources by refusing to simply take the story as the man presented it. The paper had gone the extra mile and dug into the plaintiff's background, showing he had a history of such cases. No one said it outright, but they hinted broadly enough that the man fabricated as many unpleasant incidents as he could, so he could bring lawsuits. He spent so much time in court, he didn't have a job and had been denied unemployment because he *wouldn't*, rather than *couldn't*, hold a steady job. He basically made a very good living suing other people. He drove a Cadillac and had a cabin cruiser on Lake Erie. Xander drove a five-year-old Mustang that he bought used, lived in a sparsely furnished condo in Medina, and his only recreational vehicle was a ten-speed bicycle he rode through the Metroparks three times a week.

"Judge Hooper has made quite a few statements to the press about the questionable ethics of Common Grounds. Some people have accused him of being snatched from the Dark Ages, when innocence was determined by tests like dunking. If you didn't drown, you were a witch, and if you drowned you were considered innocent. He's made it clear in his actions and his speeches from the bench that if someone can't afford representation, that means they're not contributing members of society, meaning they're lazy and selfish, along with whatever crime they're accused of. That makes Common Grounds an enemy of the common good, because we help people who can't afford anything but overworked, assembly line public defenders. He was pretty upset he didn't get the case—I think he wanted to slap me around. Legally, of course," Xander added with a grin as they settled down at the table. "You eat like this all the time?"

The waffles were stacked twelve high, steaming on a platter in the middle of the table. The Holwoods didn't eat waffles the traditional way, with butter and syrup, as Dr. Holwood demonstrated when he proceeded to make a sandwich out of his, with fried ham and cheese.

"Not all the time, no. But sometimes a little feast is good for the soul," Doria said.

"You know, something is starting to come back to me. We just don't have the time to read all the briefings that come through the offices at Arc," Anne said slowly. She contented herself with applesauce, butter and maple syrup for her waffles. "Somebody tried to sue you one other time. About two years ago, just when you were starting out? For misuse of public funds?"

Xander nodded, grimacing a little. She had asked her question just as he had filled his mouth with his first bite. Anne grinned and shrugged apology. She liked the way his eyes sparkled with laughter and his face didn't turn red as he hurried to chew and swallow.

"The suit alleged that we had no right to deny representation to anyone, even though records clearly showed the plaintiff was... sorry, I guess I'm gearing up for this afternoon. The woman who wanted our help had a long criminal record. Even before my staff started to investigate, we were pretty sure she would turn out to be the guilty party, not the victim."

"Like the guy who broke into someone's house in the middle of the night, tripped over some toys, and then tried to sue the homeowner because he broke his leg?" she hazarded.

"Exactly. We refused, and she went screaming to the papers that since we were funded with government money—her money, as a taxpayer—we didn't have the right to refuse."

"You got a lot of good publicity with that story," Dr. Holwood rumbled from his end of the table. He saluted Anne with his mug of tea. "When the story broke that the clinic was privately funded by contributions from churches and charitable organizations, and not a drop of public money, that raised quite a fuss. The lawyer bringing the case was also ridiculed for not doing his homework before filing and wasting the court's time."

"And the plaintiff was thrown into jail a month later for not paying her taxes for the last ten years," Xander added with a chuckle. "Someone at the *Picayune* got ticked off at her constant referrals to 'wasting my money as a taxpayer,' and investigated."

"Sounds like the *Picayune* causes a lot of firestorms," Anne said.

"No," Dr. Holwood said, frowning at his waffle sandwich and moving slowly, with the precision of a surgeon as he opened it and spread more mustard on it. "Andrew and Angela Coffelt are truly dedicated to truth, and they are heartily offended if someone suggests they only report the pleasant or sensational half of the story, and leave the uncomfortable or boring parts out."

"That usually sends them digging deeper," Xander added with a grin.

"From what Joan and her father have told us," Doria said, "that's somewhat how Arc works, isn't it? If there's even a hint the whole story isn't being told, or something is too good to be true, you start digging."

"We dig whether we suspect something is being buried or not. It's our policy. So no one can accuse us of favoritism," Anne responded.

"Like with me." Xander looked around the table. "I know Joan's dad said they had already been investigating me and considering supporting my dream before she joined the Arc Foundation, but sometimes I feel a little odd over all the support I've been getting. You know how nice it is to be able to hire some people to help with the load? And now that I've had Hannah working with me for nearly a year, I can't imagine how I managed without her. She's a miracle-worker."

"And you'll be able to hire more miracle workers once I do a thorough report. We aren't going to treat this investigation like a formality. That's how we do it at Arc."

"Hands-on and low-key," Dr. Holwood said. "Admirable. I've met only four or five of you now, and I'm still amazed at all the work you do. And, with so little fanfare."

"That's the way we prefer it. The more people who are watching and commenting on what you do, the slower it goes and the less you get done. We work quietly, we work in the background, we get things done, and we get out with as little fuss as possible. Do your good deeds in secret, so only your Heavenly Father knows and rewards you in secret."

"Which is why Arc supports Alexander the Great, here," he added, with another salute of his tea mug.

"Alexander the Great?" Anne decided she liked this. Especially when Xander blushed.

"A nickname that got hung on him this past spring, when my evening composition class was discussing a community project that Xander supported with free legal advice. Hannah Blake is in the class," the big man explained. "Xander's first full-time employee."

"Without Hannah, where would I be?" Xander said. "I just wish she... I wish she wouldn't put me up on a pedestal so often. I have this nightmare of falling off and hurting her one of these days."

"Just as long as you don't land on her," Anne muttered. That earned chuckles from everyone.

~~~~~

Xander insisted on taking Anne to a general practitioner friend of his, just to make sure she really was all right after the excitement of the night before. She agreed, but only after he swore he had work in his briefcase to keep him busy while she was in the examination room, so he wasn't losing valuable work time. That meant changing her long soak in the bath to a quick shower, but she felt much better with fresh clothes and didn't silently complain too much. It helped that she and Nikki seemed to be the same size and shape, and pretty much shared their taste in clothes.

The doctor pronounced her fine, other than a few bruises and not enough sleep. Xander reluctantly dropped her off to settle into her apartment, after making sure she had all the numbers where he could be reached if his cell phone didn't work. Then he headed back to his office to get some work done before his afternoon court date.

Two hours later, after finding Heinke's, stocking her refrigerator, and finding the bus schedules and routes, Anne settled into the front seat of the bus that would take her down Pearl Road and leave her in front of Xander's office. She was pleased and slightly uncomfortable to discover either her landlady or Doria had filled her cupboards with canned and boxed food, so all she had to buy were fresh fruit, vegetables, and milk. There was bread and frozen dinners and even ice cream in her freezer, and whoever had done the shopping made very good guesses as to what she liked. Then she called Quarry Hall and found Su-Ma on switchboard duty. She had to report on Xander, whom some members of the Arc Foundation had yet to meet.

"He's kind of overbearing," Anne reported. There was a faint echo when she spoke, meaning her report was being recorded. "But a good overbearing. He cares and he wants things done right and he's not going to let etiquette get in the way, you know?"

"Sounds too good to be true," Su-Ma responded, with a hint of chiming laughter in her voice. "Elizabeth says for today, just take it easy. If you're bored, you can hang around the clinic, talk to people. Pay more attention to what people say to and about him than what he says or what he's doing. That's the real test of how his ministry is performing."

"She's had questions about him?" Anne frowned, not liking the flicker of apprehension that went through her. She always second-guessed her first impressions of people, but she didn't have the slightest doubt about her impressions of Xander Finley. That was odd. She usually never let herself like anyone without reservation on the first meeting. Maybe she accepted Xander at face value just because he was Joan's friend?

"The Advisory Board wants to grow Common Grounds to the point that it can offer internships for law students who think as Xander does, to train them, let them get their hands dirty before they lose their ideals. Let them see that what he says and what he does are the same thing. That his standards and practices do work."

"That's great," she breathed. Then Anne had to repeat herself. It was hard to be heard over the grinding and roaring of the big bus as it bounced down a section of Pearl Road where repair work was in progress. "So this is more than just the standard check, before we give him money to bring on more staff."

"Well, you've been away, so you haven't overheard some of the most recent stupidity," Su-Ma admitted, her voice dragging.

"I can guess. Ex-members of the board are making trouble again?"

"That self-appointed financial accountability group has been sniffing around again. We're dotting I's and crossing T's that aren't even there, to keep them from raising a ruckus where they have no right. Uncle Harrison made some remark about using Brother Andrew's tactics against these Pharisees. Do you have any idea what he was talking about?"

Anne had to wrack her brains for a few moments. It took an effort of will to get past the surge of fury at the group that had appointed themselves watchdogs for any charitable organization that called itself Christian. Whenever they demanded an organization open its books for their examination, and were refused, they set up an all-out campaign to discredit the organization and encourage Christians everywhere to boycott them by halting all donations. Such tactics didn't affect the Arc Foundation because all funding came from the Carters' private funds and multiple trusts, and they had enough legal layers and loopholes to protect that money for the next century. They didn't take donations, and were careful to send back checks they received, rather than simply tearing them up. However, any interest from the press was considered a problem, a nuisance, and a threat to the safety of the people who worked for the Arc Foundation. Quite a few had dark pasts, dangerous secrets, and previous identities they preferred not to have investigated.

"I hope Sophie follows through on her threat and starts digging into their backgrounds," she said, while still trying to remember the story of Brother Andrew.

"Wouldn't it be great if she uncovered all sorts of stupidity and hypocrisy, and rocked their foundations for a change? Give them a taste of what they're trying to do to us," Su-Ma said, her words warped by her chiming giggles.

"Not too much, though. Just enough to shut them up and teach them some humility. The last thing we need is more in-fighting among Christians to get into the press. Oh—yeah!" Anne nearly laughed, as the information she wanted popped to the front of her mind. "Brother Andrew smuggled Bibles into Communist countries. He prayed for the border guards to be blind."

"Oh, pooh. That's no fun. I was hoping it'd be something more drastic."

"Like what?"

"I don't know. Make them mute. Give them mono for a year. Raise up another organization that would hound them. The principle of who's watching the watchers, you know? Keep them so busy they wouldn't get in our way anymore." She sighed. "The board's lighting up. It's probably one of them calling back to insist on an appointment, even though everybody is tied up until next week. Please tell me you have something you want to add to your report?"

"I'm done, and you need to answer the phone. Shame on you. Give my love to everybody." Anne let herself laugh softly as Su-Ma made her farewells and hung up. The laughter died as she looked at her phone and thought about a phone call she needed to make, wanted to make, yet dreaded.

Chapter Eight

Finally Anne called the vet in Stoughton. The call was short by necessity, because he had a waiting room full of patients and their owners. Argus was stable. He was also fighting the sedatives. That didn't surprise Anne at all. She needed to spend some time with her companion, stroking him and talking to him, to convince him she was all right. What bothered her more was the strong impression the doctor was still torn between relief at Argus's survival and believing he had wasted his time and effort. Anne wasn't about to waste her time explaining that Argus was not just her dog but her bodyguard, her confidante, her guardian angel, and a big, warm teddy bear to hold and keep her nightmares away. If she could have, she would have donated her own blood.

All that mattered, though, was that Argus would live. The vet didn't want to move him for at least a week. If the problem had just been a shattered bone, he would have let Anne take him home to Quarry Hall in a few days. If it had just been the blood loss, the same. If it had just been the broken ribs, maybe a week. But Argus had multiple injuries and he wasn't reacting well to either the anesthetic the doctor had used, the antiseptics and antibiotics, or the tranquilizers needed to keep him from aggravating his injuries. He was one sick dog.

Anne dug through her backpack for the thick sheaf of bus schedules she had picked up at the customer service counter at Heinke's when she bought her bus pass. It didn't take long to figure out the bus schedules to take her south to Stoughton. She had to get to Argus, would probably need to go spend time with him on a regular basis, and she didn't want to ask Doria to shuttle her around. Why did George have to be so finicky right now, and insist on giving her a truck exactly outfitted like the stolen one?

"Duh," she whispered, after stopping to close her eyes and press her fingers against her temples to ease the pressure of a growing headache. The movement reminded her of praying—which she hadn't been doing often enough lately. How many times did God have to hit her with the proverbial two-by-four before she sat up and paid attention?

Anne bowed her head and pressed her knuckles into her eyes. She focused her thoughts on Argus, the way she had seen him just after the vet's first anesthetic shot began to work relaxing the shivering dog's clenched muscles. Her companion had never made a sound, never snapped at anyone, but watched Anne the entire time they loaded him into the police van and drove them to the vet's and unloaded him. The movement had to hurt, but he stayed focused on her, trusting her to help him.

Just like Anne had to trust God.

"Please, Lord?" she whispered, breaking out of the cycle of her fear and anger for her companion. The sound of her own voice startled her a little. Anne was never very good at praying aloud. She always stayed silent during group prayer, and tried to duck behind others when someone was looking for a volunteer to lead.

Rubbing more threats of tears from her eyes, she sat up and looked around. This certainly looked like a shopping area on both sides of the street. There was the Einstein Bros bagel shop Xander had told her to use as a landmark, indicating she was getting close. There was the sign showing the intersection of Pearl and West 130th. A big wooden sign with the symbols of various civic groups announced the bus had just entered the city of Padua. Anne got up and made her way slowly to the front of the bus, holding onto the bar that ran from front to back. She nearly panicked for a moment when she couldn't find the cord to pull to request a stop. They didn't expect riders to verbally request a stop in this part of Ohio, did they? Then she spotted it, tucked up against the top frame of the sliding windows, both materials nearly the same shade of gray. She pulled it and relaxed a little when a chime rang through the bus and red lights appeared over front and back doors and the driver's seat.

Just as Xander said, the bus stopped directly across the street from the furniture-store-turned-office. Through the big display windows, Anne saw cubicles and divider walls blocking the rest of the office from view, and a few people at work. She walked a dozen yards or so to the intersection and waited for the light to change.

A young man who looked more like a college student than a practicing lawyer hurried up to the front, clutching several envelope folders to his chest, in response to the rusty-sounding bell that rang out when Anne walked in the front door. He glanced at the big desk tucked into the front portion of the office. It was empty, and from the neatness of it, Anne guessed the person who normally sat there wasn't in the office. She had heard a few things about Hannah Blake, Xander's paralegal and office manager, and assumed she was out running errands.

"Can I help you?" the man said, letting his folders slide down onto a table set up between Hannah's desk and what looked like a makeshift kitchen tucked in the corner of the front area. It had a cube refrigerator under a table, hot plate, coffee maker, and boxes of cookies on the table, and cups, spoons, and other supplies on shelving next to the table.

"I'm here to see Xander Finley." She went blank for a moment, not sure if it was all right to tell people she was from the Arc Foundation.

Quite often, knowing they were being observed and assessed made people uneasy and unable to function normally. At the women's shelter, everyone but Jocelyn had thought she was just another volunteer, earning college lab credits for her social work degree. But this situation was different, Anne decided. She held out her hand. "I'm Anne Hachworth, from the Arc Foundation."

A moment later, a bubble of laughter escaped her when he looked her up and down. Dressy jeans, sneakers, backpack, a lavender-gray shirt and a sporty gray jacket obviously didn't match what he expected from the foundation that helped support Common Grounds. Or maybe it was because she was around his age.

"Sorry," he said, finally, grasping her hand. He colored just enough to be noticeable against his dark blonde hair and eyebrows. "Xander told us what happened, but I just didn't make the connections. How's your dog?"

"Better, thanks." She bit her tongue against adding that she'd feel better about Argus's chances if he wasn't being tended by a veterinarian who seemed to attend the Kevorkian school of veterinary medicine. Why did people always take the "put the poor thing out of its misery" attitude with injured animals? She wanted to ask the vet if he would recommend putting a human being with the same injuries "to sleep."

"Come on back," he said, releasing her hand. "It's just the two of us in here right now. I'm Rick Solomon, by the way." He turned and gestured down the long hallway between divider walls. "The other four part-timers are out filing motions, doing research and interviews or heading to classes. Case Western has a great law school, so it's good positioning for Xander to be set up here. Lots of cheap labor."

"Cheap doesn't mean sloppy or second-rate," Xander called from a cubicle that was four times the size of the others, at the edge of shadows and open space, with a red-lit exit sign lost in the shadows. He half-rose from his desk, beckoning for Anne to come in. "They get hands-on experience toward their degrees, and I get work done by people still excited about the law. It's a win-win for everyone."

"Keep talking like that, boss, and you'll never get rid of any of us." Rick tipped a salute off the end of his right eyebrow and headed back down the hallway.

"Who says I want to?" he called, getting a snicker in response. Xander settled back down at his desk and picked up a handful of papers. "He's the first one I'm offering a job, once this current crop graduates. If he can afford to keep working for me full-time. Not that I'm putting any pressure on you to give me a good evaluation, of course."

"Of course." Anne grinned as she settled into a chair in front of his desk and let her backpack slide to the floor.

"Hannah is busy downtown, following up on paperwork that should have been delivered by courier yesterday. Otherwise I'd have her give you the grand tour, give you an idea of who's working here, their duties, our plans for the rest of this cavern of ours."

He hooked a thumb over his shoulder into the empty darkness behind him. "This is a prime location. I can't remember how many years I've driven down Pearl, watching this spot, seeing one business after another come in, open for a few months, then close up. It wasn't a good spot for their businesses, with the location of the parking lot and the traffic and everything else, but I realized it was perfect for me. And the landlord was so desperate for someone to be here, to keep up the property values, he took my low bid and hasn't raised my rates. Yet."

Xander pressed his hands together in a praying gesture, earning a grin from Anne. "I wanted this spot even before I realized I might have a chance of making a go of Common Grounds. Heck, before I even had the name. Did Joan tell you how we came up with it?"

"She mentioned something about staying up too late, the three of you working on a killer paper for some professor you all referred to as Attila. You were all blitzed on fancy coffees and chocolate, staying up too late, and when you woke up the next morning, you had the name written across the front page of your paper."

"Ouch. Forgot that detail. I barely had time to print up a new first page," he said, his grin widening. "Yeah, those were great days, evening classes, Joan and Matt and me. Now, I'm too busy for... well, God is making it pretty clear my dream is inside His plan for me. We're overflowing with work."

"Let's see about increasing the funding, so you can add more people and fill up the rest of the building." She shook her head when he opened his mouth to speak. "I know, we have to be completely by the book. I won't let the fact that you're Joan's pal influence me. However, once you meet Argus, his reaction to you will influence me."

"Yeah, I've seen Ulysses at work, and I've heard how your dogs work, reading people, guiding you away from trouble. Too bad our judges don't have Arc Foundation dogs on the bench with them, helping them make the right decisions."

Rick left, taking all the folders with him, by the time Xander finished giving her a tour of the office and explained how the revolving shifts of volunteers, interns and part-timers combined into a smoothly functioning whole. Two interns came in to pick up research assignments and talk with Xander over some questions they had found in several cases while Anne familiarized herself with the financial records. She forgot their names ten seconds after they introduced themselves and headed out again. She found it amusing that there was a definite divide between when Xander kept the records for the clinic and when Hannah took over, in terms of neatness, organization, and clarity of notations in the ledgers. She decided Xander wasn't kidding when he said he didn't know how he would survive if Hannah ever left him.

The afternoon passed quickly, with voices seeping over the divider walls from time to time as clients came in for meetings. Hannah called just after two to report that the police in Hyburg had contacted her about one of their clients. A man claiming to be the client's fiancé—after only four dates—had violated the latest restraining order and tried to take her son, as he was walking home from kindergarten. There was never an engagement, but he insisted the mother owed him for "emotional damage" and wanted the boy as recompense. Hannah was taking the two victims to a shelter in Columbus. She would meet Xander Downtown in the morning.

"She does a lot of hands-on work, doesn't she?" Anne observed, as Xander went over the bare bones of the case. She shuddered, wondering what kind of debt that mentally sick man would have demanded if there had been more than four dates.

Their client had broken it off with the man when he decided to move in with her, broke into her house, and started tossing everything into the yard that he didn't want to have in "his" household. He insisted that they were soul-mates, then counter-sued for slander and libel when she filed the restraining order against him.

"Hannah is a gift from God. I'm good at reading people in the courtroom, sensing when there's information someone is trying to hide, that could change the case. But Hannah... she senses what they need. She gives our work a personal and personalized touch. More than just the legal aspects of our clients' lives. She's so good with people, it's a miracle I got anywhere before she showed up and became the face of Common Grounds." Xander shrugged. "Lucky I didn't send people running, when I was the face."

"Don't sell yourself short. Nobody trusts lawyers who look like movie stars with ten million dollars of plastic surgery. They figure pretty boys spend all their time looking in the mirror and worrying about more money to pay the bills, instead of their clients."

"Uh huh. Never thought about it that way." He slouched in his chair. For a moment, when his smile wavered, Anne glimpsed a bone-deep exhaustion. If Hannah gave extra for their clients, Xander gave ten times as much.

He didn't complain. Didn't wave a flag to get people to notice just how much he sacrificed. Anne made a mental note of that and resolved to have a long talk with Joan and compare notes on what she had observed. For the sake of fairness, she couldn't slap the file closed and declare

Common Grounds had passed the evaluation, just based on what she had seen today. But she wanted to.

Xander had a meeting in Stoughton at 4:30, and offered to take Anne to the vet to spend some time with Argus. She gladly accepted, needing to get out of the office and clear her mind of all the paperwork she had been examining as much as she needed to see her dog.

The vet assured her Argus was doing better than expected. Anne sat in front of the cage with the door wide open, her hand resting on his head while he slept under sedation, positive he would feel her presence. She scribbled notes to herself about everything she had seen and learned about Common Grounds, the questions that had come to her, and tried to outline the beginning of her formal report. If she could start putting it together now, that would save time later, at the end of her assessment.

At five, the vet apologetically asked her to leave, since he was shutting the doors for the night. An intern stayed at night, monitoring the animals in various stages of treatment and recovery, but for security reasons no one else was allowed in the building. Anne could understand that, but that didn't help her fight the need to grumble. She was still silently complaining when she got off the bus and walked from Sackley down Church Street to her apartment.

Vincent sat on the front steps, talking on his cell phone, watching her as she came down the sidewalk. He hooked his thumb over his shoulder, gesturing down the driveway. Anne looked, half-expecting to see her truck, miraculously recovered overnight. A little dark green sedan sat in the gravel parking area behind the house. He waved for her attention, tossed the keys to her almost before she had turned back to him, and kept talking on the phone. Anne grinned and shook her head and went to investigate the car.

A suitcase sat in the back seat. Someone had gone through her closet and drawers, harvesting the few clothes she had left in her room at Quarry Hall. Even more important, a round, dark green storage tub the size of a small hat box sat on top of the suitcase. Brooklyn had sent along some bakery. Anne yanked the door open and pushed the seat forward to get at that tub. Buckeyes, chocolate chip and citrus coolers, and shortbread dipped in chocolate. All her favorites and as effective as a long, warm hug from Brooklyn. She sighed in satisfaction, and the aroma wafting up from the container made her stomach rumble.

Anne hauled the suitcase and tub upstairs to her apartment and made sure to stash the bakery where she couldn't get at it easily. She was more than capable of devouring the entire inventory of treats in one sitting if she wasn't careful. The stairs creaked and the door groaned open as she spread the suitcase on her bed, preparing to put away her clothes.

"Where did that car come from?" she asked, turning around to see

Vincent lean into the doorframe, watching her.

"George." He gave a little shrug. His gaze rested on her, heavy and assessing.

"Xander made me go to a doctor this morning."

"Good. How's your head?"

She knew he wasn't talking about physical damage. "Still processing." Anne tossed down a handful of white tube socks and turned to settle on the edge of the bed. "I know last night is exactly why Argus is with me, what you train all our dogs for, but it still makes me so mad. And makes me feel so helpless. I just..." She shuddered, and prayed Vincent could read what she meant in her face.

"The police report said you got some licks in on the guy."

"Not enough."

"That's a matter of opinion. It's a good bet he won't go after supposedly unarmed little girls in dark parking lots without having second thoughts. George has taken it into his head you're going to get your truck back, so it's a waste of time to fix up a new one for you. He says to just keep your eyes open and wait." He shrugged with a "what can you do?" expression of fond exasperation.

"Does he have prophetic dreams like Kathryn?"

"Nope. George is operating on childlike faith. Nothing more and nothing less." He finally pushed off the doorframe and stepped over to grasp her shoulders. It took all her self-control not to close her eyes while he studied her. "Sometimes it's hard to remember what he was like in the bad old days, when he wouldn't take anything on faith, not even the fact the sun was going to rise in the morning."

"Bad old days?" she prompted, nearly dropping to a whisper.

"Extremely bad no-good rotten awful bad old days." He winked and gave her a single shake before releasing her. She had passed whatever test he had conducted. "The bottom line is that George got badly hurt by people who tried to kill him to stop him from doing some pretty horrific things. Bad enough to give him brain damage, so when he woke up he was a child in a man's body, and looking about thirty years older, to boot."

"You were friends, back then?"

"Little bird... George and me, we were so evil, so far from God's grace, there wasn't anything worthwhile in us to be friends *with*. Closer than brothers and hating each other almost as much as we hated ourselves." He offered her a thin smile and wrapped an arm around her shoulders, guiding her out of the bedroom. "The thing to remember is we're both on God's team now. How we got there ... doesn't matter." They headed down the stairs. "In a couple days, George will forget whatever makes him think you don't need a new truck, and he'll get back to work. Sophie's going to take a few days to replace your computer. She's tied up with another hacking attempt."

"Maybe the guy who took my truck is using... no, the moment he turned on my computer," she said as they stepped outside, "the GPS would lead you right to it. Meaning he hasn't found it in the hidden compartment." She shrugged. "Blame the really long day."

"Long day and night," Joan said, from almost the same spot where Vincent had been sitting. She held out her arms, and Anne gladly stepped into them for a long, hard hug.

Looking over Joan's shoulder, she saw several children playing in the front yard of the Holwood house with Ulysses, and Joan's Jeep parked in the driveway. That made sense. Joan had driven up with Vincent, and while he waited for her to come back to the house, she had visited with the Holwoods, probably updating them on the search for Nikki.

Joan didn't ask about the progress of Anne's assignment. She was more concerned with Argus and whether they should leave him with the vet or risk his stability and take him home to Quarry Hall to recuperate there. By the time the three of them finished catching up and going over the carjacking, Doria had come over to invite them all to dinner. Vincent and Joan declined, because of evening meetings at Quarry Hall and left soon after that.

Anne hurried upstairs to wash up and change her clothes, and then crossed the street to help put dinner together. She assembled a salad, as Doria flitted back and forth between the stove and the table, supervising Asian twin sisters doing their homework, while a senior high boy with Down's syndrome tried to set the table around them. From time to time, she stepped into the living room to check on two more boys playing Risk on the floor, right in the traffic area.

"Just like home," Anne said with a grin, when Doria came back into the kitchen, wiped her face with her sleeve and sighed.

"What was your family like?"

Chapter Nine

"Oh, I'm not... I'm talking about Quarry Hall. It's huge and we don't have much of a staff. Everybody pitches in and does the office work, as well as the cleaning and cooking and taking care of the critters. Joan's told you what it's like, hasn't she?"

"A little bit. We've met her father and stepmother. Of course, most of our communication deals with following up on leads about Nikki." Doria shrugged and made a visible effort to be cheerful. "She has said a few times that it's better to experience the house than to hear about it."

"That's true. You ought to see the place when most of us are there. For a house so big, it really does get crowded. And the noise!" She caught the twins watching her and stuck her tongue out at them. They giggled and turned back to their homework.

"How many of you are there?" she asked a few seconds later, after bringing the bowl of strawberry gelatin and fruit cocktail out of the refrigerator.

"Well... the last time I took a head count..." Anne frowned over the cold, boiled potatoes she was slicing into neat little circles. They would be fried in Italian dressing, and she found she looked forward to trying them.

"Something wrong?"

"Hmm? No, it's just that... well the nearest I recall, there are about two dozen of us. The numbers vary. Not many of us are based out of Quarry Hall. Some are full-time investigators, practically living on the road. Some are couriers. Some things are just better handled by hand-delivered packages, rather than trusting to email or faxes, or even the post office. We have liaisons with some major evangelistic organizations, and they're based at those headquarters rather than here in Ohio.

"Of course, we haven't been in existence that long. I know Joan and Uncle Harrison are talking about expanding, having representatives in every state, finding out where help is needed most, being ready to jump in and lend a hand during a crisis, like after floods and earthquakes and such." Anne picked up the cutting board to slide the last of the potatoes into the pan. "Start cooking these?"

"Please. Rance will be home soon, and the boys have to scoot over to church for basketball practice. I truly do miss summer, even though I had the children underfoot most of the time. At least we had some time!" She winked and stepped over to the door into the living room to check on the game players once again.

Despite the very obvious welcome and the sense that she wasn't an inconvenience, Anne breathed a sigh of relief when she could retreat back across the street to her quiet apartment. The day had been utterly too long, too full of new places and faces she would have to learn and navigate around. She didn't have the freedom of knowing that in a day or two she could leave and the people around her would forgive her mistakes as soon as she left. Until her assignment with Common Grounds had ended and Argus was on his feet, she was effectively anchored here in Tabor. She didn't realize until that moment how secure and free her truck and her mobile assignments made her feel.

Xander showed up twenty minutes later with bikes on a rack attached to the back of his Mustang. He had changed into faded jeans, hiking boots and a black Petra t-shirt under a gray fleece jacket. Anne nearly giggled, remembering her last conversation with Su-Ma. Xander did have a certain ugliness about him, yet there was a charm to the ugliness. Maybe it was his honesty and caring. Maybe it was the tiny, neon green propeller attached to the top of his baseball cap, which he put on backwards when he led her outside. Maybe it was his sheepish grin when she saw the cap and propeller and stopped short.

"Having second thoughts?" he said.

"About riding bikes?"

"You're going to be stuck with me for the next few weeks, so tighten your belt and endure."

"Do all lawyers talk this way?"

"Stick with me, girlie, and find out."

He let her choose which bike she preferred to ride. Anne had already gathered from Joan's remarks that Xander was one of those guys who would bend over backward to help, and yet be mortally embarrassed if anyone noticed his extra effort. She assessed his build and the size of the bikes, decided which one would be most comfortable for him, and chose the other.

They rode their bikes down two side streets to reach the Main Street entrance to the Metroparks. Anne thoroughly enjoyed the blacktop trails, the old sandstone quarries that had been made into lakes or fishing areas or allowed to silt in through the action of the Rocky River flowing by, to make wetlands for hundreds of waterfowl. They rode slowly down the trail, hardly speaking, which suited her fine. She appreciated the fact that Xander was talked out for the day, and that he had shared his relaxing time with her. She kept quiet and enjoyed the scenery and fresh air. She was almost disappointed when he signaled it was time to turn around. The sky seen through gaps in the thick foliage of the trees lining both sides of the road showed the long fall sunset was ready to fade into dusk. It would be dark by the time they got back to Church Street.

When Xander finally drove away, full night had fallen and Anne was pleasantly tired. Tomorrow, she would go Downtown to the Justice Center with him and watch him at work.

~~~~~

Morning brought panic, when Anne realized she had nothing even remotely businesslike to wear to the Justice Center. Jury members could dress as casually as they wanted – they had the jury box to hide them. She had Xander to worry about, though. What kind of impression would she make on his peers if she showed up looking like a college dropout or a refugee?

Those thoughts kept intruding on her morning routine, along with missing Argus lying next to her within convenient reach for petting. Anne realized with a grin that she did talk to the big dog quite often during her devotions, reading aloud bits of scripture or quotes from her devotional book, or working through ideas until she came to a conclusion. She stopped herself at least a dozen times from speaking aloud. Yes, it was a school morning and yes, she could hear the children moving around in the apartment below her as they washed up and got dressed, but that didn't make it all right for her to disturb them with a stranger's voice at 6am. Especially when that stranger didn't talk in complete sentences.

When she finally stumbled through her closing prayer for the morning, Anne opened her eyes and looked straight across the street at the Holwoods' house. At the square windows tucked up under the eaves, where she imagined she could look straight into Nikki's room. Was it too early to go knock on the door and –

The front door opened and Dr. Holwood herded the gaggle of foster-children down the steps ahead of him. They all wore backpacks, probably loaded with textbooks and lunch bags for school. That was one question answered. Now she had to get across the street before Doria left the house, and pray some of Nikki's clothes both fit her and looked business-like.

~~~~~

"You're lucky – or maybe not," Xander added with a grin, as they pulled into the parking garage on the other side of Ontario from the Justice Center's twenty-six-story tower. "I don't have any cases today. Just a series of hearings preparing for upcoming cases. Some of them will be short, because I've been negotiating with the lawyers on the other side for settlement, or we're refining details and hammering out difficulties with discovery. All the housekeeping chores."

"Should I have brought a book?" Anne shrugged once more, trying to adjust the fit of the blazer around her shoulders. When she tried it on two hours ago, she thought she and Nikki were of a similar size, but the blazer didn't quite hang right. Maybe she just wasn't a blazer type of person. The dark green plaid skirt hung a little longer than Anne liked, but the pleats gave her plenty of room to move when necessary. She preferred her clothes loose to let her run or kick if she had to. She considered the borrowed brown loafers on her feet. There was a half-size difference between her feet and Nikki's, and she had a sudden vision of a loafer going flying if she ran or tried one of Vincent's roundhouse kicks on someone.

Why was she thinking about self-defense? Yes, the Justice Center would be full of criminals, either in the jail or going to and from hearings, but they were under control. Or, at least Anne hoped so.

"Hmm? Sorry, what was that?" Anne said, tearing her thoughts off her clothes and back to Xander as he continued explaining the day's schedule to her.

The ride Downtown on I-71 had been full of conversation about the area, things to do, events coming up in the Singles group at Tabor Christian, which Xander recommended she get involved in while she was in town, just to have a pressure release valve. It struck her that they shouldn't have been discussing their social life on the ride to the Justice Center but should have concentrated on the day ahead of them. Why had they done that?

Xander ran down the list of colleagues and opponents and judges she would be meeting and the bare bones of most of the cases they would be discussing, so she wouldn't feel totally lost. That took them out of the parking garage and across the street and the wide, paved, open square in front of the Justice Center, past the modernistic sculpture that looked like nothing more than some pipes a Paul Bunyan-sized plumber had propped up and never retrieved. The building wasn't half the size of the Terminal Tower or the Key Bank Building, but Anne still had to stop a moment and lean her head back to look. Maybe it was the open sky beyond the Justice Center and the glimpse of Lake Erie just past Cleveland City Hall and the Cuyahoga County Courthouse. The tiny streaks of black in the clouds rolling across the sky were rather impressive, too. What would happen if lightning hit the building? She hoped she wouldn't be stuck on the top floor during a power outage.

Anne had to sign in with Security, and needed a pass that indicated she was not plaintiff or defendant or lawyer or jury member. Some of her access was limited, but she had access other visitors to the center wouldn't have. Halfway through the security officer's explanation, Anne mentally shook her head and resolved to go nowhere without Xander.

"It's about time you showed up," a young woman called as they got off the elevator halfway up the building, fifteen minutes before Xander's first meeting. She hurried around a group of chatting bailiffs. "I was afraid you got stuck in traffic or lost a tire or something."

The assured sound of that alto voice gave Anne a sinking sensation, and the certainty that she looked like a shabby schoolgirl. Hannah Blake was supposed to meet them here this morning. Who else could this be?

Turning around, Ann anticipated a sleek, silvery-gray business suit that would make her feel dumpy in her plaid skirt and loafers. Hannah just sounded like she had the figure for an outfit off the pages of *Vogue*, that would hug it without looking seductive, fashionable and yet utterly business-like and efficient. Hannah could probably move fast in high heels without clumping or stumbling. She probably carried a black, soft-sided briefcase that bulged at the sides and hung open on top, full of folders and books, all the things Xander had forgotten to bring, necessary for today's meetings—yet never looked sloppy. Her long hair would be pulled back in a knot that looked brisk and business-like, not severe—and when Hannah let down her hair at the end of the day, it would be thick and wavy and hang nearly to her waist.

Her misery-generating thoughts shot through her mind, tangling her gut into knots, in the time it took to turn around. For two seconds, Anne blinked and wondered where Hannah had vanished to. Then her gaze caught on the young woman striding toward them. Confident—check. No long hair—an auburn, chin-length bob. Instead of a silvery-gray business suit, Hannah wore navy pants and blazer with an orange-red blouse, and her figure...

Hannah's figure made Anne feel very good about herself. She wasn't fat or dumpy, but she had an extra thirty pounds on her hips and thighs, and the colors she wore were all wrong for her peaches-and-cream complexion. She needed pastels. The battered brown leather of her clunky shoes and that soft-sided case that bulged with books and folders did indeed look sloppy. Not that Anne knew much about colors and style, but she had enough lessons on accessorizing and image shoved down her throat by her guardians, she could navigate on instinct. Maybe the outfit she had chosen for today wasn't that bad. As long as she was clean and neat, she didn't need to worry about fashion. Too much, anyway.

Anne's estimate and analysis went through her head fast enough to give her a headache. For some reason, she just didn't like Hannah. Judging by that momentary thinning of Hannah's lips when their gazes met, she didn't like Anne.

This is stupid, Anne scolded herself. *Why don't you like her? She's supposed to be a Christian, too. Dr. Holwood likes her. Xander thinks she's amazing.*

Maybe it was that slight narrowing of the eyes. Or the pause for consideration as Hannah looked her up and down. Or the sense that her smile was forced as she held out her hand and introduced herself to Anne before Xander could handle it. Certainly he had told his assistant much more about Anne than he had told her about Hannah.

"Be prepared to be bored," Hannah said with a delicate shrug and a smile clearly meant only for Xander. "It's all prep work today. Maybe we can take the time to ditch the coffee shop here and hike up to Tower City to eat." She glanced at Anne, barely meeting her gaze as the three of them headed down the hallway in the direction Hannah had indicated. "Maybe if you've figured out the bus lines, or the Rapid, you'd like to stay and take in a movie at Tower City before you go home."

"That's the big shopping center that the train lines come into, right?" Anne nodded and followed them down the hall to the double doors half-hidden in shadows, visible around the corner. It made no sense, but she instantly resented the way Hannah moved in to walk next to Xander, leaving her a step behind and to the right. And why was she so certain Hannah wasn't offering to go to the movie *with* her? "Good. I need some new clothes. These are all borrowed."

Now, why had she said that? She liked Nikki's clothes when she put them on that morning. She had been grateful for the loan.

"Oh, that's right. Xander said you'd been robbed."

"She beat the tar out of the guy who did it. If she hadn't stopped to take care of her dog, she probably would have held onto him long enough for the police to show up and take him away," Xander said.

"Wait a minute, I didn't tell you—" Anne began.

"Lawyer's privilege. I read the reports from the witnesses," he said, giving her a grin over his shoulder as he pulled the right-hand door open. Anne couldn't say anything in response, because just past him she saw the room was full of people, all waiting, watching them come in.

~~~~~

Xander breezed through three of his scheduled meetings, but one was postponed until that afternoon when all parties concerned agreed it would take more than the allotted hour to finalize the proceedings of the trial.

Anne didn't like the opposing lawyer. That didn't make sense, because the muscular, Hispanic man reminded her strongly of her adviser in college, and he had been a good friend—the first male she had ever totally trusted after the Ogre killed her parents. He was the one who insisted something was wrong when she started her long slide down the self-destructive slope. He had kept track of her, when other teachers had turned a blind eye, writing her off as another rebellious, self-centered freshman. He had called for help. Because of him, the Black Prince had come and rescued her when her guardians threw her into that "treatment center" that did nothing but drug her into dazed docility.

This lawyer facing Xander across the negotiations table looked so much like her beloved adviser, the contrast in his attitude, his very manner of speaking made her feel nauseous, so she almost had to look away during the meeting.

Maybe it was the way he looked over everyone as if sizing them up for purchase. He looked Hannah over twice, and then dismissed her as if she didn't belong. Anne felt a flicker of humor at that, but then felt ashamed. Especially when Hannah ignored the man's inspection, as if it didn't matter to her. Anne suspected she was probably used to it, and some sympathy intruded on the discomfort thickening between them. That dismissive attitude spoke degrees about this lawyer, Martinez.

He barely gave Anne half a glance. She was sure it was because she sat in a corner instead of at the table where the lawyers and judge sat with their clerks, assistants, personal recorders, and piles of books, briefcases, and notebooks. She wondered if it had to do with her clothes, because Martinez dressed like a slick, rich movie lawyer, all sharp edges and pinstripes and a gloss to his shoes that certainly didn't come from Vaseline. He had four assistants, all bright and eager, and glaring at Xander and the judge as if they had no right holding the meeting in the first place.

The case, as Anne understood it, dealt with slander, involving forged documents and stolen evidence; Martinez's client suing Xander's. The defendant worked for the plaintiff and had turned state's evidence when approached by federal officials. The irony was that if the defendant had been a whistleblower, if he had realized what was going on *before* the government investigators approached him, he would have been covered by the whistleblower laws and would be suing the plaintiff for retaliation at the workplace. Xander and the judge certainly seemed inclined to tuck it all under the whistleblower laws, but Martinez had a talent for twisting everything and turning it into a vendetta, employee against employer, with his client the victim.

The criminal trial was still in the assembly stages – discovery, Xander called it – but Martinez had pushed to get this trial going fast, so a favorable outcome could be used as leverage to have the government's case thrown out of court. Xander didn't say much about his client to Anne, other than that the man and his family had moved out of town because of threats and harassment from people who worked for his former employer. Of course, nothing could be proved.

Anne wished she had brought a book to read, as the meeting dragged on for three hours. But that would defeat the purpose of her being here, observing Xander in action. No one raised their voices, but she heard the daggers in the air just in the tones used. She felt tension like a storm brewing, prickling her skin and raising the hairs on her neck and on her arms. In among the claims and counterclaims and disagreements, she caught barely veiled personal comments and condemnation from Martinez and his assistants, which could have been against either Xander or his client. Probably both. Listening to her gut, Anne decided they were threats. Martinez had the skill for weaving words so that the target knew they were threats, mockery, abuse, but had no ground to stand on to protest. The judge's lack of action supported that perception while his expression revealed thinly veiled disgust as the meeting dragged on. There was nothing for which he could clearly call foul on Martinez. What irritated her was that she could almost admire his skill with words. Just not the way he deployed that skill.

Anne despised people like Martinez, who used the law for their own profit, instead of defending others. She had faced men like him before, who slandered and attacked the innocent because the guilty had deep pockets and paid better.

She mentally slapped herself when she realized she should have been praying for Xander all this time. This couldn't be easy for him. She had a mental image of Martinez as a snake and she had barely met the man. How hard was it for Xander to work with him, work against him, and keep his temper? No one was looking at her, so she tucked one leg under herself and bowed her head, resting her face in her hands to block out the sights of the room, even if she couldn't plug her ears, and she prayed. The sound of her breath brushing against her hands helped muffle the sounds of the voices at the other end of the room.

"You okay?" a deep, gravelly voice asked from over her shoulder. "Sorry," the man continued with a slight chuckle when Anne jerked and sat up straight. He stood in the row of chairs behind hers.

She glanced at her watch, amused to find she had been praying for nearly half an hour. How time flew when she really had something on her heart and mind.

"Yeah, I'm fine." She nodded toward the table where chairs were being pushed back as people stood and gathered up their books and papers. "I was praying."

Chapter Ten

"Yeah, that bunch really needs it." The big, balding man in a bailiff's uniform winked at her. "If you're religious, you must be on Finley's side, huh? He's a great guy, isn't he?"

"Well, what I've seen of him, yes. I'm Anne Hachworth." She tried not to lean back when the man leaned a little closer, the garlic on his breath mixing with a whiff of beer. What had he eaten for lunch? Were bailiffs allowed to drink during the day?

"Kyle Simons." He shook her hand. "You another paralegal?"

"Ah... no." Her natural inclination was to hold back until she really knew more about the man. But, Anne considered, he liked Xander, he worked for the Justice Center, he seemed like a fairly nice person. He had that heavy kind of face that had a five o'clock shadow at ten in the morning and turned red when he laughed or got angry. "Actually, I work for the Arc Foundation. We support Xander's legal clinic, and I'm here sort of on an inspection tour." No need to tell him she had been carjacked and she was wearing borrowed clothes.

"Yeah?" Simons settled into a chair and looked her up and down. His once-over look didn't make her bristle as Hannah's and Martinez's looks had. "Kind of young for that type of work. Hey, Finley, how's it going?" He stood as Xander and Hannah approached.

"It was going kind of rough until about twenty minutes ago," Xander said, and mimed wiping nervous sweat from his forehead.

"You were doing great. It was a stalemate for a while, that's all." Hannah gave him a playfully scolding look. As soon as Xander laughed and turned to fasten his overloaded briefcase, that expression slid into adoration. Just for a moment, before she put on her professional, right-hand-gal mask.

Oh, heck. Anne bent her head to hide any expression that might betray her and pretended to straighten her blazer and skirt as she stood. *She's got one huge crush on him.* Dr. Holwood's remark about Hannah calling her employer Alexander the Great took on a totally new dimension. No wonder she hadn't been warmly welcoming when she met Anne. She had to see her arrival as a threat to Xander's continued support from Arc.

"Stalemates always look like a problem for your side, no matter what side you're on," a man with a smoky voice said. Hannah stepped aside to reveal the other lawyer who had been sitting on Xander's side of the table.

"Anne, this is Frank Winslow," Xander said. "He's sort of representing the government."

"Sort of?" A shiver from deep in her gut went through Anne, making her grin weak and her chuckle tremble as she shook hands with Winslow. She knew him. From somewhere.

Back when his eyes weren't so sunken, when his hair was more brown than gray, and he had more of it. When his voice wasn't a wreck from cigarettes. *When he leaned over a nine-year-old girl with a smoldering one in his hand, shoving it nearly in her face as he snarled and grilled her and never let her finish a single sentence.*

For two seconds, she was a child again, terrified and sick and dizzy and alone, despite the court-appointed guardian and counselor standing beside her.

Anne felt the hardness of the seat in the judge's chambers, smelled the cigarette smoke blown into her face with every gusting breath. She felt herself tremble with anger and fear and the sense that she had done something very wrong. She didn't understand all the words, all the questions the man asked, but she understood his voice. He was angry with her. He smirked when she burst into tears and got angry with the lady from social services who told him to stop being so mean.

Anne never understood how he could look at her, with burns and cuts on both arms, and tell her that she lied about the man who killed her family and molested her.

"Well, the government isn't an official defendant in this case, but it's coming. Better to shoot down Martinez and his thugs before it gets that far, right?" Winslow chuckled and raked a lean, long-fingered hand through the remains of his hair. "Breakfast meeting tomorrow?"

"We'd better," Xander said, nodding. He touched Anne's arm, startling her. "Ready to go?"

"Hmm? Sure." Anne turned and headed for the door, trying not to listen as the three walking behind her made arrangements to work on the case in the morning.

"You okay, kid?" Simons asked, following her to the door of the meeting room.

"Long day, I guess."

"You been listening in on what they were talking about?" He gestured back over his shoulder at the knot of devotees gathered around Martinez. The big man glowered at Xander and his two associates.

"Trying not to. Most of the legalese lost me, but..." Anne shrugged, trying to smile as she jerked her thoughts back to the recent past, instead of more than fifteen years ago. The man who killed her family was in prison, despite Winslow's attempts to present her as a self-destructive child with no concept of reality, who lied to protect her abusers and blamed the man who had defended her. Why was Xander working with him? Didn't he know what Winslow had done to her?

No, he didn't. How could he, when Anne had deliberately forgotten the man's face and name and a large portion of those horrific, nightmare months, until now?

"Yeah, Martinez is high-priced scum, working for slime. He must own the whitewash concession for the whole state." Simons looked like he wanted to spit but didn't dare with all the wood paneling and carpeting and the gleaming floors outside the hearing room. "I've been a bailiff a long time, and it still makes me want to puke at all the lawyers who make a living protecting criminals from justice. We got the witnesses, we got the evidence—what more do we need? Take 'em out and shoot 'em. No more fancy prisons to pamper them like they're the victims. Make 'em earn a living, or put them out, permanently. Know what I mean?"

"Yeah, unfortunately." Anne fought not to sidestep as soon as she got through the door. Something about Simons suddenly made her want to get out of there. It had to be the after-effect of recognizing Winslow after all these years.

"Sometimes, I swear lawyers just waste money, instead of helping people who really need help."

"But what about the people who are falsely accused?" she had to say, even as she slowed her steps so Simons walked on ahead of her, increasing the distance between them. "Don't they deserve justice? What about the people who might get killed before they can prove they really are innocent?"

Simons glared at her for a few seconds. Anne looked at the outline of his uniform jacket, trying to figure out if he had a gun. She mentally slapped herself for that when the man's scowl softened into a grin and he shook his head.

"Yeah, got to think about the innocent people who get trapped. Like this poor joker Finley is defending. But you know something, kid? He wouldn't be in this trouble in the first place if the real crooks didn't think they could get away with using the legal system."

"Here we go again," Xander said with a grin and a sigh as he stepped through the doors into the hallway. "We're on different sides of the same argument, Simons. Neither of us is going to budge, so why waste time going over it again? Anne's a visitor, so don't pull her into it either, okay? She doesn't know much about the legal system."

Anne bit her tongue. She knew far more about the legal system than she cared to.

"Everybody can't be the whiz kid," Winslow said. He strode past her, heading for the elevators. "Bright and early tomorrow, Xander?"

"Unfortunately. Why do I always go and mess up my Saturdays with work?" Xander asked with a sigh and a wistful grin.

"You're just a giving kind of guy," Simons said. He shrugged and turned his back on them and walked away.

"He makes my skin crawl," Hannah said under her breath, glaring after the bailiff.

Anne kept her silence while the four of them walked to the elevators. Winslow rode with them until the tenth floor. Anne stayed pressed into the corner, trying to make herself smaller than she actually was. She didn't move out much further when the other lawyer left, because Hannah moved over closer to Xander.

There is something really wrong with me, Anne told herself repeatedly, to fight an urge to ask Hannah what her problem was. She knew she wasn't pretty. Her education was a hodgepodge, her nights on the road filled with reading, and classes on CD that she played while she drove. She probably had enough studying under her belt for several degrees, but never enough to qualify for any one in particular. She certainly had proof this day that she wasn't a sparkling conversationalist. What made Hannah think she was a threat? If she had a relationship with Xander that went beyond the office, then it was up to her to nurture it, not fear every newcomer who wore a skirt.

Unless Xander didn't know what Hannah thought and felt about him?

Don't be an idiot. Leave it alone, Anne scolded herself, as the elevator doors sighed open and she followed the other two out into the main lobby of the Justice Center. In maybe a week, Argus would be well enough to move and she would take him home to Quarry Hall and the kennels there, and all the coddling the big dog could ever want. His absence and her worry over him were the main reason for feeling so off-balance. A few weeks after that, her assessment would be finished, her report written and turned in. She would be out of Xander's life and never see Tabor again. She kept her mouth shut and contented herself with smiles and nods when Xander included her in the conversation as they walked across the street to the parking garage. Anne congratulated herself on putting up a pleasant front.

"All right, what's the problem?" Xander asked, as they climbed into his car less than five minutes after leaving Hannah.

"Problem?" Maybe her expression hadn't been impenetrable after all.

"You were acting like Winslow had the plague. He's a little dry, but he's really a nice guy once you get to know him."

"Maybe you don't know him," slipped out before Anne could stop herself.

"And you do?"

"I... I've had experience with his cross-examination style."

76

"Uh huh." He turned the key in the ignition, then loosened his tie before he looked at her. "He didn't recognize you, so it must have been a long time ago. You were a kid?" Xander waited until she nodded. "Want to tell me about it?"

She opened her mouth to say no, but the word caught in her throat. She wanted to explain but feared breaking into tears. Anne had promised herself not to cry about it ever again. Not to feel the hatred and fear and pain. It was in the past, and she had given her agony and nightmares and sense of helplessness to God. Multiple times.

Anne knew *how* to tell him. Her counselors had taught her to distance herself from the pain while bringing it out into the open, so it could be dealt with. Would Xander think she was weird? Would he think like Winslow had all those years ago, that she was mentally unbalanced, unable to accept reality?

Some pains could not be faced, could not be spoken, without shields.

"Okay." She forced the tension in her chest to leave on a long, deep exhale and gripped the armrest as Xander pulled out onto Lakeside Avenue. "Once upon a time, there was a princess who lived in a castle. There was an Ogre in the basement, but nobody knew he was an ogre because he had magic to make himself look like a kindly wizard in the daylight. The princess knew he was an ogre because she had seen him at night—but she didn't know what an ogre was. He hurt her and told her he would kill everyone in the castle if she told anyone. He took away the words she would have used to ask for help. One night, even though she kept silent, the Ogre killed her parents. The princess found her words again, and she told everyone. But hardly anyone believed her. They said she was too young to understand. But she understood."

"Anne." Xander reached over and caught hold of her wrist, startling a squeak out of her.

They were caught in the crawl of rush hour. He could take his eyes off the street to watch her for several moments at a time. Anne watched him from the corner of her eye while she interlaced her fingers and tried hard to keep the trembling from her voice.

"I'm sorry." He squeezed her hand. "But what does this have to do with Winslow?"

"There was a wise man," she continued, after swallowing hard. "He came to learn the truth. He asked the princess what had happened. She told him. He asked her questions with big words she didn't understand. She didn't know what he wanted. She couldn't answer him. And so he called her a liar. He told her the Ogre was a good man. He told her someone else had killed her family, and the Ogre had fought to protect them. He said when she told lies and blamed the Ogre, she was helping the people who killed her parents, and that made her a very bad girl. Just like the Ogre told her she was a very bad girl. The princess wanted to die. She believed the whole world was cruel and wicked. Until a wizard came who could reveal the truth. He took the princess away to a far-off land and healed her heart and body and mind. But he couldn't take away her memories." Anne took a deep breath and swallowed hard. "So she lived fairly happily ever after. The end."

"I'm not defending how Winslow treated you back then —"

"But sometimes the innocent do get run over in the search for truth and justice. I know." Anne strained her eyes for the signs showing the way back to I-71. Once they were on the highway, Xander would be busy driving, navigating the interweaving of traffic. He wouldn't be able to watch her with sympathy in his big, shining eyes.

~~~~~

Saturday morning, Anne couldn't stay in bed, no matter how much she wanted to. No matter how late she had stayed up the night before, thinking and praying and reading one of the books from the stack she picked up at the Tabor Heights Library, all in an effort to get her mind off Winslow. The deaths of her parents happened long ago. Winslow didn't recognize her. She suspected if she confronted him with his cruelty, he wouldn't even remember her or the case. Anne laughed at herself for the fury and exasperation that came on the heels of that bit of honesty. She had to forgive him. She had to put the past behind her. The important thing was that someone had believed her. They had listened and found out the truth. They found the proof to put her parents' murdering, molesting tenant in prison for the rest of his life. They made sure she went to live with people who would believe her and help her heal and give her the love she needed. They worked to convince her that she really was a good girl, that it wasn't her fault, that her parents hadn't been murdered because she was a bad girl.

"Please, Jesus, help me to forgive them all," Anne had whispered often during the night.

She whispered it again when she woke with the sunshine slanting in through the window, instantly making her head ache.

Anne had discovered early in her years of struggle with her anger and guilt that if she got busy with something else, totally unrelated to whatever kept the feelings and thoughts churning, she found some escape and peace — and a solution eventually rose to the conscious part of her mind. So, armed with a map of Butler-Williams University, provided by Doria, she went exploring.

She liked small colleges, privately run, more than a century old, with some history and character to their buildings. Butler-Williams had a large section of classes, buildings and teaching staff devoted to literature, music, theater, and visual arts. Walking past the theater building, she saw signs proclaiming performances scheduled to start in two weeks. Maybe she would try to see one, if she was still up here on assignment.

Her legs started to feel tired after nearly two hours of walking, by the time she crossed the intersection at Sackley and Church, turning back toward her apartment. Sackley Road seemed to be the main thoroughfare, and its intersection with Main Street marked the beginning of the business and municipal heart of Tabor Heights. She made a mental note to always keep herself oriented to those two streets, and she wouldn't get too far lost.

She continued down Church, past the Holwoods' house and her apartment, toward the post office, past several tiny sorority and fraternity houses, toward a long string of buildings labeled as art studios. Anne liked art. For a long time she had lived with a few colored pencils tucked behind her ears and a sketchpad always in her hand or under her arm. It had been her refuge, her main means of communicating with the world, making it make sense. Then she realized that her artwork had become a trap, putting a wall between her and reality and finally healing. She had drowned herself in her art during those first horrible weeks of sliding into self-destruction at school. The few times she emerged from her drugged haze at the treatment center, she had been given paper and colored pencils. That was enough to make sketching repulsive, once the Black Prince whisked her away to the safety and healing of Quarry Hall. In the last three years, she had healed enough that art didn't repulse her as it once had. Every once in a while, she took up pad and pencils and tried her hand, just to see if she still had her artist's eye.

The eye for art remained, but the passion for drawing and blocking out the world with her imagination had cooled. Anne designed the Christmas and Easter and birthday cards Quarry Hall sent out every year, but that was about it. That assured her she wasn't wasting her talent, but art was no longer the focus, the means and breath of her life.

That didn't mean she couldn't or shouldn't stick her head into the art studios and see what up-and-coming young artists were producing and feeling and seeing nowadays.

"Silly girl," Anne muttered with a grin, when that thought came to her. "You're not a decrepit old lady yet. Heading toward thirty is nowhere near the rocking chair stage. You have to wait at least fifty years after Elizabeth finally sits down before you can consider it."

Quietly laughing at herself, Anne pushed open the door into the narrow, two-story, sandstone brick building, and stepped in. The smell of wet clay and the sounds of a radio playing oldies rock'n'roll drifted out of one open doorway—there were three in the tiny lobby, and a narrow, squared corkscrew of a metal stairway to the second floor. The other two doors were closed, no lights showing through the tiny slits of their windows. Anne leaned through the door into the pottery studio and saw no one at work. There were scraps and spatters of wet clay on the floor all around the wheel, and the kneading trough was full of murky water. She suspected someone had just finished throwing a pot and had taken it somewhere to dry before firing. She went upstairs.

The door into the lobby slammed open just as she reached the metal grid of the landing of the second floor, which was little more than a wide loft with doors opening off it, two on either side. Fragments of beams and broken brickwork in the walls showed where the original floor had been removed and the metal grid installed. Light streamed through the only open door, facing south. Anne nodded, knowing there had to be a painter in that studio, just to get the right light all day long. She paused, feeling the vibrations from someone stomping up the metal stairs. A pale-haired young man, dressed in gray sweats with the college logo in navy blue on one arm, climbed the stairs. He barely glanced at her as he leaped onto the landing and hurtled through the door.

"Todd!" The girl inside the studio didn't sound at all happy. She didn't sound surprised, either, Anne realized. Something told her to stay there and listen. She stepped back against the far door at the end of the landing and leaned against it.

"What was that message for?" Todd demanded.

"What message?" There was a sound like a drawer sliding shut, sticking and creaking.

"The one you left me last night. The one that said you weren't going to church with me tomorrow, and to forget about lunch for the rest of the semester." There was a bang-thud, like a fist on wood, followed by a muffled hiss of pain.

"That sounds pretty clear to me. Your roommate left out the part about not calling me until you learned how to apologize, didn't he?"

"No." His sullen tone made Anne grin. He sounded like a little boy caught doing the very thing he had been scolded not to do only a few moments before.

Chapter Eleven

"This doesn't sound like an apology to me. So go away."

"Come on, Lisa! I forgot about last night, that's all."

"You forget a lot, and somehow *I'm* always blowing it out of proportion if I get angry. But, if I'm even ten minutes late for something that matters to *you*, I get scolded. With witnesses. The only reason I went to that party at *your* professor's house was because you wanted me to come. I sat there for over an hour, waiting for you, trying to make small talk with people I don't even know. And you know what I found out when I left? You were at Dwayne's place — two doors down! — the whole time. Did it ever occur to you to come get me, or just tell me you were there?"

"No." More sullen and muted than before.

"Did anybody tell you I waited for you?"

"Yeah."

"They thought it was funny, when I finally couldn't take any more and left."

"Aw, they're just a bunch of jerks, Lisa."

"They're *your* friends." Another drawer slammed. "I have better things to do with my time than sit around waiting for you or getting lectured because I *wasn't* there the very second you wanted me there. I have a life of my own!"

"Yeah, sitting up here drawing cartoons all the time. There are real people outside. A real world to live in."

"What would you know about real people? Now get out. This is my studio and I have work to do. I have to live up to the terms of my grants. I don't have a rich daddy to pay my way every time I lose my merit grant, or I don't feel like doing work study."

"Lisa... " The groan turned into a snarl.

Anne flinched as the gray-clad Todd stumbled backward out of the little studio.

Lisa appeared a heartbeat later. She was a thin, dark-haired girl dressed in ragged jeans and a blue plaid flannel shirt, barefoot — and armed with four sharp pencils, which she held like double daggers in both hands, forcing Todd to retreat. Anne bit her tongue to keep from cheering on the girl. She pressed into the corner of the landing and held still to keep from being seen. Judging from the rehearsed reasonableness of Lisa's voice, this confrontation had been building a long time. Anne guessed Lisa was normally a patient person who had to be pushed very far before she fought back. Meaning she would stop the assault in her own defense if she knew she had an audience. And Todd would probably make her pay for that same audience seeing his humiliation. Whether he was a physical or mental brute, he would make the poor girl pay.

Anne hoped this break-up became permanent. Unless they got some things straightened out between them, this would keep happening for the rest of their lives. She had seen this happen until one side or the other broke from the strain, far too often with bloody consequences.

"All right! I'm going!" Todd flung his arms up in the air and nearly fell as he turned and leaped down the first two steps.

"And don't go running to Daddy this time to fix the problem!" Lisa called after him. She gripped the frame of her doorway, fingers turning white and threatening to snap the pencils still in her clasp. "So help me, if he lectures me one more time about how I don't treat you right—"

Then she stiffened and turned and looked straight at Anne. Her mouth dropped open and her triangular little face turned ice white.

"Men can be such jerks, can't they?" Anne flinched as the metal door slammed closed on the floor below. "How many times has he stood you up like that, and refused to admit he was wrong?"

"Too many," Lisa said, her voice rough. She swallowed hard, and the color flooded back into her cheeks.

"Come right down to it, there's only one person in this whole wide world you can depend on." Feeling fairly sure she had taken the right track, Anne stepped out onto the landing.

"Don't give me that self-reliance crap," the other girl said, her voice coming back to normal. "I've been on my own since I was seventeen. It's not all it's cracked up to be."

"Nope. I was talking about Jesus." The door opened again and she stepped over to the edge of the landing to look down. She caught the tail end of someone dressed in black shorts and sandals stepping into the pottery studio directly below. Anne mimed wiping sweat off her forehead. "Whew. I was afraid I'd have to borrow some of those pencils for a second. I've been trying to retire as a dragon-slayer for years."

That earned a giggle from Lisa. She stepped back into the studio with a little nod of her head, inviting Anne to follow.

"Are you a Christian?" Lisa asked, settling down on a rickety wooden stool in front of a tilted drafting table.

"The work I do, I'd be one huge idiot to go anywhere without my eternal life insurance." She found an empty chair, a reject from a faculty office, to judge by the torn padding on the arms and the stuffing coming out of the institutional green vinyl seat.

"What do you—this is crazy." She finally put down her pencils, on a narrow little table pushed up against the wall that held boxes of colored pencils, chalk, and colored markers. She held out her hand. "I'm Lisa Collins."

"Anne Hachworth. And my job is basically going around and sticking my nose into everybody's business and helping them. So if you want to hire a bodyguard, or maybe find some cute jock to make Toddy-boy jealous, I can probably arrange that."

"Jealous? Mr. Oblivious Montgomery?" Lisa snorted, shaking her head hard enough to make her straight locks swing sharply.

"Bodyguard?" she asked, softening her voice.

"No. He's not the hitting type. The most physical Todd gets when he's mad is to go run laps until he's sick. The last time he did it, I was sure he was just trying to make me feel guilty."

"Did you?"

"For about two seconds." A tiny snort of laughter escaped her. "It made a couple great panels in my strip," she added, gesturing at the papers attached to her drawing table, "and Todd never figured out it was about him. That's pretty oblivious."

"Strip?" Anne focused on that word, sidestepping the rest of the issue. She had encouraged Lisa to talk, but it couldn't go on in that vein very long or the airing of her wound would just make it deeper. "You're L.N. Collins? You do the strip in the college paper?" From Lisa's short nod and the blush traveling up from her neck to her forehead, she was indeed the creator of the cartoon strip. "That's great stuff! Joan showed me a bunch — she gets the school paper because she's an alumni — alumnus? Can she really be an alumnus when she only took classes and never graduated with a degree?"

"Search me." Lisa visibly relaxed another ten degrees.

"And then I borrowed the latest paper from Dr. Holwood and I'd really like to fill in all the episodes I missed and... Slow down, huh?" She shrugged in apology to Lisa's slightly confused look. "I'm staying across the street from the Holwoods. They're kind of looking after me. I work for the Arc Foundation." Anne wondered if that meant anything at all to Lisa.

"Oh. Okay. Those are the people who are looking for Nikki. Our student prayer group is praying for her. Dr. Holwood is my advisor, and I kind of knew Nikki for a little while. Before she ran away." Lisa's gaze traveled to a closed sketchbook sitting on the end of her table, next to the pencils and crayons and chalk waiting to be used. Anne knew immediately what that particular look in the other girl's eyes meant.

"Sorry. You wouldn't be inside on a gorgeous day like this unless you wanted to get some serious work done." She got up, intending to leave.

"And hide from Todd. It's amazing he came to find me. He must have been ticked. Or his roommate razzed him about my message. Usually he just leaves a bunch of messages and waits for me to come running. Not anymore." She flipped the sketchbook open, revealing what Anne guessed were preliminary drawings for her next panel.

"Ah, one suggestion." Anne stepped a little closer to the drafting table and lowered her voice. "If Todd is finally paying attention to you, he might realize your next couple panels are about him. Be careful that you stay the innocent party in all this, or he'll never let you forget it."

"Oh, no, this isn't for school." She actually grinned and let out a breathy laugh. "I'm working on this new cartoon series. I have this great idea — well, I think it's great anyway. If I could just figure out who to connect with to present my ideas, I have this comic strip that would be just perfect for the Christian magazines. The ones for families, for pastors, that sort of audience." She lifted several sheets of paper off the top of her table, revealing neat drawings, three panels, each one four blocks wide, showing what appeared to be people unloading a moving van. "I call it 'PK,' about a huge pastor's family." She stopped with a chuckle. "The family is huge, not the pastor. I figure, there has to be a lot of material in there about the kids and growing up and dating and making a pastor's tiny salary cover a whole lot of hungry mouths. You know?"

"It sounds great. And you have a lot of talent. I used to think I was an artist, but looking at this..." Anne whistled softly and shook her head, earning a blush of pleasure from Lisa.

She couldn't wait until she was out of the art building, so she could place a call home and ask if Elizabeth knew any agents among her many and varied connections. Lisa was good, and the idea was fresh and unique — at least in her experience.

"Mr. Montgomery thinks I'm just wasting my time, scribbling." Lisa let the papers slide back into place.

"Who?"

"Todd's father. You should have seen him, coming to check me out, as if Todd was intending to marry me just because we had three dates. When Todd finally took me home for dinner after church one Sunday — oh, he just made me so mad! The way he looked at me. Like I was a bug that needed squashing."

"Like a threat to him, a threat to you, or he looked at you like someone who wouldn't accept you unless you conformed to his standards?"

"Huh?" Lisa sat back, blinking hard for a few seconds. Then her mouth dropped open and she nodded, a slow smile wiping away the confusion. "No, he really can't hurt me, can he? He's doing the other thing — he wants me to think and see things his way, or I'm not good enough for him." She snorted. "Not good enough for his little boy."

"Look, I've probably been sticking my nose in where it doesn't belong —"

"After the way I've been dumping on you, it's a little late now!" Her giggle sounded like bells. "Anne, do you believe in angels?"

Now it was Anne's turn to step back and try to regain her balance. Fighting back a flood of stories from the other daughters of Quarry Hall that she could have told Lisa, she just nodded.

"Maybe an angel brought you in here. I sure needed someone to talk to — or talk at, maybe." She shrugged, adding, "I don't have many friends. The art students around here are kind of self-absorbed, unless you sign on for the mutual admiration society. BWU is a great place but there are so many little cliques... It's all surface friendliness, unless you're willing to take risks and spend a lot of time on cultivating people."

"I never was much of a gardener myself." Anne rested a hand on Lisa's shoulder, squeezing. "What church do you go to?"

"Oh, I've jumped around to all of them. Tabor's lousy with churches. They almost outnumber the college buildings. Most of my church time and Bible study comes from the student prayer group, not from a church."

"Find one, and find friends there, and anchor yourself." She waited as Lisa took in that bit of advice. "Any particular church you really liked?"

"Tabor Christian."

"That's Dr. Holwood's church."

"I know. It's great, but..." She shrugged.

"Mr. Montgomery goes there?" Anne guessed. She felt a flicker of anger against the unknown man when Lisa nodded and looked away. "Well, there are a lot of Pharisees out there, but don't let them stand between you and God, understand?"

When Anne left the art building half an hour later, she had Lisa's name and address, copies of a few panels for 'PK' that her new friend had revised, and a promise to meet her at Tabor Christian on Sunday morning.

Anne laughed quietly as she walked up the tree-lined street and considered how thoroughly her thoughts had been taken off herself. Nothing like someone else's problems to put her own in perspective. She walked as far as the corner, where two college buildings faced each other. Stone benches in front of both and thick trees just tinged with the first scarlet of fall, towering over them, created a restful place for sitting and thinking. She sat on the first bench she came to and pulled her phone out of her pocket. It was a matter of moments to reach Quarry Hall and ask for someone to find the names and addresses of three agents to send Lisa's artwork to. After all, with all the connections the Arc Foundation had with various Christian organizations and businesses, it was a given someone knew someone who had the inside track in the right place. When she explained Lisa's comic strip and the general idea behind it to Su-Ma, she got an enthusiastic response. It was nice to know she wasn't the only one who thought Lisa's idea had some merit.

Anne spent the rest of the morning borrowing the copier at Dr. Holwood's office, explaining what she was doing and showing the panels to the man, writing cover letters, and then running up to the post office to mail the sample pieces to the three agents.

Dr. Holwood knew about Lisa and Todd's on-again, off-again relationship, as well as Mr. Montgomery's opinion of her. He had at first condemned Lisa because she was studying in the "frivolous" art program, and then because she wore pants to church — no good Christian woman, according to Mr. Montgomery, wore pants. A career meant she wouldn't devote herself to serving her husband and raising children. That meant she wasn't good enough for his one and only son.

"Did he actually tell Lisa that?" Anne asked, settling down on the wide arm of the old-fashioned easy chair tucked into the space between Dr. Holwood's desk and the deep wooden windowsill. "Wow, the guy sounds like a couple dozen self-righteous creeps I've tangled with, all wrapped up together."

"No, Saint Arthur told me that. Since I'm her academic advisor, I should tell Lisa how to live her life, and yet I don't have the sense to see what a disaster her relationship with Todd would be. This doesn't leave this office, understand?" He gave her a stern look that came close to making Anne shiver, but she sensed the compassion behind his somberness. She nodded. "I'm telling you this because I can see you care about Lisa. She needs all the prayers on her behalf she can get. Honestly, the disaster would be for Lisa to bind her life to Todd's. She's too sensitive for the casual disregard he subjects her to, day in and day out. If it was just his neglect she had to deal with, they might have a chance. However, she needs to consider the family that comes with Todd, if they should ever marry." He sighed and settled back further in his chair. "Lisa needs a friend. Someone who will listen and help her think things through. It would be easy to sit her down and present all the arguments to purge Todd from her life, but the heart doesn't listen to facts, does it? A friend would help her discover the truth gently."

"Was Nikki her friend?"

"I think they could have been, given time. And, they could have been a good influence on each other." A flicker of sadness dimmed his big, dark eyes. "Lisa is a sweet girl who will let people walk all over her while she attempts to lead them to the Lord. You're right, though. She doesn't really have an anchor." Dr. Holwood nodded, a slow smile brightening his face again. "Is this the sort of thing you girls do all the time?"

"We try," Anne said with a shrug. "We're told to listen twice as much as we talk." She held up her hand as if taking a vow. "And keep our lips sealed about things like this."

"Well, if your idea can give Lisa that big breakthrough in her career,

I'd say God definitely sent you to Tabor to be her guardian angel. Validation of her art and storytelling abilities would give her strength to stand up for herself, and a higher opinion of her own worth."

"Meaning Todd and his father wouldn't be able to walk all over her." She nodded, feeling even better about her plan. She would ask everybody at Quarry Hall to pray for Lisa and her career. Even if this evaluation assignment turned out to be a waste of time as far as Xander and Common Grounds was concerned, she was glad she was here in Tabor.

~~~~~

Anne went to visit Argus that afternoon, and when she returned to Tabor, she felt as if the sun had vanished from the sky altogether. The big dog had a respiratory infection, ready to turn into pneumonia. The vet was just as frustrated as Anne. Her only comfort was that this had become a matter of honor to him, a test of his knowledge and skill. He wasn't going to let Argus die now.

She spent a quiet hour sitting on the floor of her tiny living room, praying and letting a few tears come. Holding her fears and misery and guilt inside wouldn't do anyone any good. She called Quarry Hall and reported on the prognosis.

"Was I wrong?" she concluded, when she had listed everything the veterinarian said was wrong with Argus or could go wrong next.

"Anne, fighting to save a life is never wrong," Elizabeth said, entering the conversation. There was an extra echo to her voice, meaning somewhere in the conversation Lori, who was working the switchboard that afternoon, had switched her over to the speakerphone.

A sense of weariness washed over Anne, along with a loosening of all the tense muscles in her back and head and gut. Elizabeth's voice always seemed to do that. Low and soft and cultured, it reminded her of bedtime stories with the summer sunset changing from scarlet, purple, and gold to silvery gray. All was right with the world, and there was someone bigger and stronger and smarter to drive away the monsters under the bed — and the ogres in the castle dungeon.

"I just think about Argus suffering," she admitted. "Am I being greedy, refusing to let him go? How much does he understand?"

"How much does a newborn baby understand? Yet in the midst of their crying and fear and pain and the utter strangeness of the world they've been born into, they know where their comfort and shelter is. Sometimes, though, we forget."

"Like maybe I've forgotten?" she whispered.

"Distracted." Elizabeth's voice held that wistful, loving smile that always seemed to strengthen the hurting and make the guilty blurt whatever lay heavy on their souls. Anne had no idea how she had learned that particular talent, but it was useful. She hoped someday God would give her that gift. It was far easier than grilling some unwilling soul until they broke down sobbing and confessed or spilled their hatred and fear in a most unpleasant way.

When she went across the street in response to an invitation to dinner, Anne felt tired but clean and empty inside, and ready to face whatever came next. When the twins asked her to take them to the theater just a few blocks away, on Main, she was more than willing. Then she saw the gratitude on Doria's face, and Anne knew she was here with the Holwoods for a reason, too.

"Everything works together, Lord," she whispered during Dr. Holwood's blessing over dinner. "Please help me remember that."

~~~~~

Lisa was waiting at the side door of the church, when Anne walked up with the twins the next morning, followed by the Holwoods with the other foster-children. She enjoyed the convenience of being able to walk down the street a few blocks to get to church. It was hard not to blurt to her new friend what she had done for her yesterday. Anne contented herself with anticipating Lisa's joy and surprise if one of the agents contacted her. How long would it take for an offer of a contract? She probably wouldn't be in town when that happened. Maybe she shouldn't even tell Lisa what she had done, just leave it a big mystery and blessing. Anne decided she preferred it that way. Doing good deeds, leaving gifts, and getting out before anyone knew it was her — she wondered if that was how Zorro, the Lone Ranger, and other mythical heroes got their satisfaction after they rode off into the sunset.

They all sat together on the left side of the wide, brick sanctuary, about halfway up, on the outside wall, close to a bank of windows. A tiny breeze came through the window just behind her, making Anne smile. She turned to Lisa, who looked beyond her. Her smile faded. Anne turned to see what she was looking at.

Chapter Twelve

The man coming down the aisle by himself had square features, dark wavy hair with gray at the temples, wide shoulders, and the slow elegance of stride that quietly declared "aristocrat" to Anne's way of assessing the world. The type of "aristocrat" she always associated with the Stuart Granger version of *The Prisoner of Zenda*. Yet where Stuart Granger had warmth and a sense of humor, there was ice in this man's eyes. He looked neither to the right nor to the left, ignoring the church members who greeted each other with smiles and handshakes as they filled the pews. Someone called him — Arthur — and held out a hand. He shook it slowly, his stony reserve untouched despite the other man's hearty handshake and warm smile.

"Who's the stiff?" Anne whispered. That got a snort of muffled laughter from Lisa, and helped the other girl break the spell the cold man's appearance put on her.

"Mr. Montgomery."

"Eww. Sorry. If I had known he'd be at this service, I wouldn't have pushed."

"Well, he never notices me unless I'm with Todd. And I figured just because he's a grump doesn't mean everybody else here is a Frigidarian."

"A what?" Anne nearly squeaked. She got a few giggles from the twins sitting on her right and a curious glance from Doria at the other end of the pew.

"A friend of mine wrote a poem for a contest, called *First Church of the Frigidaire*. He just fits the picture, icicles hanging from his ears, skating down the aisle on a sheet of ice." Lisa's eyes sparkled. "It'd make a couple great cartoon strips... "

"Don't draw him, specifically. I bet he's the sort of Grinch who'd recognize himself."

Lisa nodded, but the sparkle didn't leave her eyes. She pulled a blank notebook from her purse and sketched quickly, alternating words with stick figures and squares of roughed-in backgrounds. Anne sighed a moment in regret for those lost days of throwing herself into her artwork. She had never been so well-prepared and devoted as Lisa, but when she took the time, she had thoroughly enjoyed losing herself in hours, sometimes whole afternoons of sketching and dreaming.

Someday, she knew, God would give that back to her — when the time was right.

Pastor Glenn Carson reminded Anne of a lumberjack from the moment he stepped up onto the platform. There was something rugged about his appearance, a wideness and strength in his shoulders and upright carriage. He wore a neat, dark suit, with a tie painted to look like a fish. Something about him told Anne he would be more comfortable in blue jeans and flannel shirt, with a tool belt around his waist and work boots on his feet, building something. She liked him. His sermon had meat to it, shaking his congregation by their collars and making them sit up and think, instead of just spoon-feeding a "feel good" gospel.

At the end of the sermon, she kept a watch on Mr. Montgomery, fighting a mental image of the man coming down the aisle, seeing Lisa with her, and breaking his reserve to speak an unkind word. Anne remembered what Lisa had said, accusing Todd of running to his father to fix the problem between them. She suspected Mr. Montgomery would make Lisa the criminal and his son the innocent, misunderstood victim. Anne wondered if he hit his wife. Where was she? What kind of marriage-husband-father role model was he for Todd?

She turned with Lisa, herding the twins ahead of them. Anne caught a glimpse of what seemed like a wide blue wall coming up behind her. Then she blinked and re-focused, and saw the glimmer of badges and handcuffs, the matte black of guns and holsters.

"Mike, Todd, how nice to see you!" Doria called out. She shuffled down the length of the pew to the end where Anne and Lisa stood. "Anne, these are Mike Nichols and Todd James."

"Word gets around fast," Mike admitted as they shook hands. "We heard someone from the Arc Foundation was here, and we wondered if there was any word on Nikki."

Todd barked laughter when Anne backed up a step, wondering why the police would be interested in a girl who had run away last year. What exactly had Nikki done, besides break her foster-parents' hearts?

"No, not like that," he hurried to say. "Mike and I are sort of her honorary uncles."

"Sort of, nothing," Mike said, grinning down at Anne. "And I'm really skeptical about it being an *honor*. We saved Nikki's life when she was a baby. You know that old African tradition, you save someone's life, you're responsible for him, or her, for the rest of your life."

"Uh huh." She decided these two officers were just as concerned and hurt by Nikki's absence as her foster-parents. "Well, sorry, but there hasn't been any word yet. We sent her description and all the information Joan and Sophie could find on Brock Pierson to all our contacts across the country. And we're praying for her every day. You might be able to escape us, but you can't escape God."

"Uh huh," Todd echoed, his eyes narrowing and his smile cooling. "You Arc girls really are kind of scary. But it's a good kind of scary. Nikki doesn't stand a chance."

Anne decided to laugh at that. The two officers stayed to chat with the Holwoods while they waited for the traffic jam to clear from the sanctuary. The opportunity to slide out of the pew and down the aisle had been lost, and it was simply smarter to wait. Both officers were on duty, evidenced by their uniforms, but they had permission from their chief to come inside and listen to the sermon when they pulled Sunday duty, as long as they kept their radios with them. Almost the minute Mike admitted that, the radio at his belt crackled and hissed and a woman's voice rattled off codes and an address. He nodded to his partner and they waved farewells as they hurried down the aisle, both of them holding their radios to their ears.

Mr. Montgomery caught up with their group as they stood on the sidewalk by the side door, trying to convince Lisa to come with them for Sunday dinner.

"Lisa?"

That voice sounded just as chill and reserved as Anne imagined. She looked up as she felt her friend stiffen.

"What are you doing here?" Mr. Montgomery stopped with five feet of space between himself and the Holwoods' large, chattering group. "Todd told me you were sick and couldn't come to church today."

Anne wished for Argus to growl and frighten the man when she saw the quick, dismissive glance Mr. Montgomery gave Dr. Holwood before focusing on Lisa. Did she imagine it, or did his lip start to curl before he brought it under control? What could the man have against Dr. Holwood? Unless he was a racist? He maintained a distance between himself and their group, as if the liveliness and sheer numbers irritated him.

"Why isn't Todd here? He's certainly not looking after me," Lisa said after a moment of hesitation. Anne silently cheered how she kept her voice calm, almost cool. Well, almost uncaring.

"He said he was going to check in on you and bring you lunch. Don't you think you'd better head back to your dormitory and wait for him as you agreed?"

"I didn't *agree* on anything with Todd, Mr. Montgomery. I told him yesterday I didn't want to see him until he learned how to apologize when he's wrong."

Score one for you, Anne silently crowed. She bit her lip against a grin as the man's straight posture went ten degrees stiffer and his chin tilted back a little, as if he had been punched in the jaw and refused to admit it.

"I think you'd better talk to Todd about lying, while you're at it. I'm not sick, except sick of him trying to tell me..." Lisa caught her breath, her

91

cheeks flushed. "This is no place for discussing Todd's rudeness, is it? I don't imagine I'll ever see you again, so have a nice Sunday."

Lisa didn't exactly turn her back on the man, but she didn't wait for a response from him before turning her head to focus on the twins, who, with exquisitely perfect timing, latched onto both of Lisa's hands and demanded she draw a cartoon for them, right that moment. Anne avoided meeting the man's eyes, though she caught movement from the corner of her eye when he looked at her. Probably gauging her reaction.

"Good day, Miss Collins," he murmured and walked away.

Lisa let the twins lead her over to one of the benches set up along the sidewalk leading up to the church door. She sank down, knees wobbling. It was a good thing the bench was so close, Anne decided, because Lisa might very well have slid down to the blacktop pavement instead.

"I can't believe I spoke to him like that," she whispered, her voice straining. "Even if Todd did want to apologize, his father will never let him now."

"Then good riddance to them both," Doria said, coming over to join them. She winked at Anne and stepped over behind the bench to rest both hands on Lisa's shoulders and lean over the girl. "Arthur Montgomery is someone who will never admit he's wrong, and never admit that there are ways to walk the Christian life other than his own. He doesn't say anything against Pastor Glenn, because it isn't proper to criticize the clergy—his words—but everyone knows how much he resents the new life that's come into our church since Glenn and Rita came here. The man's a stick in the mud." She sniffed and a tinge of anger touched her voice. "You should hear some of the sermons he's given, never directly to our faces, but always when we're in hearing distance. Nikki's mistakes are our fault, because God could never bless a mixed household. Each race belongs with its own kind, don't you know?"

"Just where did all the races come from?" Anne blurted. "If we all came from Adam and Eve, then racists are wrong. Especially, the creeps who use the Bible to justify racism."

"Unfortunately, the more exclusionary people are," Dr. Holwood said, coming over to join them, "the better Bible scholars they are, and the more new interpretations of scripture they find to back up what they say. As Chesterton said in *Orthodoxy*, and I paraphrase, they are trapped in the clean and well-lit prison of one idea, their minds sharpened to one painful point."

"Uncle Harrison keeps saying we need to read that one. Then he warns it will take at least three tries before it starts to click and make sense." She leaned down to catch hold of Lisa's hand. "Are you going to be okay?"

"I think I should thank you," Lisa said, trying to smile. "Before we talked, I wouldn't have dared stand up to him. Even though Todd lied, I would have made up some excuse and taken the blame. That's just the kind of effect that horrid man had on me. I was afraid to think for myself or contradict anything he said." She glanced up at Doria. "He's said such horrid things about Nikki. Laughing about all the church ministry work she was involved in before she ran away, like he was glad that she had destroyed any future in missions work."

"If God threw away everyone who made big, foolish, selfish mistakes and never let them serve Him again," Dr. Holwood said, "nine-tenths of the Bible wouldn't have been written."

"Well, one good thing has come of this. Todd will be so busy explaining himself to his father, he'll never come after me anymore."

"You're better off," Doria said. She gestured, urging Lisa to get up again. Their group came back together and headed across the parking lot to the street. "Modern wisdom says marriage is just between the couple, but old folk wisdom says you marry the whole family."

"Marriage?" Lisa choked. She went pale, then blushed bright red, rivaling the tiny flowers in her dress. "Todd's never —"

"I overheard him discussing buying rings, with some of his buddies just last week," Dr. Holwood said.

"If Todd Montgomery decided we were getting married, he never told me."

"He'll have to *ask* you, won't he?" Anne observed.

Lisa stared, her mouth hanging open for a moment. Then she grinned, tears in her eyes. A tiny sputtering chuckle escaped her. Then one of the twins stumbled into the puddle in a low spot in the blacktop, and they had to pull her out before she got too messy to go out for dinner.

~~~~~

As soon as she and Xander arrived at the Justice Center Monday morning, Anne called the veterinarian to check on Argus's battle with the infection. She settled on a bench in the hall while Xander stepped into Judge Tomlinson's office to check on something before they headed up to what promised to be an all-day negotiation with Martinez. Anne pulled out her cell phone, determined to make the call before Hannah or Winslow joined them. The thought of either of those two hearing her problems and worries over Argus sent a bristling feeling through her.

Maybe it was the wrong attitude to have, but after bad dreams about Argus dying on her, Anne was in no mood to care about her attitude until she got some good news for a change.

The news was bad. The vet had changed the antibiotics and increased the sedatives, just to keep Argus from opening his wounds worse than they already were.

"I'm coming down. It'll take a while, but he needs me." Anne hesitated, hearing a step in the hallway, but saw no movement. "I'm the only one who can control him when he's really bad."

"I know we discussed this before, but considering the downward turn he's taken — " the vet began. His tone of voice had gained a magnitude of sympathy. Anne was in no mood to appreciate the change.

"No. There is no way I'm going to give up on him. I'll take him to another doctor if I have to, but I'm not giving up."

When she hung up a few moments later, Anne had no recollection of what she had said, what the vet had said. She clenched her fists, threatening the case of the cell phone. She had to get control of herself or she would never find her way from Downtown to the vet's office in Stoughton. But if she did that, taking the bus all the way, she would have to find her way to Xander's office in Padua. Would it take more time to take the bus to the office to get her car? She couldn't seem to wrap her brain around the logistics, and that wasn't doing Argus any good.

"Problem?" a man asked, his voice accompanied by the sound of approaching footsteps. "Need some help?"

Even before Anne turned to face the newcomer, she knew what had happened. He had hidden around the corner to eavesdrop. She wasn't surprised when she raised her head and saw Martinez looming over her. Anne fought the urge to stand up and move away. He was invading her personal space, taking advantage of her emotional turmoil.

"Yes, but this is something way beyond your abilities."

"Oh, I don't know." His smile had a coolness that made her think of the Ogre when her mother caught him trying to lure her into his apartment.

The Ogre had pretended to be friendly and concerned about the "little gal" who seemed lost in a house so big her parents had made the lower floor an apartment to rent out.

"I have connections," Martinez continued. Anne could just imagine the type of connections he had. "I'm a very influential man. Whatever your friend needs, I'm sure I can find a much better doctor, better medicine, a better hospital somewhere else."

"In exchange for what?" Anne stood now, quickly, her sudden movement making Martinez step backwards. She took advantage of his momentary retreat by stepping into the spot he had vacated.

"Exchange?"

"I haven't heard much about you, Mr. Martinez, but I've met plenty of people just like you. I'll wager you never offer anyone a helping hand unless it profits you. What do you want me to make Xander do?"

"No one makes Alexander Finley do anything," Hannah said, appearing abruptly from behind Martinez's bulk.

"Yes, so I've heard." Martinez looked back and forth between them.

His smile widened. "I know what you really want, Miss Blake. And you, Miss Hachworth. Is that your real name, or an alias for your line of work?" He waited for a response, and the tension in the air rose three degrees when Anne just smiled and tucked her hands into her pockets. "You work for the Arc Foundation, don't you? There's something not quite right about you people. Too many secrets. Too many fingers in too many pots. You're going to make a mistake someday and the whole house of cards is going to come tumbling down."

"No, there's nothing wrong with us. There's everything right about us." She took a step forward, making him retreat. Anne felt breathless with the sense of power washing over her. "We don't have any secrets. Everything is open. And that's what's wrong with people like you."

"Oh, really?" He smirked, but the corners of his lips twitched, and that wounded part of Anne that had turned so self-destructive in college latched onto it with a fierce howl of joy.

"It's beyond the imagination of your teeny, tiny, greedy, twisted mind that someone could operate without any lies or secrets. So you think we're even filthier than you. Anything you want to know about Arc, all you have to do is ask."

"Oh, you can be sure —"

"But you won't ask, will you?"

Hannah stared, too stunned to smile.

"You don't trust openness and freedom, do you? You hate people who willingly help others. All you care about is power and hurting as many people as you can." Another step forward — mirrored by another step back for Martinez. Anne marveled at how she kept her voice low, even if intense. "And sick minds like yours have a lot of fun trying to make it legal. You use the law to strangle anyone who tries to obey the law, who tries to live right. Well, you won't win. You'll never win. I hope you go down in flames! And I'll be sitting there watching, the day Xander whips your butt out of the courthouse. How about that?"

One pair of hands slowly, loudly clapped, echoing in the hall outside the conference room. Anne turned, with a sick twisting that went up from her stomach and stabbed into the back of her head.

Xander stood in the doorway with Bailiff Simons, and two judges, three more bailiffs, and Winslow in the hallway beyond him. Simons and the other bailiffs grinned. Xander's face was a stony mask. The judges seemed more amused than anything. Hannah's face twitched as she fought a smirk, and Anne could only dare hope it was directed at Martinez, who was speechless and taking another step back even before he realized they had an audience.

"Are you done?" Xander asked. "We have some work to do. If you're ready?"

"I can't." Anne flinched as Martinez stepped around her and stomped down the hallway. She couldn't see his face, but from the sudden struggle to hide grins and the way everybody stepped aside, Martinez was a black cloud of fury. "Argus—"

"Is he okay?" His face instantly defrosted. Xander put out a hand, as if he would grasp her shoulder.

"I have to go to him."

"Who?" Hannah asked.

Everyone moved on, leaving Xander, Anne, and Hannah alone in the hallway. For the moment.

"It's complicated, but he's sick and fighting the sedatives, and I'm the only one who can control him. If he doesn't lie still..." She swallowed hard, hating the nausea twisting through her gut. Anne wished it was simply worry for Argus and not shame for her too-hasty mouth.

"Here, take my car." Xander started to dig into his pocket.

"No. I can't. I'm probably not in any condition to drive." Anne stepped backward, holding up her hands. "I'll take the bus. I'm getting pretty good at figuring it out."

"You sure you can find the way?" Xander didn't look totally convinced when Anne nodded. "Okay, but I want you to call me when you get back to the Holwoods."

"The meeting's starting, Xander," Hannah said, her voice soft. She stepped toward the doorway and glanced inside, then back over her shoulder at Xander and Anne. "I'll be saying a prayer for him," she added, sympathy warm in her eyes.

"Okay, but—"

"I'll be fine. Go grind that jerk into mincemeat for me, would you?" Anne said.

A grin split his face. "I don't know how many times I've wanted to tear into him like you just did. It probably did him some good to get that character assessment—especially from someone he doesn't know."

"No." She shook her head, even as she backed down the hall. "He says he does know me. Could that be a problem?"

Chapter Thirteen

Xander could only shake his head. Anne turned and hurried around the corner. She had to get to Argus. She was halfway to the elevator before she realized someone followed her. Turning, still walking, she prepared a dozen arguments for why Xander couldn't come with her, despite how much she really wanted someone to lean on right now.

"That was great," Simons said, his eyes almost bugging out wide enough to match his grin. "I really expected you to pop him one. Finley shouldn't have stopped you like he did."

"No, that was the kindest thing Xander could have done." Anne ran the last few steps to the elevator and slapped her hand against the call button. Fortunately, they were in the part of the Justice Center where she didn't need a bailiff to program the elevator for what floor she wanted to get off. Anne didn't like the idea of riding down with Simons — he wasn't going to offer, was he?

"What do you mean? Martinez needed a good slug in the kisser a long time ago. Maybe a broken nose. A black eye, at least. And what could he do? Everybody could tell he brought it on himself, giving you a hard time. Man, I'd give anything to see that."

"Well you won't get it from me."

"Yeah?" Simons stepped back and frowned. She could believe his disappointment was honest. "I had you pegged as the kind who settles your problems with your fists. At the very least."

"Not anymore." Anne felt a few bands of tension leave her chest as the elevator pinged and the middle set of doors rumbled open.

"What do you mean, not anymore? I heard you tore into the guy who stole your truck and killed your dog."

"Argus isn't dead!" she snapped, as she stepped into the elevator. "And I don't settle things with violence — it only brings on more violence."

"Yeah, well if anybody deserves a knife between the ribs and his *cojones* chopped off and stuffed down his throat, it's Martinez."

Anne almost asked what Simons meant by *cojones*, but understanding came to her at the same moment the doors started to close.

"God is the only answer for creeps like Martinez," she called, raising her voice a little to be heard above the squeak-rumble of the elevator. She caught movement beyond Simons and wondered who had come up to join the conversation. She had the awful feeling she would be the topic of discussion in the bailiffs' room for a few hours, at the very least.

That was not a very good witnessing moment, now was it?

It didn't matter that all the counselors she had gone to over the years said her tendency to punch first and demand an apology later was a result of the trauma of her childhood. Being polite and obedient, and a good girl hadn't done her any good. No one had come to her rescue, so her subconscious insisted she had to defend herself and depend on no one. Anne knew better, however. She constantly prayed God would give her more self-control—or better yet, protect her from instances where she lost her self-control. He didn't seem to be listening. Or else she was failing Him miserably again, after months of good behavior.

"Please, Lord," she whispered. "Please, heal us both."

She managed to get her aching need for tears under control by the time she reached the bus stop.

~~~~~

Argus whimpered like a dying puppy when she came through the door into the back room of the veterinarian's office. He kept trying to get up, but his legs folded before he got more than five or six inches off the ground. Each fall slammed his weight down on his wounds. Every time he put weight on his injured leg, Argus let out a yelp. Anne let the tears come as she hurried across the room and threw herself down on the thick mat where he lay.

"It's okay, mutt," she whispered, and wrapped her arms around Argus's neck.

He went instantly still. For two long seconds, Anne held her breath, positive he had waited until she got there just so he could die in her arms. Then she felt his labored breathing, his struggling heartbeats. Argus let out a long, deep sigh and his half-open eyes closed completely.

"That's amazing," the veterinarian whispered from the doorway. "I've seen some pretty astounding shows of loyalty, but this is incredible."

Her mind slid back to the rainy spring morning when she had come down to the kennels to check on the newest batch of puppies. She had only been at Quarry Hall a few days, still getting her balance and working all the medication out of her system. Kathryn had insisted on her getting up every morning and moving, doing something, anything to keep from curling up in a corner and dreaming her life away.

Argus sat perfectly still when she came into the wing of the greenhouse that was given over to the dogs of Quarry Hall. All his littermates continued squeaking and struggling and crawling all over each other. Argus squatted on his chubby legs and looked at her, his head tilted to one side. Then he let out a yelp and leaped, straight at her. Anne had to throw herself to her knees to catch him in time. Panic at the thought of the puppy getting hurt gave way to the overwhelming joy of realizing that

Argus had chosen her. It took several more days to grow more aware of the world around her before she realized the significance. She had her miracle before she even knew to ask, to be jealous of the other girls with their lifelong companions.

"I'm not letting you leave me," she growled, and rested her head on top of Argus's.

~~~~~

When she got back to her apartment that afternoon, Anne looked across the street, hungry for a friendly face, and found the Holwood house too quiet. On the outside, at least. After being taken under the family's wing, she could guess the lovingly regimented routine inside, children helping with preparations for dinner while others finished up their homework. She shivered, feeling like an outsider, and immediately scolded herself for being foolish. If she was lonely, all she had to do was call Quarry Hall to talk or jump in her borrowed car and drive to Akron in less than an hour. Or ask one or several of her adopted sisters to meet her halfway between Akron and Tabor, to have dinner, go to a movie, or do some shopping. She could even go home for the night—but an ache immediately shot through her chest at the thought of going home without Argus.

She thought of all the drive-through restaurants and grocery stores she had passed on her way from Stoughton to Tabor. Why hadn't she stopped at one, so she wouldn't have to stretch her brain around the task of making dinner? Anne was glad she had decided it would save time to take the bus to Xander's office and drive to the vet, but now that she was safely back at her apartment, she wondered at the wisdom. She had been in a haze from the moment she let go of Argus and walked out of the vet's office. Driving as if on remote control was not safe.

A sticky note in fluorescent pink waited on the door of her apartment when she got upstairs. Anne's mouth relaxed into a grin even before she recognized Doria's handwriting, inviting her for dinner, or for dessert if she got home late. She went into her apartment long enough to drop off her purse, put her keys into her pocket, change her shirt—it was covered with Argus's hair and dotted with slobber—and then hurried back down the stairs. She nearly skipped as she crossed the street.

When she stepped through the door, most of the foster-children greeted her by name, and with smiles. She gladly stepped into the hectic pace and did whatever needed doing. There was homework to supervise and dishes to take out of the washer and a table to set and salad to make. In the middle of the noise and questions and people going in three different directions at once, a sea of quiet enclosed her. Not just weariness, but the quiet that came from praying long and hard until she had run out of words and even thoughts, and there was only a sense of waiting and listening for God to speak. She gladly welcomed that sense of contentment in the waiting. Anne appreciated it when Doria asked about Argus and wisely kept from going any further when Anne admitted that he wasn't good, but she had hope for his recovery.

Xander showed up just before dinner was ready to go on the table. Anne was outside, trying to persuade Ricky to leave the neighbor's dog alone and come inside to wash his hands. She noticed the car parking in front of the house but paid it no attention until Xander got out and called her name. Then she jumped. That made Ricky laugh — and took his attention off the dog long enough for the creature to get away.

"You have no excuse," Anne said, and caught hold of the boy's shoulders, turning him toward the house before he could head after the fleeing dog. "Get inside before Mom Holwood comes looking for you."

"Wanna play," Ricky whined.

"Don't you want to eat dinner? Aren't you hungry?" She flinched at the sound of Xander's shoes scraping on the flagstone sidewalk, approaching from behind her.

"Starving!" the boy crowed and ran up the steps into the house.

"Wish you could handle everybody that easily?" Xander asked. When she turned, he was grinning at her. Anne released a breath she didn't know she was holding.

"Hi. Uh — sorry about this morning."

"Justified. I've wanted to ream that arrogant bozo a couple dozen times myself."

"How many years have you been working against him?"

"Well, not him exactly but... well, other people like him, almost from the moment I had my letterhead and a web site spelling out what made Common Grounds different."

"And you've never blown up at him, at any of them, no matter how much he got in your face?" Anne stepped back until she could settle down on the wide steps of the old-fashioned, sandstone and wood porch. He shook his head. "Then I come along and in only two days I self-righteously slap him around just because he makes fun of my dog."

"He was threatening you and Arc. Yes, he was," he pressed on, when Anne shook her head. "I know Martinez. He starts out pretending to joke, then the jokes turn nasty. Notice he said he knew about you? Want to bet he spent most of the weekend looking you up, asking the wrong people about you? Want to bet he was scared badly enough to mess his pants when he found out you worked for Arc, and what the place has done? Hey, technically, you're my boss!"

That startled a sputter of laughter from Anne. She shook her head and closed her eyes, shoulders shaking. Then she felt the air shift around her and the step she sat on creaked and Xander sat down next to her, close enough for their shoulders and hips to touch. The breath caught in her throat. She opened her eyes and found him grinning at her.

"That's better," he said, his voice softening. "How's Argus, anyway?"

"He finally slept while I was there. Just keeping him still without drugs is helpful." She fought a thickening sensation in her throat. "We just have to keep praying. Funny how it's always our last resort, when it should be the first thing we think of."

"I've been praying for you all day." He slid an arm around her shoulders. "Kind of hard to concentrate on all my depositions and opening arguments and plea bargains."

"Thanks," she squeaked. Anne fought not to stiffen, or even run away. She didn't want to hurt him, but it was hard to sit still with the electric jolt running through her at his touch. And the image of Hannah scowling at her. Did this count as trespassing on another woman's territory, if she wasn't the one making the first move? "Uh—how did it go today with Martinez after I left? I mean, I didn't make things harder, did I?"

"I think you put him off balance for a while. He sure didn't like it that bailiffs were snickering. And he knew the rest of us were just better at hiding it. He's really got it in for you."

"Oh, no..." She welcomed that dropping sensation because it decreased that humming from Xander's arm around her.

"Hey, you did me a favor. Martinez seethes and doesn't do a good job of covering it. Kind of a one-track mind, sometimes. If he's busy trying to figure out how he can get back at you—and he can't, so don't worry—he'll be distracted from our case."

"Oh, great, God sent me here as a distraction." Anne was able to laugh, though, when Xander did.

Doria stepped out on the front porch and wasn't at all surprised to see Xander there. Anne wondered if he had called to check on her before he came over, and her hostess knew the whole story of what had happened. She invited Xander to stay for dinner. Anne couldn't decide if she was relieved or disappointed when he refused.

"Sorry. Big day tomorrow and we're pulling an all-nighter at the office to prepare."

"Anything I can do to help?" Anne offered.

"No, but thanks. I think Hannah and Winslow and I can handle it." That flicker of something undecided in his eyes made her suspect he refused her help because of Winslow's presence, not because he didn't need her help.

Anne hoped that wasn't the reason.

She was quiet during dinner, which wasn't hard with everyone else chattering about their day at school, and activities at church and the university. Anne was glad, because it let her get used to this new revelation about herself without trying to navigate a conversation.

What exactly did she feel about Xander? He wasn't athletic, but he wasn't a couch potato, either. He certainly wasn't handsome, but there was something appealing about his rough, unfinished looks. He could be stern and business-like, but sympathetic. He had dignity, but it didn't get in the way of common sense.

"It is definitely not romantic, but maybe I'm... drawn to him?" Anne asked herself, daring to speak the question aloud more than two hours later as she walked through the sunset-streaked woods in the Metroparks. She was glad her apartment was so close to the park system, with its walking paths and hiking trails.

Maybe the first step of attraction. As long as it didn't go any further. Not that Hannah had first dibs on him. More like Anne knew it wouldn't be fair to Xander to even try to go beyond friendship.

If he wasn't aware of how Hannah felt about him, should she tell him? Would that ruin things for Hannah by making Xander uncomfortable around her? For all Anne knew, they had a relationship they didn't reveal to anyone.

That didn't fit the image of Xander she had already built up in her head. Not a guy who wore his heart on his sleeve. Nor was he the "strong, silent type," who kept everything hidden.

"This is just friendship. For now, anyway," Anne told herself as she strode briskly down the winding blacktop path. At this point, it ran along the side of the wetlands where ducks and geese drifted and tall marsh grasses nodded in the gentle evening breeze. This was certainly a lovely place to be alone and get some fresh air and breathing room. "Am I just lonely because Argus is missing, and I'm latching onto anyone who shows me some comfort? What's really going on in my head?"

Tires crunched on the gravel at the edge of the asphalt of the road just behind her. Only four cars had passed Anne since she started down the pathway from the Main Street entrance to the Metroparks, and they had all been going the opposite direction. She glanced over her shoulder and her heart did a flip at the sight of the police car pulling up behind her.

The next moment she wondered why it was a black and white cruiser, and not the brown sedans with green emblems on the door that the park service rangers drove.

"It's getting on toward night," the officer said, after rolling down the window. He tapped the gas and coasted up alongside Anne. She stopped.

"There's another couple hours of light," she said after a moment's hesitation. "The signs say the park closes at eleven."

"I know, but you're alone. Not good to — oh, hi, Anne."

Anne blinked, then she recognized Mike Nichols. She felt a couple more knots of tension untangle and took two steps closer to the car.

"Is it really that dangerous?" she had to ask.

"Used to be kids could be out here in the park until way after dark, no problem, but we've got muggers now and carjackers even in Tabor. Sometimes I think they like to come out to the quiet, safe little towns just to show us we're not immune. If you need a ride back to Holwoods' place, just let me know."

"Thanks, but... I really need to get out and stretch my legs. I'll be careful, though. I can take care of myself." Anne waited for him to say he had heard how she beat up on the carjacker in Stoughton, but he didn't. He looked her over once, then nodded, his frown indicating he didn't like the idea of her being alone. He also couldn't force her to ride with him or make her go back to the Holwoods' house.

"I'll be heading back this way in another twenty minutes. If you change your mind, just flag me down."

Anne promised she would do that. She stayed where she was, watching until he vanished around a bend in the tree-lined road before she resumed walking. It took her a few minutes to realize that her pace was twice as fast as it had been before he showed up.

Deceptive images, she thought. *No matter how nice a place looks, no matter how safe it feels, it can hold a lot of danger.* She looked at the thick clumps of bushes set back from the road, the gaps in the trees where she could get glimpses of the lake on the other side of the road, the shadows stretching out over the wetlands.

She studied the ducks and geese dozing on the water, the birds nesting in the trees all around her, twittering softly and settling down for the evening. If the birds were relaxed and quiet, was there any danger? She could listen to the birds for signs of potential trouble.

Then again, what should she or could she do, if the birds did suddenly startle? Twenty minutes was a long time before Mike came back. Even with her flying fists and feet and sessions in self-defense with Vincent, what were her chances against someone with a weapon? Anne knew better than to put God to an unwarranted test. She turned around and headed back for the entrance to the Metroparks.

~~~~~

Anne spent Tuesday morning at the Justice Center, then went back to the veterinarian to spend the afternoon with Argus. He didn't show much improvement, but she knew he was doing better when he slept, real sleep instead of drugged sleep. During those quiet hours of sitting next to him on the floor, one hand resting on his back and reading in the dim light, Anne's thoughts drifted to the problem that Xander presented.

Or more accurately, the problem he created for her by showing so much concern over Argus. Hannah had been pleasant enough when they met at the office that morning, but a flicker of hurt touched her face when

Xander asked how Argus was doing. Then a few moments later, he mentioned a friend who was a vet, who might be able to help if there wasn't improvement. Maybe Hannah thought Xander cared about anything that hurt Anne because he cared about *her*. As more than a friend. That could explain a lot. Did Xander show signs of interest in her that she hadn't caught? Maybe his behavior had changed enough for someone who knew him to notice – and to suspect his concern was more than just being a nice, caring guy.

"I'm not ready for that kind of relationship. Especially not when it means poaching in another woman's territory," she muttered, still chewing on the questions and attendant problems Wednesday morning. "But how do I tell her that?"

"Problem, kiddo?" a rusty-voiced woman asked from behind her. Anne turned to see Bailiff Vogle sidling along the row of seats right behind her. She grinned and nodded toward the long table where Xander, Hannah, and two other lawyers were haggling over the conditions of a settlement in favor of Xander's client.

"No. Not really." A sigh slid out between her lips, surprising her.

"Take my advice, honey, and don't date a lawyer. They're as bad as doctors and firemen combined."

"Date?" Anne felt that dropping sensation again. So, other people were noticing besides Hannah. Wonderful – not.

"That Finley's a great guy, but he's a little dense. Girls throw themselves at him, and he doesn't even notice. So when he shows some interest... people notice." She patted Anne's shoulder and continued down the row with a note probably intended for the bailiff keeping watch over the haggling at the table.

That summed up the problem in a nutshell, Anne realized, both there in the conference room and later in the kennel Wednesday afternoon, keeping watch over Argus. Hannah didn't strike her as the type to throw herself at anyone, but she had displayed enough interest, even when Xander didn't notice, other people did. Someone probably said something to Hannah, either teasing her or commiserating, which just made the situation worse. Then along came a total stranger, and Xander made the effort to pull his head out of his work to look after her. It wasn't fair to Hannah, but Anne had no idea how to help, what to say, without embarrassing all three of them.

Chapter Fourteen

"I never thought the legal profession would fall so low," Martinez said, stepping into the elevator two steps behind Anne as she headed upstairs to join Xander and Hannah after lunch on Thursday. He chuckled when she looked at him and didn't bother answering. "Never thought I'd see someone as ugly as Finley with a groupie. Must be pretty good for his ego, huh? Or — no, I know!" He leaned back against the opposite wall and looked her up and down.

Anne knew he had to be disappointed. The day was chilly and damp and she had worn a dark green corduroy jacket, khaki slacks, and a long, pale green cotton sweater borrowed from Nikki's closet. Nothing to outline her figure, nothing for him to gawk at.

Why had she decided Argus was feeling well enough she could spend the whole day away from him? It was like Satan was just waiting for her to make a bad choice so traps could spring up all around her.

"He's doing this to make the rest of us jealous. How much is he paying you to hang around? Are you any good in — " He stopped short as Simons stepped into the elevator.

There was a dangerous glint in the bailiff's eyes that made Anne feel protected. Then the next moment, she wondered if the glint was just a little too bright. Extremes in anything couldn't be good. Weren't bailiffs supposed to help keep the *peace* in the Justice Center?

"Any good in where?" Simons asked softly. He turned his back on Martinez and nodded to Anne. "Have a good lunch? The Fruit-n-Cream is a great place. I saw you over there just a little while ago."

"Oh. Yeah. Fantastic." Anne fought the urge to wipe at her lip and see if any of her drinkable lunch remained to be seen. She had walked over to Tower City during the lunch break to get away from Xander and Hannah, and to get some exercise. She wished she had followed her routine of the last few days and taken the bus to Stoughton. Or stayed at Common Grounds' office to look through records today. Anywhere but here.

They didn't say much else during the short ride up to their floor. Anne hung back while Martinez stomped off the elevator and down the hall.

"He's a real slime, ain't he?" Simons hooked a thumb over his shoulder at the departing lawyer. "You watch out. He'll try something next, just to get a reaction out of you. Won't he be surprised when you punch his lights out? Or worse, maybe?" He grinned, nodded to her, and headed down the hall in the other direction.

"I wouldn't do anything like that," she said, clearly and distinctly. Several passing people in uniforms turned to look at her, then glanced at Simons. Anne felt rather ridiculous, though she knew they had to understand she was talking to him.

What was Simons pushing for?

Problem: she *wanted* to take a few good swings at Martinez, black his eye, give him a bloody lip, mess up his perfectly coiffed hair. She didn't like her violent impulses.

She needed to be back in her truck, touring the country with Argus.

How mature does that make me? She headed down the hall and reached the conference room just before another bailiff stepped out to close the door. *How strong am I against temptation and bad impulses if my way of handling them is to take off across the country?*

That thought kept her mind off Martinez, even though she did catch him looking at her and leisurely licking his lips a few times. She caught Xander frowning at the man, then glancing her way. Anne didn't look forward to the grilling she was going to get on the ride back to Xander's office. Maybe she should take Hannah up on her offer of a ride home, since she lived just a few streets away from the Holwoods?

Maybe she should have a heart-to-heart talk with Hannah on the ride home? Several times today, Hannah was clearly concerned about work she needed to do at the office. At every break, she checked the answering machine and relayed messages between Xander and the other lawyers. Breaking her usual routine had probably alerted Martinez and gave him fuel for his insinuations.

Anne wished she were alone so she could bang her head against a wall, to hopefully knock some common sense in and oblivion out.

After their meeting let out an hour later, Xander, Winslow, and Hannah elected to have a short strategy session in the snack bar opposite the waiting area for the jury pool. Anne could either sit with them or wait outside, maybe downstairs somewhere. She almost announced she wanted to sit by herself for a while, but she looked down the hall and saw Martinez at the elevator. Waiting for her, if Simons was right.

She sat next to Winslow. There really was no way to avoid being so close to the man. It was either sit next to him or opposite him at the four-seater table. Winslow was more vocal and active in his discussions than she remembered from the hearings when she was a child. He kept bumping her knee with his or stretching his long legs under the table and stepping on her feet or nudging her in the shins. To her chagrin, she jumped every time. Hannah noticed, and her little frowning glances of real concern just proved what a nice person she was under her aching heart.

Anne distracted herself for a few seconds, thinking about grabbing Xander by his collar and getting nose-to-nose with him to point out that Hannah was in love with him. Or, if not in love, then seriously, warmly "in like," with a strong possibility of something much deeper.

Yeah, as if she had any claim to being an expert in relationships?

Besides, she was supposed to observe Xander at work, relating to people, not playing Cupid. Pulling her mind off solving Hannah's problem just meant she jumped the next time Winslow nudged her by accident. Why did he have to have such long legs, and suffer from restlessness this late in the day?

Finally, she couldn't take it anymore. It was one thing to run away to avoid challenges to her spirituality and maturity, but it couldn't be wrong to leave an uncomfortable situation before she started to scream. Besides, she had to use the bathroom. Anne muttered an excuse and got up.

Winslow waited for her when she came out of the women's restroom. He stood against the opposite wall, hands jammed into his pockets, briefcase at his feet.

"Something about me makes you uncomfortable," he said, when Anne kept her head bowed and tried to pretend she hadn't seen him.

He reached out as if he would catch her by the arm and she couldn't take that. He would always be linked in her mind and memories with the Ogre. Touching was not allowed, or she really would hurt someone.

"I'm not a very good actress, am I?" She leaned back against the wall on her side of the hallway and clasped her hands in front of herself. Just in case she felt the urge to leap on him and scratch or slap or do something more vindictive.

"I have this feeling Xander knows. He kept trying to make excuses. Your dog. The trouble with Martinez." A rare smile lit Winslow's face for a moment. "You know he's just giving you a hard time because Xander likes you."

"I like Xander, too. What does that have to do with any of it?" She tried to shrug. Inside, she shriveled. Did the entire Justice Center know?

"Nothing. That's the problem. I'm a problem for you for some reason, and I want to know why." He crossed his arms and shifted his stance, preparing for a long wait.

"You want to know why," Anne murmured, nodding.

She had to release some of the pressure, and going for a long, sweaty run with Argus was not an option. The question was if she could release enough, and not too much.

"Why not? I'm really curious, first of all. Is this a sudden change for you, defending the innocent?" A bitter chuckle burst from her when Winslow frowned and blinked and shook his head. "The first time we met, you seemed to enjoy defending the criminals and trying to make the innocent victims carry all the guilt."

"What are you talking about?" he said, his voice low, harsh. "I've never met you—"

"A murder case in Buffalo. The trial started in July." Anne remembered vividly how she had sweated and suffocated in the thick, scorched air in the tiny room where she waited during other testimonies. "The double homicide happened in late February. A wealthy couple, slaughtered by the man who rented out the lower level of their house. The only witness was the nine-year-old daughter, whom the old man had been molesting from the day he moved in downstairs. The night he moved up to physical torture, punishing her because her parents realized something was wrong and started asking questions—"

She choked and bent her arms to hold them behind her back, pressed against the wall. The burn scars from cigarettes and scalding hot tea actually itched, for the first time in years.

"The mother caught him. She heard something, she felt something was wrong, even though the little girl was gagged to keep her from screaming. He killed her, then killed the father when he came in answer to her screams."

If her heart hadn't been racing, loud enough to deafen her and her knees hadn't threatened to fold under her, Anne would have laughed at the shock that turned Winslow's face corpse-white for several seconds. She swallowed hard and struggled to get her breath back.

"You stood there, insisting that I was lying, that I was making up everything that man did to me, nearly shouting at me to tell the truth. I was in tears. I had burn marks all over my body. I wore a sleeveless dress to court, so the lawyers could show the scars on my arms and legs. There were doctor reports stacked three feet high, proving what he did to me — and you called me a liar." Anne swallowed hard and took three deep, strangling breaths, fighting to keep her voice soft and to fight the sensation she would vomit right there in the hallway.

"My family was dead and I saw it happen, and you said I was making it up. They found bloody clothes and the axe he used to kill them in his apartment. They found photos of me, naked and tied up. I was nine years old. I didn't know enough to make up all the disgusting things he made me do. But you called me a liar," she finished on a whisper.

"He was a pillar of the community," Winslow said, his voice dragged out of his chest by some force beyond the stunned weariness that made his face sag and turned his eyes into burned pits. "Someone captured him and knocked him out and delivered him to the police with most of the evidence. They called 911 after they stopped the real murderer. It was too neat. It had to be a set-up. Someone put those words in your mouth, the ideas in your head. He was framed."

"Even with all that proof?"

"It was impossible. He was a good man with fifty years of public service and charitable works behind him. He lost his wife to cancer. He had nothing but his reputation and his memories."

"A false history. Just like the makeup and wig he wore, to make him look old. Created to let him move from town to town, gaining the trust of his targets before he slaughtered them." Anne felt something snap in her chest, releasing half the pressure, and she sent up a silent prayer of thanks for the Black Prince, who had provided her proof that she wasn't insane, that she was fully the victim. "That was the fun part for him, tricking people, making them think he was their friend. Letting him into their homes. Giving him access to their children for his games."

"You can't prove—"

"I have documents." Anne hesitated a moment, wondering if it was going too far to reveal that her father had been the Ogre's target, and she was just the fringe benefit of a job well done.

Like she always did when she thought of the Black Prince, she asked God to keep him safe in the filthy, diseased, dark world he traveled, rescuing the abused and wounded. She fervently believed God had sent him to break her out of the pitiful excuse for a mental hospital where she had been a prisoner. He later provided the files to help her heal, to destroy the last lingering doubts and fears that maybe, yes, she was to blame. Just as the Ogre's defense lawyers had claimed all those years ago.

"But—how was I supposed to know?" Winslow's voice wobbled and thickened, and he visibly fought pain. "All I knew was what everyone else in that courtroom knew about him. He was a good man, a friend to everyone."

"I was a child with my whole life ahead of me and he tried to destroy it." Anne swallowed hard, hating the strangling feeling moving through her throat, threatening to choke off her words. A quiet portion of her mind noted the irony that she finally had a chance to tell off the man who, in some ways, had hurt her worse than the Ogre, yet she didn't enjoy it. The words were bitter, the emotions scalding as they surged through her.

"Do you have any idea what it was like, to be hurting, inside and out, to be an orphan, and to be called a liar when you tried to tell the truth? He told me no one would believe me, and he laughed at me. He threatened to kill my parents if I ever told anybody what he did to me. He said I was a bad girl, and he was going to punish me until I was a good girl. And then my mother—she caught him. I never told anyone, but he still killed them."

"I was wrong," Winslow said, his voice cracking. The wrinkles seemed to deepen all across his face, making him look twenty years older. His shoulders stooped, as if pressed down by a horrible weight.

"Yeah, everybody's wrong." She coughed, trying to clear her throat of the sensation that more angry words would pour out.

This wasn't right. She *thought* she had released her anger years ago. She *thought* she had forgiven the Ogre and the wise man who was only now admitting he had been a fool.

Harrison Carter had told her, in her first few days at Quarry Hall, when she was still shaking off the effects of long-term sedation, that her healing was up to her. She was responsible for stepping away from the path of anger, vengeance, and self-pity. She had to choose every day to deny the hunger to dwell on her injuries. She had to turn her thoughts away from her wounds, or they would never heal. She had to consciously hand the pain over to God every day, and then keep her mind and soul busy so she wouldn't take the pain back inside her. The secret to healing was to bring healing and help to others who also suffered.

Sorry, Lord. I should have kept my mouth shut. Anne swallowed hard against a sob that tried to burst from her throat. *I should have told him he was wrong and walked away.* She had to change the conversation. She had to get her mind—and Winslow's mind—off of her. Off their shared history. Even if it hurt, if it felt hypocritical, even sanctimonious, she had to say the words. Saying the words aloud was half the battle in making herself believe them.

"But you know something?" Her throat felt like it was full of sand. "What I suffered is nothing compared to what other people have gone through. I have to remember that every day. I have to get up every morning and go out and help them. I only hurt myself when I curl up into a little ball of pain and demand the world pay me back."

Winslow stared at her, his mouth working a little but no words escaping. There was something almost comical about him, with a few thin tears gleaming on his leathery cheeks, his bloodshot eyes wide, and his mouth gaping like a suffocating fish.

"Keep helping the innocent against the rich creeps who can hire people like Martinez to make them look good. Maybe someday you'll be able to forgive yourself." Anne shoved off the wall and moved down the hall. Her legs didn't quite wobble like she had feared. Maybe she could even get downstairs without someone accusing her of being drunk or on drugs. That certainly wouldn't look good for Xander.

"Can you forgive me?" He didn't reach out toward her, could barely lift his head to look at her. Anne stopped, glancing back over her shoulder once at him.

"I thought I had," she admitted after a long silence, when she thought she could hear his heartbeat through the hiss of the ventilation system and the far-off echoes of voices somewhere around the corner. "I guess I have to keep praying about it, huh?"

Her legs grew steadier with every step she took. Anne felt like she had emerged from a dark, slippery tunnel when she stepped out of the restroom hallway.

"You're something else." Simons grinned, a tight, mirthless expression, when Anne jerked and let out a startled squeak. The bailiff leaned against the wall. He tilted his head to one side, hands stuffed into his pockets, shoulders hunched, and studied her. "I'd be tearing into Winslow if he'd ever defended someone who hurt me."

"Lots of innocent people have been called liars before, and more will in the future. Lies are a whole lot more fun and profitable." She shrugged and continued down the hall.

Simons caught her by the elbow. Anne jerked, hissing, and twisted around. She spread her arms, fists clenched, body bending into the first defensive posture Vincent had taught her.

"Yeah," he said with a grin. "You're trained. You're a pro. You know how to take out the bad boys with your bare hands. I bet you're some kind of vigilante, huh? Go hide in dark alleys and just pound the slimes when they try to hurt some poor, innocent, defenseless old ladies. Or little girls," he added with a knowing wink.

Anne wanted to throw up. *Lord,* she prayed, *give me the words. Quiet my mind. Something good has to come of all this pain.*

"Xander's way is better. Everyone deserves to have their say. If we resort to violence to solve our problems—"

"Cut the crap!" His voice echoed off the polished walls, the metal doors of the elevators.

Anne wondered for a moment why they were alone, why people didn't come running at the sound of their voices.

"How can you talk about justice, after what happened to you?" he spat.

"Because I've profited from the biggest injustice of all." A cool calm settled over her. She felt the tense lines in her face relax, and knew another spirit was working over and through hers.

"What the heck are you talking about?"

"Mercy is when we don't get what we deserve. Grace is when we get what we don't deserve."

"Look—"

"Crimes must be punished, right?" She waited until the big man thought for a moment, visibly trying to find the trick in her words.

Winslow chose that moment to step out into the lobby. He looked like he had been through the wringer in just a few moments. He tried to avoid looking Anne in the eye, but it was like a line had been strung between them, pulling them toward each other. She spoke to him as much as she did to Simons.

"Someone has to pay for what was done. That's justice. God said so.

Every evil, every crime, every tear comes from rebelling against what God set up as the standard. God said that's sin. Sin is punished by death. Nothing but blood will pay. So Jesus took our punishment. Only a totally innocent man could carry the weight of all the evil in the world. The debt was paid. Our punishment was cancelled. Now, an innocent man dying so the guilty could go free, that's the biggest injustice in the entire world, don't you think?"

"You're crazy," Simons growled.

Winslow nodded, a light beginning to dawn in those burned-out, sorrowful eyes. He didn't smile, but Anne thought maybe some weight crumbled off his shoulders. It occurred to her to wonder how many unjust cases he had been involved in, where he realized later that he had been on the wrong side. Maybe the man didn't really enjoy defending the guilty. Maybe his anger against her, during all those hearings, had come from sensing, fearing, that he was in the wrong.

She wished she had thought of that years ago.

Lord, forgive me, and help me to forgive.

"You and Finley deserve each other," the bailiff spat. "He's wrong. The scum gotta pay. They got no right to justice. He's just wasting time, trying to make things right. They gotta pay. And you're gonna get hurt if you keep helping him," he finished, pointing a finger like a gun at her and stomping out of the lobby.

Anne slumped against the wall, eyes closed, feeling like her knees would fold now.

"So that's why you're not an axe-murderer," Winslow said.

That startled a breathy snort of laughter out of her. She kept her eyes closed and was grateful when she heard his footsteps tapping on the floor as he left the lobby.

Chapter Fifteen

Anne walked in the Metroparks that evening, losing herself in the rhythm of her rapid pace to try to bring her racing thoughts and the unwanted images under control. Every time she thought she could pray, start to sort things out, a new thought would branch off like an unwanted sucker on a sapling that needed to be trimmed. She paid little attention to her surroundings, just kept going on the asphalt walking/biking path through the Metroparks. Down past the covered bridge. Across Pearl Road. A sign for tobogganing chutes brought her up short and cut off the thread of her thoughts so abruptly she stopped, breathless, and burst out laughing.

Sunset had turned into twilight. She turned and looked back the way she had come. Even though she couldn't remember the twists and turns, she had a very long walk to get back to Tabor and her too-quiet apartment. Traffic was heavy, but there didn't seem to be many walkers on the trail. The few she saw around her were heading down the trail at a quick pace. She suspected the cars she had seen parked in various turn-offs along the park road would be gone when she retraced her steps.

"Lord, please protect me from my stupidity," she whispered, and turned around.

Her legs ached. Anne suspected they had twinged for a while now, but she had been too busy thinking to pay attention.

The light seemed to fail a degree with every step she took. Anne tried to hurry without appearing to hurry. Why attract predators? Sharks were attracted to thrashing and the tang of blood and fear in the water, not simply to the presence of an intruder. Walking with confidence wasn't much protection, but if she acted like she wasn't afraid, someone looking for a target might leave her alone.

"I'm not alone, Lord," Anne whispered. A gasping little laugh escaped her as she hurried across Pearl Road. The light turned yellow just as she passed under it. "Now is one of those times when it would be nice for an angel to turn up. Even if I can't see them, let my enemy see."

She picked up her pace and stepped into the thicker shadows of the trees near the covered bridge crossing. Anne smiled at her momentary flight of fancy. Angels with flaming swords weren't part of her equipment package. Some people got the flash, some got the struggle—but it all evened out in the end, she knew. She didn't want the heartache and roller

113

coaster of joy and terror, or the danger that came with those who saw angels. Look at all Sophie and Joan had gone through, and they had met an angel face-to-face. Big miracles were granted to those who needed something to hold onto in the middle of big, dangerous problems. She preferred to be someone who struggled along, nice and steady on the sidelines, growing slowly with no backsliding. Doubting was fine because it kept her climbing.

A twig snapped somewhere behind her. Anne thought she heard a shoe scraping on asphalt. No cars waited in the parking area she had just passed. No branches or side paths led into the woods off the trail she followed. That feeling of being watched, the weight of attention focused on her, pressed against her back. She concentrated on moving smoothly, briskly, confidently, landing on the balls of her feet. She could break into a run in a split second if she had to and keep it up for however long it took to find other people. She just didn't care to prove it, thanks very much.

A flashing red light caught her eye. Anne grinned tightly and breathed a little easier. Ahead was the crossing for the covered bridge, on her left. The road led up out of the Metroparks. Maybe she could follow it to some place where she could use a phone—she had left hers behind, to ensure quiet to think . At the very least, there might be some houses where someone would make a call for her.

Neck hairs prickled. That sense of being watched changed, intensified, as she imagined it would when someone sighted down the barrel of a gun at her. Footsteps penetrated her thudding heartbeats. Anne turned, hands rising automatically, warding off the hands that reached for her neck. She put all her weight on one leg and brought the other up. The man shouted as her knee caught him low in his gut. Shock turned into anger and he swung with both arms, trying to hit her. He was built like a fullback, dressed all in dark jeans and sweatshirt with a hood pulled low over his head.

A length of rope dangled between his hands. The perfect position and length to wrap around her neck. Something snapped inside Anne. She ducked the swinging arms and butted his chest with her head, hitting just under the juncture of his ribs. He yelped, the breath knocked out of him, and stumbled backward. Anne followed up with a hard right swing that made her knuckles crack and sting against his chin. He went down, cursing. The words bypassed her brain and went straight to her gut and Anne flung herself at him. She landed hard, knees in his ribs, and pounded with both fists.

He rolled out from under her. She leaped backward and stumbled a few steps, struggling not to fall. Anne knew better than to lose her footing, even for two seconds.

In those few seconds she was off him, suddenly he had a gun in one hand, the rope still in the other. He snarled at her, blood streaming from his nose, his hood yanked down far enough to reveal his balding head, stringy blond hair, and the scar running from his right temple across his cheekbone. Anne would recognize him anywhere now. Those muddy brown eyes burned — she preferred them dull with shock and the first sparks of fear.

"What do you think you're doing, you —" A stream of cursing followed.

Anne wanted to laugh, but it was sick laughter that might make her throw up. It would infuriate this man, and she had faced this kind of fury before, his type of self-righteous brute. He was enraged because she dared to defend herself. As if it was his right to attack her. He looked nothing like the Ogre, but she had seen the old man's face as she pounded him.

Don't ever let your emotions run your defense, Vincent had said hundreds of times during self-defense lessons. *Use your emotions as fuel. Use your hurt and anger as fuel. Even use your fear as fuel. But don't let it run your defense. Think. That's why God gave you your brain instead of just hormones.*

"That's enough!" a voice boomed over a bullhorn.

Headlights flashed across the scene, striped by the few trees standing between the car and the two of them. A man's silhouette moved into the headlights. It had the bullhorn in one hand and a gun very visible in the other. Blue and red lights turned slowly on the top of the car.

The cursing continued, but now the gunman turned it on the police officer who approached them. Anne trembled, dizzy with a moment of disbelief. If her attacker ran off into the woods and the police officer and his car vanished into thin air moments after she was safely out of the Metroparks, she wouldn't be surprised at all.

Why didn't the idiot shoot at the officer or try to run into the darkness of the woods? It was only a few yards behind him. He just stood there, cursing, blaming Anne, his gun hanging at his side in his limp hand, the rope still clutched in his other hand, and blood smearing his face.

The cruiser started its engine and came around the bend in the road where it had stopped. Anne wondered how long the car had been there. Had the officers seen her coming, and decided to wait for her? Had they just stopped there? How much had they seen of the fight?

When the angle of the light changed, she recognized the officer: Todd James. Anne took a stumbling step toward him.

"You okay, Anne?" Todd smiled tightly when she nodded and offered her his hand. Then the headlights of the oncoming car fully illuminated the gunman. His eyes widened and he whistled softly. "What did you do to Bruiser Olson?"

"You know this jerk?" she blurted, her voice cracking.

Olson's face crumpled and he looked like he would start crying. His stream of profanity stopped in mid-curse and he dropped his gun.

"Man, this ain't anything like it should be," he grumbled.

"The college girls getting too smart for you, Bruiser?" Todd gestured with his gun for the man to step back, and kept an eye on him as he bent to pick up the dropped gun.

"College girls?" Anne repeated, feeling rather numb suddenly.

"His favorite trick is to slash some tires or take a distributor cap from cars in the parking lots at the university, then offer to help the poor stranded girl—if he's lucky enough to get a girl's car," Mike Nichols said, stepping out of the car to join them. "Then he tries to get her to go to a bar with him, and if she won't go he tries for some groping in the front seat of his car to pay for the ride home. The ones he takes to the bar can't remember much the next morning."

"You got no proof," Bruiser muttered through his swollen lips. "Can't prove it's me."

"No, but we have enough witnesses that put you at the scenes, enough of a pattern, we can warn people what to watch out for. Must be hard to get around on campus when a sketch of your face is on every dormitory bulletin board."

"So now he's in the park, trying to mug defenseless joggers?" Anne said. There was something almost comical, almost pitiful about this.

"Well... not defenseless," Todd said, grinning. "That was quite a show."

"How much did you see?"

"Enough to testify he attacked you, and it was all self-defense."

"Man, all I did was ask her for directions!" Bruiser blurted. "I was just walking along and she was coming at me and I said, hey, do you know where this road's going to, and she just screamed and came at me."

"You came up on her from behind with a rope aimed at her neck," Mike said, sounding bored. "Into the car, Bruiser." He nodded back toward the cruiser. His partner took the would-be mugger by the arm to guide him. "You can't ride in the front seat—against regulations—but I think I can promise he won't try anything if you ride in the back."

Anne giggled. The last dregs of her adrenaline high sent a shivering through her body that made her feel dizzy and nauseous.

Bruiser glared at her and muttered under his breath during the mercifully short ride to the police station. Mike took the bruised and bloody mugger inside to process him while Todd took Anne home. He pulled into the Holwoods' driveway. Some parental instinct must have alerted the Holwoods. They came to the front door before Anne could start down the driveway to retreat to her own apartment. Her friends were understandably upset at hearing what had happened to her, but as Todd described what had happened, he managed to shine a humorous light on the situation.

"Hey, for all we know, God put Anne there to teach the creep a lesson," he finished. "The next time he sees a lady walking alone, he'll think twice before he tries anything."

"I know the campus will feel a little safer," Dr. Holwood remarked.

"This attack might be enough to convince the prosecutor to press charges, finally. It's hard to gather evidence or get girls to testify when everything is a drugged blur."

"Circumstances like this do tend to make us chafe against the system, but if we made ourselves judge and jury without due process, where would we be? Innocent people could be punished, even killed, before the truth came out. If, it ever came out."

"Still, it'd be nice if we could do something about idiots a little faster," Anne muttered.

She thought of Simons. Wasn't that his complaint? Justice wasn't served faster on people who were obviously guilty. Lack of evidence meant no charges could be filed. But where would operating without evidence and rules lead? To vigilantes? Posses and witch trials, kangaroo courts and people killed because they had the wrong skin color or saluted the wrong flag, wore the symbol for a secret society, or belonged to the wrong country club.

~~~~~

Lunchtime, Friday. Xander, Hannah, and Anne stood in the lobby by the revolving doors out of the Justice Center, debating where to go eat, when a cluster of bailiffs came toward them. Anne didn't recognize the woman who walked at the head of the line, and by now she thought she was getting to know all of them on sight.

"I know her," Xander said, and gestured at the oncoming group with his chin. Then he looked up as Winslow approached, holding out a handful of papers.

"What's a bailiff from Tabor Municipal Court doing here?" Hannah added.

Simons walked with the woman and pointed at Anne as they approached. Five other bailiffs followed them, all focused on either the woman or Anne. What did they know?

Tabor Municipal Court? A light, relieved sensation swept through her when the pieces came together in her head. They wanted her to testify against Olson. Maybe she should have stayed at the police station to lodge her complaint. Mike had said he would file the report, and to be prepared to be called for a deposition. Why would they send a bailiff for her?

"Anne Hachworth?" the woman said, her voice husky but soft. She was a rail, all pale hair and silvery blue eyes and that fragile complexion that most models would kill for. She waited until Anne nodded. "You're being served with a summons to appear in Tabor Municipal Court in one week's time."

"To testify against the guy who tried to mug me." Anne held out her hand for the paper.

"Mug you?" Xander blurted, stopping the conversation he was holding with Winslow. "When did this happen?"

"Last night." She tried to shrug it off. The woman's stillness made her hesitate with the paper just an inch from her fingers. "Something wrong?"

"You're being accused of entrapment."

"Entrapment?" Hannah echoed. She sounded like she wanted to laugh but didn't dare. Anne refused to look at her.

"And assault and battery." The woman's composure slipped. Her lips twitched and disgust darkened her eyes. "Olson claims he was unarmed, despite the testimony of two officers that he came after you with a rope, and then a gun."

"When were you going to tell me about this?" Xander demanded, stepping up next to Anne.

"It's nothing. At least," Anne corrected, "I thought it was nothing. I suppose this guy claims I was working with the police, luring him out into the open?"

"That about sums it up," the bailiff said. Now she did smile; crookedly. "I have to tell you, a lot of us have been wishing for months someone would do a number on Olson. He's been the main suspect for a long, long time in these park muggings, but no one could prove anything."

"What do you mean exactly by 'did a number'?" Simons asked. He had an eager grin like a kid about to rush into the grandstands for the championship football game.

"Black eye, cuts, bruised ribs, bloody nose. He's also claiming whiplash, but you would have had to pick him up and swing him around and slam him against something to do that, and he's way too big for someone your size."

"Not too big for Anne to beat him bloody, though," Hannah said, her voice rich. She rested a hand on Anne's shoulder, making her flinch. "What's the story?"

"I was out too late in the park last night, getting dark, everyone gone, and this jerk jumped out of the trees and tried to mug me. I defended myself. The first thing they teach you in self-defense is if you can't get to safety, you make sure the guy can't chase you. Then he pulled a gun. Some cops were there in time to see the whole thing. End of story." She looked down at the paper limply clasped between two fingers. "Except for this."

"Well, if you need a good lawyer..." Xander shrugged, but a spark of laughter in his eyes made Anne think maybe it wasn't as embarrassing as it felt right now.

"Knew you had it in you." Simons winked. "Good job. Keep it up."

"Self-defense is one thing," Anne said, her voice rising a little more than she intended. Other people walking through the lobby slowed or turned to look and listen. "Deliberately going out and beating up on somebody just because you disagree with them is wrong."

"Is that a slur against my client?" Martinez purred, stepping out of a blur of people passing by just at the edge of Anne's vision. "I have plenty of time for more slander cases."

"That's a general statement of character," Winslow offered. "Look it up in the dictionary sometime. The concept might be enlightening."

Martinez glared at the man, looked Anne up and down once, and continued on his way. She had the awful suspicion he knew what had happened, and it amused him.

"If you need any help," the other lawyer continued. He started to reach out a hand as if to grasp Anne's arm, a purely supportive gesture, but he stopped and looked at his hand as if he had never seen it before, then let it drop to his side.

"Thanks," Anne managed to say, her voice breaking into a whisper.

"Okay, folks." Xander made shooing motions with one hand. "The show's over. I'm sure you'll hear all about it through the grapevine. Could we get going and get our lunch before we're out of time?" He hooked his free hand through Anne's arm and guided her out the revolving doors. Winslow and Hannah were close behind, like bodyguards. Anne appreciated that when she could finally get her mind out of neutral gear.

The past few moments caught up with Anne, crashing down on her. She wanted to curl up and sleep somewhere, but she knew she wouldn't sleep. She had the rest of the day to get through. She had a summons to appear in court. What were her chances of being thrown in jail? She tugged free of Xander's grip and started to open the folded papers.

"Here, let me take care of that. I'm your lawyer, after all," Xander said, neatly snagging the paper from her fingers.

Nobody said anything until they reached the relative safety and anonymity of the food court at Tower City. Winslow and Hannah went to get their lunch. Xander guided her to a table in a far corner of the noisy mezzanine jammed with tables and diners. He read through the summons and another piece of paper that wasn't attached but folded up with the first. Xander snorted and smiled a little as he handed it to Anne.

"Sorry," he said. "Personal mail."

It took three tries to make sense of the words on the paper. Then a flush of warmth and relief and a longing to cry worked through her. The paper was from Mike and Todd, a note of encouragement, detailing the sordid history of the lawyer Bruiser Olson had hired and the reactions of various people throughout the Tabor Heights Police Department.

"This might make things a little harder to disprove, though," Xander said, when she finally closed her eyes and put down the paper.

"Huh?" Anne rubbed her eyes and didn't bother looking at him. She knew the concerned expression he wore now – the same expression he wore for every client.

It was ironic that the last thing she wanted right now was a good lawyer. She wanted a friend. She wanted a hug. She wanted to wake up and find out this whole ugly week was just a bad dream.

She wanted to go home to Quarry Hall.

"Most of city hall is delighted about what you did to Olson. Did you know the two officers had a video camera going? They got suspicious when they saw a young woman out alone. They saw a shadow moving in the trees, turned on the dash-cam, and before they could move to help you, you pulverized the mugger. They say you moved like a professional."

"Well, heck yes!" She sat up straight and opened her eyes now. "Vincent won't let any of us hit the road until he's sure we know some basic self-defense. It'd be kind of stupid to send us out without any means of keeping ourselves in one piece. Even the new girls on courier runs know how to take care of themselves. We carry pepper spray and have our dogs, and every time we go home Vincent beats up on us for a refresher course. Sure, we trust God to protect us, but we don't walk into danger on purpose and we sure don't put God to the test."

"Olson and his lawyer also say you moved like a pro. That could work against you. More proof it was a set-up. That you deliberately went out tempting someone to mug you. They may just say that Olson was the target, that he had been watched for weeks to find his pattern, and you went out specifically to lure him into a compromising position."

120

Chapter Sixteen

"Isn't that sort of *confessing* that he did attack? That he was lying when he said I attacked him? He chose to attack me. He had a rope and a gun. He sure wasn't asking for directions or a quiet conversation." She closed her eyes for a few seconds, reliving that short struggle. "He pulled the gun on me after I had him down on the ground. If he was innocent, what was he doing carrying a gun into the park, anyway?"

"He and his lawyer probably haven't thought of that yet."

"With his reputation, nobody will believe him if he claims he was scared to be alone."

"Reputation ... that could be motive for setting up the trap. Knowing he wouldn't be able to resist a poor defenseless little girl out after dark all by herself."

"Whose side are you on?" she demanded. A strained little laugh escaped her. "He came after me with a rope, aimed for my neck. When I defended myself, he got mad. He tried to use deadly force. He's not an innocent victim in this."

"No, he isn't. What about this reputation of his? What did the police tell you?"

They discussed what she had learned from Mike and Todd while they waited for Winslow and Hannah to come back, and then while they went through the lines to get themselves something to eat. Winslow volunteered to check into Olson's lawyer, to see what could be brought to bear on him and predict how he would turn during the proceedings. Hannah took the task of checking with all the girls who had been stranded by slashed tires or engine problems, and either got pawed by Olson or had blanks in their memories later. Xander said he would check Olson's schedule, to see if he really did go to the park every evening as the lawyer claimed. Anne appreciated their help, but their enthusiasm irritated her a little. Later, she realized how ridiculous that was. They were helping her — what more could she ask?

Martinez managed to get in a few more snide remarks during their few encounters that afternoon. Anne passed him in the hallway once, and he made a pretense of stepping out of her way, then loudly remarked that she was the kind of girl to get nasty if someone looked at her cross-eyed. Then another time he brushed against her while she was sitting next to the aisle, coming into the conference room, and pretended to be worried that she might be angry with him. He followed up on that by some snide remark she didn't hear, but which caused his several assistants to snicker and grin at her.

"How can you just sit there and let him keep doing that?" Bailiff Henderson asked, sliding into the chair behind Anne in the conference room. The tiny, red-haired woman was a judge's personal bailiff, meaning she wore a security badge but no uniform.

"Being a jerk isn't against the law. Yet. It's more likely someone will pass a law against reading the Bible in public before they'll pass a law against acting like a jerk. Freedom of expression, remember?" She snorted and looked back down at the book in her lap, which she had been trying to read before Martinez's latest stunt.

"Sensitive, ain't ya?" Simons said with a grin. He popped his gum and slouched into the seat ahead of Anne's. "So, just how much training did you get before you left the Marines?"

"The—" Anne burst out laughing, and immediately clapped both hands over her mouth. Henderson looked a little alarmed, and Simons gave her a disgusted look. She shook her head. "No—the Marines? Who said that? Singing *Onward Christian Soldiers* is the closest I ever came to the military. No—wait—I take that back." A few more chuckles escaped her. "We used to play *Star Trek* in college. Does belonging to Starfleet count?"

"Honey, this day has been too much for you." Henderson patted her shoulder as she got up, and looked toward the table where the lawyers were getting into their regular afternoon haggle mode. "If you need a place to lie down where you won't be bothered by anyone, you let me know."

"Thanks. But I'm going to be okay." Anne summoned up a smile as the woman left. A few more giggles rose up in her throat, like bubbles from too much soda, but she felt very tired. All she really wanted was to go home and put this all behind her, make the whole assignment in Tabor Heights turn into a bad dream.

"Yeah, you just keep playing innocent." Simons winked as he got up to follow Henderson. "We know better. You're the kind who speaks nice and then—whammo!—you pound the roaches like they deserve. You're okay, kid. I don't know why you hang around with a wimp like Xander Finley, though."

"I thought you said Xander was a great guy."

"He is. He just doesn't know when to stop with the Christian act and start using some common sense. He doesn't know what real justice is." Simons winked again.

Anne shuddered and looked away. For just a moment, she didn't see his face. She saw the Ogre, a kindly man who gave all the children in the neighborhood candy and balloons and told them wonderful stories — during the day. When adults were around.

"It's not an act," she whispered, and bent her head over her book again. She had to lose herself in it, or she would worry and think herself into a sick headache.

Please, Lord, can't I just go home?

~~~~~

Xander insisted on Anne going straight back to her apartment when they returned to Common Grounds' office that afternoon. They could still put in an hour or two of work, and Anne insisted on helping Hannah catch up with all the office chores she neglected by spending her days at the Justice Center. Hannah asked how Anne felt, before seconding the plan. Shouldn't she be eager to get Anne out of the office and away from Xander as soon as possible?

Maybe the romance is over, and I'm the last to know, Anne mused as she got into her car. Hannah certainly no longer felt any threat from her. Or maybe she finally realized that looking out for Anne was part of Xander's nature, and not an indication of deeper feelings.

With everything that had happened to her over the last few days, Anne knew she was second-guessing herself. She called Quarry Hall that evening, to report in after supper. And get some overdue counseling.

"Maybe someone should come out and examine the situation," she said, after she finished her long recitation. "I'm making a royal mess of things, I think."

"You're not thinking of bailing out on us, are you?" Joan asked. For some reason, she had picked up the phone instead of Jennifer, who had switchboard duty that evening. Anne didn't let herself wonder why for long. She was just grateful.

"More like bailing a leaky boat," she offered.

"Well, you can't. Bail out, I mean." Joan waited a moment, but Anne couldn't respond to that. Was that really what had been in her mind? "I mean, you can get married and all that, but you'll still be a part of the family. This is one army you don't get discharged from, you know?"

"Married?" Anne squeaked.

"That's what the big problem really is, isn't it? You're attracted to Xander—not that hard at all, really—"

"Then how come you and Xander never paired up? You've known him forever, compared to the rest of us," she retorted.

"It's not meant to be," Joan responded with steel in her quiet tone that made Anne shiver.

"Sorry."

"Besides, the guy is as oblivious as a brick wall when it comes to anything outside of the clinic. Hannah and Xander would be great together, but until he can see that for himself, it's better not to intervene. Some guys can't be badgered. Kicking himself for all the time he wasted will be good for their relationship, when that day comes."

"Uh huh." She felt her face relaxing into a smile. "Is this your subtle way of warning me to back off, that he's already spoken for?"

"A guy isn't spoken for until he realizes he's spoken for. And I know you well enough to know you aren't tempted, and you aren't a real threat. Him giving you some extra attention... that's just going to make Hannah unhappy for a while, until she realizes Xander is a knight in shining armor for everyone."

"Won't that make her even more unhappy, to realize that he wasn't singling her out for special treatment for a while?"

"Well..." Joan sighed. "If Hannah is as special as I think she is, she's what Xander needs, and she'll have the strength and endurance to wait until he wakes up and really sees her."

"Okay, so... I think I'm relieved."

"You haven't been playing with the idea of just shucking all the problems in your life and finding someone to settle down with and live happily ever after?"

"Joan—I—sure, maybe I've played with the idea. Once or twice. But... I'm nowhere near ready to even think..." Anne shivered.

It wasn't about simplifying her life and staying in one place, because her life wasn't really that complicated. She kept moving, concentrated on her missions for Arc, kept her possessions limited to what would fit in her truck. She hadn't even gone to visit Argus today—what did that say about her mind and heart right now?

"Elizabeth and Brooklyn would be delighted if you ever found someone to settle down for, and with. They've always wondered when you'd start looking at men as something more than fellow soldiers or background or props."

That shiver waiting to erupt from deep inside turned into a cold, aching emptiness. Anne curled tighter around herself, sitting on her sofa in her quiet, dark apartment.

"Still haven't thought about... well, about sex yet," she admitted in a voice that threatened to drop to a whisper.

"You'll have to, won't you? And get it settled in your head before you decide if you're going to encourage whoever catches your eye. Wouldn't be very nice to give the guy ideas, and hope, and then push him away when he starts getting romantic."

"I wouldn't do that to him. Whoever he is." Anne closed her eyes, trying to conjure up an image of her modern Prince Charming, holding her close, kissing her. That alone could kill any chance of a deeper relationship, right before it started.

In the last few years, she had finally become able to watch romance movies without squirming because she could separate herself from the woman on the screen and not turn a heated moment into a violation in her imagination. Maybe she had put the wall up so high, so thick, so steady, she could never imagine herself voluntarily, eagerly going into a man's arms?

To her relief, Joan finally let the subject drop—though Anne knew it would be brought up at some future date when her family at Quarry Hall decided she needed to deal with it. They discussed the summons to appear in court and the different reactions of people around the Justice Center. Anne finally admitted the harassment from Martinez, and the innuendos about the Arc Foundation and its support of Xander. Joan got Sophie on an extension and they examined all the information Anne had about her attacker and his lawyer. Sophie promised to dig for information they could use in Anne's defense and hopefully tighten the noose further around Olson. Joan took on the job of talking to the two officers who had intervened, since she knew them.

"Maybe we can put some pressure on that creep lawyer," she said, when Sophie got off the phone. "Maybe we can get some of the girls who were attacked to testify on your behalf. You realize, as soon as it's pointed out that you're a stranger in town, the charges of it being a set-up will go right out the window? How many times did you go walking in the park alone?"

"Two, three times. I don't know."

When they finished and Joan passed along messages from those currently at home at Quarry Hall, Anne felt as if a weight had trickled off her shoulders. She would be able to sleep, and the problems of Olson, Xander, Martinez, and Argus wouldn't be quite so overwhelming in the morning. She had people praying for her, people thinking about her, a family waiting to help her, whatever she needed.

Joan was right, she knew. Even if she did decide to abandon the road and settle down somewhere, with the man who broke through the wall around her heart, she would still be a member of the family, still find a way to serve Arc and Quarry Hall.

~~~~~

Anne thought Saturday would never come. One of her messages last night was from Elizabeth, who said all three agent friends had mentioned receiving Lisa Collins' cartoon panels. That got Anne thinking about her. Lisa had mentioned she liked to spend Saturdays in her studio and invited Anne to drop in and see what else she was doing. Today was the day to do just that. After she got some groceries. Thank goodness the grocery store was only a few blocks away from her apartment.

Besides, errands and visiting her new friend would keep her mind off the people and situations at the Justice Center, and all the problems that came with them.

First, she called out to the vet to check on Argus. Anne knew it was irony and probably some twist of divine humor that Argus had improved greatly just in the last day. When she wasn't there with him. Was there a corollary between wounded dogs and watched pots that never boiled? Now that she would be stuck in Tabor for a few weeks to answer Olson's charge, of course her companion bodyguard would be doing much better.

No question, but that she would bring him to Tabor to stay with her. The Holwoods' foster-children all wanted to see the big dog. They thought he was a hero, getting shot while trying to defend Anne. Once she did bring her companion to Tabor, he would be petted and pampered and gain twenty pounds before they were free to leave. Well, let him. Argus deserved some spoiling after all he had gone through.

She just wished there was someone to spoil her, too.

"Stop that," she scolded herself, as she walked across the short bridge over the river that led to the shopping center. What had happened to her good feelings, the freedom and sense of being cared for that enveloped her last night and when she woke up that morning? With a force of will, she focused on her shopping list. She needed to get a few groceries, provisions for the weekend, some food for nibbling while she sat with Argus.

The last person she expected to see in the grocery store was Hannah. She came around the corner from the produce department to the bakery, just as a cart turned the corner around a tall display of snack crackers and cheese logs mixed with team logos for at least a dozen football teams. Anne had been distracted, trying to decipher the logos because she didn't recognize most of them. She just realized they were local sports teams, high school and college, and came face-to-face with the front end of the cart. She twisted sideways, out of the way, and reached to balance herself against a table stacked high with clear clamshell containers of cookies. When she turned to grin at the person pushing the cart, a pair of startled, gray eyes crinkled with laughter.

"Are you okay?" the amber-haired woman asked.

"Yeah. Sorry. I wasn't watching where—"

"Anne?" Hannah stepped around the cart.

"Oh, this is Anne?" the woman pushing the cart said.

"Uh. Yeah. Hi." Anne glanced back and forth between the two, wanting to ask why Hannah was in the grocery store instead of spending Saturday with Xander. From the way they were talking yesterday, they had enough work to keep them busy the whole weekend.

"Anne Hachworth, Rene Ackley," Hannah said. "Rene's my roommate."

"Welcome to Tabor," Rene said, stretching across the cart to shake Anne's hand. "We're stocking up for a weekend of studying. What are your plans?"

"I'm visiting a friend I made on campus, and then spend the afternoon sitting with Argus."

"Argus?" Rene turned the cart and tipped her head, beckoning for Anne to walk along with her. "Sorry. My business partners are coming by the apartment in about half an hour to get some paperwork, so I have to get back there. Gotta move!"

"It's convenient having a grocery store so close, isn't it?" She watched Hannah settle into place on the other side of the cart, leading the way through the bakery section and turning past the deli to the dairy case. "Argus—my dog. Bodyguard, really."

"Oh, that's right. Hannah said. How is he?"

They chatted about Argus and the progress of his healing. Anne felt a little odd, realizing Hannah had not only expressed concern for her and Argus to her roommate, but had asked for prayers for them at Bible study on Wednesday night.

"We need yeast?" Rene asked, before they passed the dairy case.

"The way we've been going through bread?" Hannah glanced at the envelopes and squat brown glass jars. "Definitely."

"Whenever we have one of our working weekends, Hannah gets her bread machine out and we just indulge in fresh bread and butter all day," Rene explained.

"Sounds great." Anne glanced back over her shoulder, wondering if she should have opted for a gallon of milk instead of the half-gallon she had already put in her basket. Then she thought about carrying it home, along with the other groceries she wanted to get. Her list had doubled in size since she walked into the store. She should have driven, instead of being virtuous and walking for exercise.

"It's a bad habit I got into in college," Hannah said with a shrug and a deprecating little smile. "We'd buy a loaf of whole grain bread from the day-old rack at this incredible bakery down the street from the dorm, and a pound of butter, lock ourselves in our dorm room, and just eat bread and butter and study until we had the books memorized."

"Sounds nice. Relaxing." Anne stepped back and snatched up a tub of whipped cream cheese. "That gives me an idea. I saw some raisin rolls in the day-old rack. Even if they're stale, warm them up and put this on." She tossed it into her basket.

Hannah looked like she was about to say something, her expression much warmer and friendlier. It would be nice if they could become friends before she left Tabor. But whatever Hannah was about to say, the moment was lost when Rene went to turn down an aisle and Anne turned back to the bakery section for those rolls. The three traded farewells and Rene said they would look for Anne in church the next morning.

After the rolls, Anne went looking for the pet supplies aisle, to get a new rawhide chew for Argus. She picked up some noodle meals and didn't see Hannah or Rene before she left the grocery store.

After she returned to her apartment and put away the few perishables, she thought about driving to Lisa's art building, then silently scolded herself for getting so soft in such a short amount of time. As long as she could walk to her destination, she would. Just ten minutes later, she headed down the sidewalk again, looking forward to spending some time with Lisa. Anne quietly laughed when she found herself wishing Hannah had been about to invite her to spend the day with them, even if all she did was sit at the table and read while they worked and studied and ate warm bread fresh out of the machine.

Silence filled the art building when Anne got there. The door of Lisa's studio hung open, letting light spill out into the gloom of the second-floor landing. She hurried upstairs quietly and paused in the open doorway. Lisa sat at her drawing table, resting both elbows on either side of a blank piece of paper, her chin in the V formed by the heels of her hands, staring with hooded eyes at a point somewhere between her nose and the paper, and likely a thousand miles away. Anne paused in the doorway and watched her a few moments, wondering if she would interrupt a creative session or break through a growing artist's block. Lisa sighed and glanced toward the curtainless window, then toward the door, effectively taking that question out of Anne's hands. Her welcoming smile removed the last hesitation her visitor felt.

"Still in town, huh?" Lisa grinned and sat back, turning on her stool so she leaned back against the wall beside her. "What's up?"

"Well, I came to ask you that question. How are things? Quieting down?"

Chapter Seventeen

"Oh, I wish," the younger girl groaned. But she ended on a chuckle. "I wonder sometimes how dense I can be. Remember what Dr. Holwood said, about Todd talking with his buddies about getting a ring?"

"He didn't." Anne settled down on the second stool on the other side of Lisa's table. "I hope he apologized before he asked."

"What Toddy-boy thinks qualifies as an apology. Oooh, I could just strangle him sometimes. And the rest of the time he really is the sweetest... jerk!" She laughed and hid her face in her hands for a moment.

Anne would have laughed with her, but she had seen too many situations like this where a man was very good at apologizing but very bad at changing enough to stop doing the things he kept having to apologize for. She was very glad to see no ring on Lisa's finger.

"So, what did he do?"

"He came in here with flowers and a pizza when I was working really late. At least he realized that I skipped lunch and supper. He said that he was sorry he forgot about me, but he's had a lot of things on his mind and I was one of them."

"He should have said you were the only thing on his mind."

"True. The man needs some lessons on being romantic, and yet sometimes he gets it so right." She sighed but smiled. "It's totally by accident when he does, though. Oh, you should be proud of me! I told Todd that was no apology. Then he gave me his standard confused little boy look, and he got down on one knee and held out this battered, blue velvet ring case."

"He didn't talk his father into letting him give you a family heirloom, did he?" Anne wondered if maybe she should reconsider her assessment of Todd.

"Hardly." Another sigh. "I refused to take that ring, and I told him he should have asked me if I wanted to marry him before he wasted all that money. Oh, he got mad!" She chuckled, a little less certain than before. "He was very indignant and made sure I knew that his father refused to loan him money for a ring for me."

"Makes sense. Fits with the man I met."

"Sorry about that."

"No, that's all right. I figure maybe God made sure I was there when he confronted you. And besides, now he knows Todd lies to him about you. Could be some of the problems you have with him are because Todd paints a completely different picture of you to his father, and then when you two meet, he's upset because you aren't what he expected."

"Mr. Montgomery is the kind of man who says, 'Don't bother me with facts, my mind is made up.' It doesn't matter what I say or do, or what people say about me, the man very obviously doesn't want me anywhere near his son."

"Why?"

"I'm a useless artist. His words, not mine." She drew one heel up on the edge of the stool and wrapped both arms around her bent leg, so she could rest her chin on her knee. "He has this image of Todd's successful future, and what Todd needs is a wife who will be the perfect hostess and mother and housekeeper — and probably housekeeper for her father-in-law, too."

"You wouldn't go live with him after you married Todd, would you?"

"I'm not marrying Todd, so that question is useless."

"So if his father didn't give him the money for the ring, where did it come from? Or didn't you even let him show it to you?"

"Considering the condition of the box, I asked him if he was giving me his mother's ring without his father's permission or knowledge. And do you know what that romantic idiot did?"

"No." Anne prepared for something unbelievable and oblivious, considering the exasperated smile inching across Lisa's face.

"He opened the box, and inside was this glass and plastic ring, junk jewelry, or a really good bubble gum machine, you know? He told me that our marriage was between us, and his father had no vote and no say in who he married." She rubbed at her eyes, and Anne suspected Lisa fought a few weary tears. "It was really hard to keep saying no after that. Mostly because I know despite how Todd feels now, eventually his father will win. He's such a thoughtless wimp, letting his father do his thinking for him most of the time."

"You love him, though."

"I know." Another sigh. "If only Todd would pay half as much attention to me on a regular basis as he has the last week, I would never get mad at him. He's here all the time when he's not in class. We haven't eaten so many meals together in a row in months. He brings his books and studies while I'm working. I swear, he's never studied so hard in his life."

"Then you're a good influence on him."

"Temporary. In another week or so, he'll go back to his old habits. He'll call me and tell me where to meet him, instead of coming to get me. He'll miss lunch, or go at a different time, or go get a hamburger in town with his buddies and forget to tell me. Then he'll lecture me because I waited all through my lunch period for him to show up and had to go to class without eating."

"Go without him a few times."

"I did! He never noticed because he was late. Or else he claims he didn't notice..." Lisa frowned, nodding a little as if that thought had never occurred to her before. "It doesn't matter. Todd can languish all he wants, I'm not giving in."

"At least, you hope not," Anne guessed, seeing the hesitation in her new friend's resolve. Lisa gave her a pitiful little smile and nodded. "Maybe we should pray about it." She had to laugh when Lisa's mouth dropped open. "What? You don't pray about your big problems?"

"It's not that big of a problem—is it?" Lisa said. "I mean, sure, God loves me, but would He really care about Todd and me and all our fighting?"

"It sounds more like Todd takes you for granted and you're finally starting to stand up for yourself. But yeah, God cares. What if you did marry him, and had kids, and those kids were miserable because of the way they saw their father neglect you? Or they decide that it's normal, and take it into their own marriages? Turns into a problem for more than just you two, right?"

"Right, but—"

"God isn't just for church and world-shaking events, you know. If He cares about the sparrows and the lilies—"

"I get the picture!" Lisa grinned again, a faint blush in her cheeks for a change. "I should use something like that in my strip. Maybe I should give Katie some boyfriend problems. It'd probably be a big problem, dating and all that, if your father is constantly changing churches every few years and you have to leave, just when things are getting nice..."

"Katie?" Anne prompted, when it seemed like her friend would drift into a creative haze over her cartoon strip and forget all about her.

"Oh. The oldest daughter in the family. She's kind of my alter-ego, you know?"

"She does and says the things you wouldn't dare, or don't think of until it's too late?" she guessed. Lisa's nod and giggle said it all.

They managed to pray before they got off track more. Anne hoped Lisa would stick to her guns and keep Todd out of her life. She saw a lot of misery for the two of them unless Lisa learned to be more aggressive in speaking up for herself and demanding more respect.

The talk naturally segued to Lisa's cartoon strip. Anne learned a little about her new friend's life. She was alone in the world, except for a few elderly relatives who basically handed her money and expected her to go away. It was no wonder she was such a softy when it came to Todd's thoughtlessness; Lisa had no one to belong to.

PK was about a large, happy, sometimes silly family. Lisa had been an only child and her parents had been quiet people who lived for their art. Her father was a portrait artist and her mother wrote music. The family in the cartoon strip lived at their church; Lisa had never gone near a church except for weddings and funerals until she came to BWU, and a group of upperclassmen art students took her under their wing. She became a Christian just after Christmas that first year, discipled by her friends. But now all of them had graduated and were busy with their own lives, and Lisa had never settled on a home church. The more Anne explored the cartoon strip, all the things Lisa wanted to do with it, all the back story and possible extra characters, the more she realized Lisa was making the family she wished she had. Katie was indeed Lisa's alter ego; the person she wished she could be.

Anne didn't know whether to worry about Lisa or be relieved her friend recognized what she was doing. Awareness was the first step in avoiding big problems, like living in her cartoon strip and hiding from the real world.

What exactly would Lisa do with Todd's alter ego in her strip? Anne suspected a little sniping at Todd, carefully screened, was already in the works. She wanted to laugh.

Then her stomach rumbled, taking her away from the fascinating new world of cartooning and all it entailed. Lisa heard and laughed with her, and suggested they go to the cafeteria for lunch. It would only cost Anne two dollars, since she was a guest of a student.

"I have a better idea," Anne said. "Let's be totally decadent. Burgers and shakes in town instead of whatever slightly nutritious glop they've got in the kitchen."

"I don't know. This early in the term, the food's still pretty good."

"My treat. And make sure you pick a great place."

"You're on!"

It was a matter of moments for Lisa to close up her studio and head down the stairs. Anne looked back once when they were half a block away and caught a glimpse of someone coming to the front door of the art building. She thought it might be Todd, but she wasn't about to say anything to Lisa. Let him learn she wasn't going to sit around waiting for him to get smart.

They decided it would be easier if Lisa drove Anne's car to the restaurant, instead of acting as navigator. Then they had a few awkward moments when Lisa needed to adjust the driver's seat and Anne didn't know how. That led into an abbreviated explanation of her adventure more than a week ago, getting carjacked and Argus getting shot.

"And if I had just held onto my keys, I wouldn't be in this predicament," Anne finished, gesturing around the borrowed car.

"What? Getting chauffeured around by starving art students?" Lisa stuck her tongue out at her when Anne could only groan. "Have you prayed about getting your truck back?"

"Well, of—" Anne stopped short. She had prayed, but how often? How intensely? And just a short time ago she had been lecturing Lisa on how God cared about the little things.

"Of course," she finished. "Just not as often as I should." She didn't add that she was waiting for a replacement to come from Quarry Hall.

"Then when you pray over our lunch, pray for your truck—and Todd's brains." Lisa sighed. "Because I do love the jerk. I tell myself I can live without him. I tell God I will, if that's what He wants. And then I add, please don't ask me to. What can I do about him?"

"Maybe you have to suffer a little now, to avoid a lot of suffering later." Anne knew she was the last person to offer lovelorn advice.

Later, she couldn't decide if it was the prayer over their burgers, or she was on the other side of the street, or she had never been down this section of Sackley before. She glanced idly into the yard of a body shop and car repair business as they passed on their way back to campus.

There was her truck.

"Lisa—pull in," she said, gesturing hard to her right. Fortunately, the body shop business was big enough to have two entrances on the street, and they had only passed the first.

She barely glanced at Anne, but flipped on her blinker and turned, hitting the brakes just enough to avoid skidding as they went from forty and pavement to twenty and gravel. Anne gestured at the nearest parking slot. They pulled in. She closed her eyes and prayed hard for several seconds after Lisa put the car into park.

"What's up?" her friend asked, keeping her voice down.

"That's my truck." Anne hooked a thumb over her shoulder at the cars inside the locked chain link fence on the other side of the parking lot.

"Your truck?"

"Dark green with the gouge in the left rear hubcap and the dent in the bumper where the white fiberglass shows through. It's a prong shape, pointing up. And that's my license plate. The idiot didn't even bother switching plates!" She finally opened her eyes.

"What are we going to do? You can't just walk into the body shop and tell the owner that your stolen truck is there."

"The crook probably brought it here to have it painted. Why is it taking so long to get it done, though?" A moment later, she shook her head, amused at how she focused on petty details. The important thing was to be grateful she had seen it. "For all we know, this is the center of operations for some carjacking ring."

"We have to go to the police."

Anne said a prayer of thanks when she arrived at the police station only ten minutes later and saw Mike Nichols and Todd James walking to their patrol car. She jumped from the car and called their names. They would listen and believe her and come with her. Anyone else would probably check the official records and take time considering their options before going out to the body shop and checking out her claim. In the time it took, the carjacker could come back and move her truck somewhere else, or the paint job could get started.

Less than half an hour later, she and Lisa walked toward the gate of the yard while Mike went into the front office of the body shop. Todd stayed in the patrol car, waiting with the radio in case he had to call for assistance.

"Those are my keys!" Anne blurted, when the owner came out with Mike. "Joey" was stitched across the pocket of his gray coveralls in red thread. Anne would know the tiny plastic German Shepherd hanging from the key ring anywhere, with the paint scratched off where Argus had chewed on it.

"Hey, Mike, I'm just doing a favor for a friend. He said he was taking care of his brother's truck while the guy was out of town." Joey glanced at Anne, then back to the officer. Mike nodded, and he handed the keys to Anne before he unlocked the gate in the fence.

"Is he still in town?" Mike asked.

"Oh, yeah. He works here. Best detailer I've ever had. You're not going to be too hard on him, are you?"

"We'll have to leave that for the judge," Anne said. She felt sorry for the man. The misery in Joey's pale blue eyes showed he liked the man who had stolen her truck and shot Argus.

It was a matter of moments to unlock the driver's side door and climb in. Anne couldn't believe it—nothing was missing. Not even the change she kept in the right-hand cup holder. Her flashlight was still in the loop in the visor, and her sunglasses. Her poncho and the floppy brown suede hat Vincent had given her after they giggled together through a Clint Eastwood marathon last winter. Her extra clothes in the neat plastic drawer unit stashed in the compartment behind the seats. Her cooler—full of melted, stale water now. Her little bag of plastic plates and cups and utensils tucked into the netting on the passenger side door. All her emergency gear.

"Okay, this is the real test," she muttered, as she climbed back out. She hit the switch in the side bottom of the passenger seat. It folded forward and then pivoted up, revealing a compartment built into the floor of the truck. Anne stuck another key from the ring into the tiny slot and turned it. Her computer was still there.

"Well, that's proof, even if the registration papers weren't still there," Mike said, when Anne brought it out. "Who'd know that was there, unless the truck was theirs?"

"Hey, I'm not arguing with you," Joey said, backing up with his hands raised a little, palms outward. "I'm just glad to get it off my property and be done with it. You want Larry's address, I'll bet."

"That might be helpful."

"We're going to have to get a warrant," Todd said, joining them. "To search his house for anything else that might belong to you."

"It looks like everything is here. Like he dumped the truck and didn't want anything else to do with it. I really think this was his first carjacking," Anne added. "He didn't even try to vacuum up the dog hair all over the floor." She stepped up into the truck again and sat down in the driver's seat and opened up her computer to test it.

"Now that's proof too, that it's your truck," Mike offered. "Compare the dog hair with your dog."

"You're not making this any easier for us," Todd said almost at the same moment.

"Easier?" She almost laughed, but she was distracted by the process of going through her computer's start-up. Nothing had been tampered with, so far.

"We use the truck as an excuse to search his place for evidence of any other robberies. To get enough to put him away so he doesn't carjack anyone else. Next time it could be a person, and he kills them, instead of just putting your dog in the hospital for a few weeks."

"Larry Tucker shot a dog?" Joey blurted. "No wonder the guy's been moping all week. That guy loves critters. He spends his free time at the APL kennel and trying to get strays adopted, that sort of thing. Man, he must have been scared if he shot a dog." He started to chuckle, but the disbelieving looks the two police officers gave him made the sound die in his throat. "Hey, the guy's kind of a loner."

"Is he having money trouble?" Anne asked. "He kind of struck me as not wanting to rob me, but he had to. At least he was smart enough to try his stunt far from where he lives."

"Whose side are you on?" Mike blurted, half-laughing.

"God's side, I hope."

A car pulling around the other side of the body shop, in the area marked for employees, caught Anne's attention. She signaled for quiet and the other three complied. The engine died, then a door creaked open and closed, then footsteps on the gravel.

Larry Tucker, aka the Nervous Carjacker, came around the side of the building. He gave the two officers and his employer a shaky grin and shuffled over to them with his hands jammed in the back pockets of his jeans. Shoulders hunched, he had to sort of tilt his head back, slightly to one side, and squinted against the sun shining into his eyes from behind

Anne's truck.

"Hey, Joey. Something... uh... wrong?"

Anne actually felt sorry for him. She shook her head, put aside her computer, and slid out of the truck to join the other four on the ground.

"Hi, Larry. Remember me?" A tiny giggle escaped her when his mouth dropped open and his face went white. The two police officers gave her sour looks, like she was spoiling their fun.

"You're—I didn't mean—is your dog okay?" Then he hung his head and offered his wrists to Mike, who stood closest to him. "Can I have a cell with a window?"

~~~~~

"There may be some hope for this jerk after all, if he's so worried about my dog that he actually asked if he could visit Argus before they put him in his cell." Anne leaned back against the top step in front of the Holwoods' house and stretched out so her heels touched the sidewalk. "What a day!"

"Tell me about it," Lisa said with a giggle. "You wouldn't believe what I found in my mailbox."

"Todd tried to give you the ring again?"

"Again?" Dr. Holwood said. He had been lounging against the pillar at the top of the porch steps, listening to her tale of Larry the Carjacker. "Todd Montgomery actually asked you?"

"I turned him down, of course. First he has to apologize and really mean it," Lisa said. "I mean, when he apologizes, he's more sorry that he made me mad than sorry for what he did, you know? Maybe it's being picky, but there's a difference."

"It's like a diamond thief being sorry he got caught, but not being sorry he stole the diamonds," Doria offered from her spot on the top step, leaning back against her husband's legs.

"Exactly." She hunched her shoulders, hugging herself in glee. "But this is a thousand times better. When I stopped in at the student center just now, I got a letter from an agent who wants to talk to me about *PK*!"

Anne contented herself with a grin while the Holwoods poured out their congratulations. She knew after the turnabout day she had and the strains of the last few days, including Bruiser Olson, she wasn't going to be any good at pretending surprise. Delight, yes. Relief, that an agent had responded so quickly. But not surprise.

Chapter Eighteen

"And it's all your fault!" Lisa threw herself across the step to hug Anne. "She said you sent the panels. You didn't tell me you knew an agent."

"I don't. I just asked Elizabeth if she knew anyone, because I knew this really great artist who deserved a chance, and a lot of really boring denominational magazines that could use a shot in the arm and it sort of... gelled," she finished with a shrug.

"I have this feeling a lot of things gel when you Arc girls are around," Dr. Holwood remarked in a dry tone. He managed to keep his expression neutral — except for a tiny spark of amusement in his eyes.

"Like finding your truck. On Sackley road, of all places," Doria added.

"Kind of weird he was more worried about your dog than about you. What if he had shot you? What kind of a jerk threatens a lone woman with a gun?" Lisa said.

"Well, I had a lot of hidden weapons too," Anne said, trying to put on a jaunty smile. Right now, she just felt tired. She still hadn't gone out to visit Argus yet or call home to let them know what had happened and thank them for their prayers, yet again. The other three gave her questioning looks. "Guardian angels. My fists. My feet. A good, heavy grocery bag." She took a deep breath and sent up a prayer of thanks. "God."

"It's not like you really needed outside help, did you?" Doria said softly.

~~~~

"Hey, Anne, could you help me with something?" Xander said, as she hurried across the parking lot behind Common Grounds to get into his car Monday morning.

"Sure. You know you can ask me anything." Immediately, she twinged, thinking of all the possibilities in that little opening. She bent her head to concentrate on fastening the seat belt and prayed she wasn't blushing.

"You've been listening to us talk about the case, right? Enough to follow during the discussions?" He put the car into gear and headed for the driveway out into early morning Pearl Road traffic.

"Sure." She tucked her purse between her feet, relieved to have it instead of her backpack. It was nice having her own clothes, her own gear again. "As long as you don't drop into a whole ton of legalese."

"Hannah called in sick. Winslow and I can handle the topics we're working on today, but if you could take notes of the general course of the discussion, that'd be great. Maybe different impressions, a different viewpoint would help us, too."

"Hannah's sick?" Xander's Gal Friday struck Anne as the type of person who was always healthy, refusing to allow a silly little germ to knock her off her feet.

"Yeah. She said she doesn't have a fever, but she spent Sunday evening on her knees in front of the toilet. I told her maybe it was food poisoning."

"You ate the same sandwich she did, Friday," Anne couldn't help offering.

"That's what she said, when I said food poisoning. The thing is, her roommate has the same thing, and they didn't get sick until Sunday. So it wasn't the food on Friday. But why in the world would she pay attention to what I eat?" He shook his head, grinning crookedly.

"She likes you. A lot." She almost laughed when he took his attention off traffic long enough to stare at her. He even took his foot off the accelerator, which earned a honk from the van behind them. "Sheesh, Xander, for such a perceptive guy, I wonder why you never noticed."

"No. Hannah's just a very active, alert, intelligent... I just thought we were good friends."

"In this day and age, every tiny emotional attachment gets turned into something big and romantic — or at least an excuse to jump into bed."

"She's not that type of girl. She's a Christian."

Anne bit her tongue against remarking that when it came to claiming the man she wanted, some women forgot about God's basic rules. Besides, while Hannah might have let jealousy get in the way, when she imagined Anne was capturing Xander's heart, she most certainly was not the type of girl to use her body and every trick in the book to capture her man. Discretion was the better part of valor, so she changed the subject. Since she would be working closely with Xander today, making him uncomfortable by discussing Hannah's interest in him wasn't smart.

~~~~~

"What are you doing here?" Simons greeted Anne when she stepped out of the conference room at the 10am break, to get something cold to drink and rest her hand. She wished she had brought her notebook computer to make it easier to take notes.

"I'm working for Xander. Didn't you hear Hannah was sick?"

"Yeah, I heard, but I thought — I heard you left town."

"Why? Just because I'm facing a stupid lawsuit?" She managed to laugh.

Why, she wondered, did Simons care what she was doing and where she was? It sent a shiver up her spine to think he might be watching out for her. But not in a protective way.

No. She mentally shook her head. He wasn't like the Ogre at all. Besides, he knew she could defend herself if anyone tried anything. Ogres targeted defenseless people.

"It's a good thing you're here, huh?" He grinned weakly and started to walk away, talking over his shoulder. "That Hannah never gets sick."

"That's what everyone says."

"Better send her to the doctor. You know, someone would expect her to poison you to get you out of the way," the bailiff added, raising his voice. "Wouldn't it be funny if it turned out she was poisoned?"

"No, it wouldn't," Xander said, coming out of the doorway around the corner and blocking Simons from doing his usual vanishing act. "Why would anyone want to poison her?"

"Besides Martinez, just to slow you down?" Simons grinned, but he began to go red. "Don't you know your two ladies are fighting over you?" He nodded toward Anne.

"Fighting?" Xander turned to Anne and took a step around Simons. The big bailiff left.

"Some people seem to think Hannah's jealous." Anne gave a faint smile, wishing she could think a little faster, maybe distract him.

"That's..." He flushed and shook his head. "It can't be true."

"She did get a little irked when you took me bike riding."

"Well, you needed a break, after everything that happened."

"Why don't you ask Hannah to go riding when she's feeling better? It might be fun." To her relief, Martinez chose that moment to come out of the room.

The opposing lawyer glared at Anne and Xander and growled, "Finley, I need to talk with you." He jerked his head back into the room, through the open door. With Xander distracted, Anne beat a hasty retreat.

Someone else commented on Hannah's unusual illness later. A third person said they heard she was poisoned and rushed to the hospital over the weekend. Anne had the awful feeling the story would warp until she would be blamed for it, maybe under suspicion of attempted murder. She beat up muggers and carjackers — why not a romantic rival?

At least Xander hadn't heard that particular insinuation yet.

Anne had other things to worry about. Martinez had some grudge making him steam — but when the big man got really angry, she learned, he stopped talking. He glared at her for the rest of the morning.

Martinez followed them when Anne, Winslow and Xander went to the Old Arcade for lunch. He made a remark to Xander as he passed their table. Anne didn't catch it, on her way back with her salad and bagel sandwich. Winslow's mouth dropped open and Xander leaped to his feet, one fist clenched and his arm cocked back to strike before he stopped himself. Martinez chuckled and walked straight to Anne.

"I thought surely you three would commandeer an empty room for a lunchtime quickie," he said, eyes sparkling and his mouth curving in the first smile all day.

Anne burst out laughing. Martinez stood between her and the table, and her two companions were thirty feet away, at the very least. She had no way of knowing if they heard. The other lawyer stared down at her, then flushed. She imagined steam coming out of his ears in a moment.

"How else are you going to keep your job? That's how little Saint Hannah keeps her cushy job with the White Knight."

"I'm the last person to let a man touch me, for any reason. And if you were as thorough as you claimed in researching people's backgrounds, you'd know that." Anne took a step closer to him, delighted when Martinez backed away, as shocked by her calm face as her pleasant tone. "And maybe it hasn't occurred to you, Mr. Martinez, but I'm Arc's representative. Xander Finley works for *me*. And if Hannah were giving 'quickies' at lunchtime, she wouldn't be in love with Xander. I've seen it often enough to know. Big difference between real love and just sex. Obviously, you only know from hearsay, not from experience." She batted her eyelashes at him as the man's mouth dropped open. Then she stepped around him and headed toward the table.

Xander and Winslow saw her coming and both got up to meet her. Anne shook her head, sidestepped around a gaggle of toddlers and their three mothers, and threw herself down into the one free chair.

"Kind of a limited imagination, huh?" she commented, and tore the wrapping off her bagel. The two men stood on either side of her a moment as she bit into the sandwich. Anne wasn't really hungry, not after what just happened, but she had to do something with her mouth and all the nervous energy running through her in the aftermath of Martinez's accusation. She didn't dare talk—who knew what would pour out of her mouth?

~~~~~

"Hey, kiddo, how's it going?" Simons said, startled when Anne came back into the conference room after the mid-afternoon break. He straightened up from searching under the row of chairs directly behind Xander's side of the conference table. He moved so quickly, and jerkily, he knocked a few chairs out of line.

"Something wrong?" Anne wished she had not hurried back. She wanted some time alone with the novel she carried in her purse. How long had it been since she had the luxury of just reading, escaping to a different world where people's safety or jobs didn't depend on her?

"Well, somebody said you lost your backpack, and I was just looking to see if maybe it got kicked under around here."

"That's nice of you..." That shiver of warning ran up her spine. Why would Simons care if she lost anything? And who would tell him such a thing?

Of course, she had overwhelming evidence of how rumors started and warped and ran amok around here. Someone probably commented she wasn't carrying her backpack, and it ended up as a story that she had been robbed.

"Put it in storage, huh?" Simons jammed his hands into his pockets, hunched his massive shoulders, and started toward the door. "Bet someone decided to tighten security for a change and wouldn't let you bring it past the elevator."

"No." She lifted her arm a little, to reveal the purse tucked against her side. "I decided it didn't go with my lawyer-in-training look." Why, she wondered, didn't she want him to know she got her truck back? Other than that her personal life was none of his business?

"Oh. Makes sense." He grinned, but there was something wrong with the expression. Something weak, perhaps. "I heard you got your truck back."

"Where did you hear that?"

"Around. You know how people like to talk around here."

"Yeah, I'm learning." There was something definitely wrong with his grin.

"Did you beat up on the guy when you caught him?"

Ah, that was it. He was hungry for something. Details. Vicarious justice and revenge. Probably one of those guys who sat at home and watched cop shows and cheered for the good guys but wouldn't lift a finger to stop someone from stealing his neighbor's newspaper.

"I didn't have to. He nearly turned himself in."

"Yeah, well, slimes like that deserve to be shoved around a little. That Martinez deserves a good right hook in the eye, after what he said to you."

"To me?"

Martinez wouldn't have told anyone about the encounter, since she certainly didn't give the reaction he wanted. That meant Xander or Winslow would have told the story, and she couldn't imagine them telling anyone. It would be embarrassing for her. Unless Simons heard them talking about it, when they didn't think anyone would listen? She shook her head, to mentally and physically clear it. What was wrong with her?

"I bet the guy would come after you if he caught you alone somewhere. Bet it'd be self-defense, open and shut case, if you tore his hide apart. Guy's got it in for you. Nothing a creep like him likes better than to take advantage of a girl out alone. Take it from me, he'd rape you if he got a chance. Guy like him deserves to be shot between the eyes before he even tries."

"You just don't know when to quit, do you, Simons?" Martinez seethed, stomping through the doorway. Xander and Winslow and several court officials were right behind him. "First you tell me Finley's going around accusing me of poisoning his little bimbo assistant—"

"What?" Xander blurted.

"And now you're accusing me of rape? That little slut doesn't need to be raped. She's practically begging for a real man—" Martinez grunted in surprise as Xander grabbed him by the arm and spun him around.

He stumbled against the chair in the aisle and both men scrambled to catch their footing. Xander let go and stepped back. Anne thought he was more surprised at his own reaction than Martinez's words.

"Hey, only telling what I've heard people saying," Simons said, shrugging, hands spread wide in a gesture of innocence. "You really got it in for this sweet little girl here, and you'd deserve it if she tore the stuffing out of you."

"I'm telling you for the last time, Martinez, you watch your mouth around Anne. You've got a grudge against me and everything I stand up for, but you leave her out of it." Xander's fists were almost white with pressure as he clenched them, tugging on the hem of his jacket—probably to keep from punching the other man.

"She has everything to do with it. She told me you practically work for her."

"I do." Xander nodded to Anne, winking before turning back to Martinez. "We have a chain of command, those of us who work for Arc. She has the boss's ear."

Martinez looked like he wanted to spit. He looked Xander up and down, then glanced over his shoulder at Anne. He growled something under his breath. Xander's shoulders stiffened, then amazingly he turned his back on the man and walked away. Martinez barked a curse. The men waiting in the doorway leaped, reaching to stop him, but were too late. Martinez vaulted the intervening space and tackled Xander. They went down, sending chairs skidding and rolling across the carpeted floor.

Judge Harrison, who was overseeing the proceedings that afternoon, stopped short in the doorway. Anne hadn't been aware of the woman's presence until then, but she prayed she had seen enough to know Xander had done nothing except resist Martinez's efforts to get him into a fistfight. She had seen it often enough. The class bully goaded the good kid until the good kid pounded him, timed just right so the authority figure didn't see the goading, only the attack. The class bully got away with a few bruises and his victim was punished for reacting.

The tussle was over in a few seconds. Xander slowly pulled himself to his feet while the other men slung Martinez across the room into one of the chairs still standing upright. He walked over to Judge Harrison and said something Anne didn't catch. The woman frowned, but she nodded and crossed the room to Martinez. The big, red-faced lawyer started to growl something unintelligible.

"You will keep a civil tongue in your head, Mr. Martinez, or I will have you thrown off the case. I have plenty of witnesses that you were the aggressor. Mr. Finley's only crime is that he didn't respond to your provocations." Judge Harrison looked around the room. Her gaze rested on Anne a moment, then continued on the momentary search. "What has happened in this room will not be repeated outside these walls, does everyone understand?" She waited until everyone nodded. "Now, there were some accusations being flung when I first walked in. Let's clear the air or we won't get any work done for the rest of the afternoon."

"Finley's accusing me of poisoning his woman." Martinez glowered when Harrison gave him an admonishing look. "His assistant," he corrected, with a sneer that clearly said he didn't agree with that label.

"Poisoning? Hannah? She's got the flu." Xander turned to Anne, giving her a helpless look.

"There's some silly gossip going around that someone poisoned Hannah," Anne supplied. "And even sillier gossip that Hannah's got something in for me. Go figure." She shrugged and attempted a smile. She caught Simons glaring at her, just a glimpse out of the corner of her eye, but the man turned away before she could be sure. What was his problem? He didn't like his pet theories being called silly? Or was there something more to it?

"Simons told me Finley is going around telling people I poisoned his little assistant to block his research on the case," Martinez said. His voice was only partially back to its smooth control. "I'll bet she isn't sick at all. It's just a scheme to discredit me."

"And everyone knows how stainless your reputation is," a man commented from the back of the small group gathered around the two lawyers. Heads turned, a few smiles, a few muffled chuckles. No other reaction.

"I never even heard about Hannah being poisoned until just now," Xander said, holding up one hand like he was taking an oath. "Food poisoning, maybe, but we ate the same food last week, and I'm fine. If it was someone involved in the case, his only opportunity to poison Hannah would be here. That destroys that theory, as far as I'm concerned. Whatever is making Hannah sick, it's affecting her roommate."

"Roommate?" Simons barked. "She never said she was living with any guy."

"She's not. Rene is a young woman from our church."

"Bailiff Simons?" Judge Harrison gestured for the man to come over to join the three of them.

Simons didn't look at all happy to be brought into the spotlight. Hands clasped behind his back, shoulders slightly hunched, he came to the edge of the invisible circle drawn around the three. When prodded by the judge, he hemmed and hawed a bit, then finally nodded and gave a big sigh, as if giving up.

"There's a lot of bad blood going down, Your Honor. People saying all sorts of nasty things. Like they're trying to win or lose the case for these two before it even goes to trial. You know how the courthouse is, all the gossip going around, all the politicking." Simons waited until the woman thought a moment, then nodded. "Mr. Martinez here has been accusing Mr. Winslow and Mr. Finley of... well, jumping into closets with his pretty little assistant and now with this young lady." He nodded to Anne. "And doing drugs, drinking during work hours, spying on him, all that."

Everyone turned to Martinez. He muttered something under his breath and refused to look anyone in the eye.

"Everybody knows they wouldn't do that, but people still wonder. It's enough to make anybody steam, you know? Most mornings, we come to work expecting to see a good knock-down, drag-out fight between these two. But we never do. Kind of admirable, you know?"

Why, Anne wondered, didn't she believe Simons?

"And now Mr. Finley seems to have joined the mudslinging?" Judge Harrison asked.

"Your Honor, I never said such a thing. I never even mentioned Hannah and Martinez in the same breath today," Xander said, holding up a hand again.

Anne wondered if he had been a Boy Scout and had made the pledge quite often. Then she dismissed that as an irrelevant thought.

Chapter Nineteen

Judge Harrison finally did what Anne considered the only sensible thing. She started asking everyone who had told them the rumors. Not one person could trace the rumor of poisoning directly back to Xander — or Winslow or Anne, for that matter. They always heard it from someone else, and the stories got tamer as they backtracked. It would have been impossible to go through the entire Justice Center, to find the source of the gossip. Some people had overheard someone talking in the line in the cafeteria and didn't know their names.

Everyone, however, could trace the nasty remarks attributed to Martinez back to the man. Most of them had heard him speak the slander. Anne listened and supposed there was some justice in the world, after all. Xander had come out clean and Martinez was dirtier than ever. Xander even apologized to Martinez for the rumors that weren't his fault. Anne doubted that endeared him to his opponent.

When they were finally able to get back to work, there was less than an hour of the regular session time remaining. Judge Harrison asked if everyone would consider staying an extra hour or two, just to get things cleared up. No one demurred. Despite working nearly to seven that evening, Anne was somewhat surprised to see steady traffic in the halls of the Justice Center when she walked to the lobby with Xander.

"I'm whipped. I don't know about you, but this is one of those nights where I just want to crash — and pig out." Xander chuckled and rested his free hand on her shoulder. "How about I make it up to you with a great dinner? You like steak?"

"Make it up to me?" Anne shook her head. "Thanks, Xander. It sounds nice, but I think I'd rather go for a really long walk to clear my head. By myself. Some of the things going on today..." She shrugged and hoped he would understand.

"I wouldn't be surprised if you didn't come back tomorrow. You know, Hannah might just be right. Maybe there's something — "

"I just want to go for a walk by myself."

"That might not be good. You might beat up on another innocent mugger."

"Very funny."

"Anne, really, if you don't come out to dinner with me, I'm going to spend the evening by myself at the office, working on this stupid case.

Save me!"

"You should take dinner—"

"Now what do you want?" Xander interrupted, his grin changing to something akin to a snarl aimed at someone behind her. "Haven't you made enough trouble for today?"

"That Martinez deserves a 44 Magnum in a dark alley," Simons said, stepping up to join them near the revolving door out of the lobby. The traffic around them had cleared out, leaving the three of them nearly alone, except for the security guard on the other side of the front desk and the girl closing up the little snack bar. "The world would be a lot better place without him, getting crooks off and sending innocent guys to jail like he does."

"The justice system has its flaws—"

"Big ones. There's a whole lot more injustice than justice anymore. What we gotta do is string up the crooks right away, instead of letting them out to hurt people again just because they say they'll make nice. If someone's guilty, you lock them away forever. Doesn't matter if they say they didn't do it, or the devil made them do it or they were crazy when they did it."

Anne stepped back, chilled by the intensity in Simons' eyes. She wondered what kind of injustice and pain the man had gone through in his past.

"Vigilantes aren't the answer," Xander said. He hooked his arm through Anne's and steered her toward the door.

"Gotta weed out the wimps as well as the crooks, Finley!" Simons snarled after them. Anne glanced back in time to see him turn sharply on his heel and stomp across the lobby, back the way they had just come. She shuddered. Then they were outside in the cool evening air.

Xander tried to make small talk on the drive back to his office and her truck. There were long gaps of silence, despite their efforts to get their minds onto other subjects. He asked her once more to reconsider going to dinner.

"Maybe Hannah is—"

"Speaking of Hannah." Anne hoped her smile wasn't too quick and false. "The best thing you can do is take dinner to her and fill her in on everything that happened today. You have no idea how much better that'll make her feel. But no greasy burgers and fries, understand? Go to one of those places that put together picnics on the spot. She'll love it."

"Anne—" Xander paused, his mouth open, a struggle in his eyes.

She took the reprieve to get out of the car—and nearly fell flat on her face, her feet tangled up in the straps of her purse. She should have stuck with her backpack.

Backpack. Something about her backpack. Something odd—

something someone had said. What was it? Anne hated it when a feeling that something was very important nibbled at the back of her mind, but she couldn't figure out what it was.

"Take Hannah some dinner and talk things out with her. You're going to hurt yourself in more ways than one if you don't open your eyes and see what's right before you," Anne said as she scooped up the scattered contents of her purse and jammed them back in.

"All right. I will. After I get some work done. That part wasn't a lame excuse."

She was four stoplights away from the office when she realized her purse felt too thin. A quick check before the light turned green revealed her book was missing. It was probably under the passenger seat of Xander's car. She hoped. If she had dropped it at the Justice Center, she would never see it again. She would check in the morning when she met Xander to go back Downtown.

Doria Holwood had provided Anne with some leftovers to make meals, so when she came home after a long day she wouldn't have to fuss, just pop the container in the microwave. Anne thought about what she had in her refrigerator, but nothing appealed to her. She considered the contents of her cupboards, and the fast food restaurants she passed on the way into Tabor, but nothing made her feel hungry. The dropped book was uppermost in her mind. She nearly stomped up the stairs to her apartment, remembering her neighbors just in time before she slammed the door. Gritting her teeth, praying he wouldn't answer the phone, Anne called to ask Xander to look for her book when he had a chance. Fortunately, he didn't answer the phone and she left the message on his answering machine. To discourage him from calling back, she told him she was going for a drive to relax. She felt a little better and peeled out of her clothes, leaving them lying on the bed as she changed into jeans, a t-shirt, and sneakers.

Moments later, she was back downstairs and heading out the door to her truck. The Metroparks, despite the growing shadows, was a sanctuary. She needed the peace and quiet, and the sense of isolation that came with evening, to get her peace of mind back and to pray. And maybe if she found enough calm, the tantalizing sensation of the answer hovering just out of reach would finally slip into her grasp.

Anne parked by the waterfowl sanctuary and walked, fast and furiously, fists clenched, her footsteps almost in even time with her heartbeats and the racing of her thoughts. Her prayers seemed to spin like a whirlpool, always going back to the same subject, the same questions. She knew she wouldn't get anywhere until she was able to sit down and listen for God's answers—but first she had to get everything out of her head and heart and unload the churning and burdens. It was long past twilight and heading into real night by the time she returned to her truck. There was a picnic table only a few feet away, between the parking strip and the waterfowl sanctuary shallows. Anne snagged a blanket from her truck, wrapped up against the chill, and sat on the table. Looking out at the water, finally she felt some sense of peace and slowing down flow into her mind and heart. She had no more words and feelings churning through her, just emptiness and waiting. At the edge of her awareness, she heard a car drive by once or twice, but no one ever stopped. She was grateful. She might beat up on someone even worse than she had Olson, if pressed on this night of all nights.

It was nearly ten when she returned to her apartment. Dr. Holwood was walking up the sidewalk from an evening class he taught nearby. He called out, inviting her over for fresh pie Doria had waiting, before Anne could get up the courage to ask if they could talk. She knew she should call home to Quarry Hall and get some advice, walk through the day's events with someone, but the problem was she couldn't decide if she needed more to talk with Elizabeth, Brooklyn, Joan, or Vincent. Talking with the Holwoods was a good compromise. Sometimes talking to people who didn't know her very well helped more, because they only saw the outer layer of the difficulties.

Anne suddenly felt ravenous, and it was a struggle not to inhale the strawberry-rhubarb pie loaded with vanilla ice cream. The Holwoods prayed with her after they talked, without her asking, and that almost brought her to tears. When she crossed the street to her apartment house, she glanced back and saw Doria watching until she got inside safely.

~~~~~

Xander knocked on the door at 7:30 the next morning.

"Somebody beat Martinez to a bloody pulp last night," he said, when Anne stumbled backward to let him into the apartment, one shoe in her hand and one shoe on her foot.

She could only stare stupidly and wish she had gotten up early to do her devotions. Her mind just wasn't in gear yet to handle such news. At least she was showered and dressed when he showed up.

"Who?" she managed to say after a moment. She walked blindly into the kitchen, where her first pot of coffee in the apartment had finished brewing.

"You and I are prime suspects," Xander admitted with a crooked grin. He nodded when she gestured at the full carafe. Anne filled cups for them both. When she handed his to him, the stunned misery in his eyes told her worlds more than he actually said.

"No, I'm the suspect," she said slowly, shaking with the feeling that she had walked through this scene already. Maybe in her dreams. Maybe this was what Kathryn went through all the time with her visions and dreams. How did she ever get used to it? "You've already been cleared, right? Why else would you come here so early?"

"They found pictures of you on his computer..." He took a quick sip of the coffee without using any of the milk and sugar she offered him. Anne suspected he didn't even taste it or want it; the move was just a delaying tactic. "It seems Martinez has a hobby of taking photos and altering them into... embarrassing scenes."

"Who in the world would believe a nudie of me?" She almost laughed, but her throat closed up around the sound. "I'm in shape, but there's nothing to look at."

Still, she remembered the way Martinez had looked her over, the remarks he had made. He would see curves and foundations for lust even if she was as flat as a fifth-grader. Then again, maybe Martinez liked pre-adolescent girls.

Stop that! she scolded herself.

"The scenario is that Martinez called you to blackmail you or just continue what he started yesterday. You got mad, went over to his place, he wouldn't erase the files or hand over the photos, so you laid into him. And you went further than you meant to."

"Me? Beat a big guy like him into a bloody pulp? He's saying that?"

"Martinez is unconscious in the hospital. He'd probably be dead by now, but neighbors heard shouting—his house is usually pretty quiet. Nobody saw anybody leave, but there are some pretty thick woods behind the house and it was dark. They called the police and broke in and found him. He's got a fractured skull, broken ribs, and serious blood loss. It was touch and go for a while."

"And they say I did it to him? What makes them think it's me?"

"He has your cell phone number written out on the pad next to his desk, and when someone jogged the computer the screen saver came off and they found some photos he was altering, and... it's a long trail."

"You've been involved in it since the start, huh?" She tried to smile. "How were you cleared?"

"I spent the entire evening with Hannah and Rene at the hospital. Plenty of witnesses, despite the tip from some anonymous, helpful soul who said two people, a man and a woman, went into Martinez's house last night."

"This helpful soul said we had a reason and ability to try to kill him?" Anne carefully put down her mug of coffee before her hand shook enough to spill the hot liquid all over her clothes. "Is Hannah all right? She and Rene didn't get the flu, did they?"

"Poisoned. Makes you wonder where the story started, hmm?"

Xander insisted that she go over to the Holwoods' house, that she shouldn't be alone. With all the strange things happening, including

Hannah and Rene being poisoned — meaning someone had gotten to them in their apartment — he didn't want Anne alone. She agreed, mostly because she suspected if she didn't comply, he would call Quarry Hall and have Vincent come up to Tabor and take charge of her. Actually, the thought of Vincent running to her rescue, to scold and badger her with his rough love sounded heavenly. Just not yet.

"It sounds like someone has a grudge against you," Dr. Holwood offered, after she and Xander had settled in the living room with him and Doria and went through the story.

"Against Anne?" Doria asked. "Why?"

"The rumors. Someone wanted poison to be uppermost in people's minds, and then kept reminding people there's a grudge between her and Hannah."

"There's no grudge!" Anne hoped her face wasn't turning red. "Yes, she was a little jealous because I had more of Xander's time and attention than she's had lately. There's nothing going on, and it was clearing up even before all this started. Is Hannah going to be all right?"

"Well, she's staying out of things for a while. It seems whoever poisoned her tried to frame Martinez." Xander gave the three a sickly smile when they reacted to that. "The police found the remains of a bottle of Lasix in his office. Hannah and Rene's symptoms match most of the symptoms for Lasix poisoning — nausea, vomiting, fever, weakness, congestion, headache —"

"That's why they thought they had the flu."

"Exactly. The thing is, Lasix is a little white pill, so there's an investigation, trying to figure out how someone got them to take the poison — the best guess it was ground up and put in something they ate over the weekend — and it would take a large amount to bring on the more serious symptoms, like bleeding and sensitivity to light."

"It was put in their food, something they kept eating," Dr. Holwood suggested.

"Something they thought they could keep eating, even when they fell ill," Doria added. "Those poor girls."

Anne shuddered, her thoughts flashing back to running into Hannah and Rene in the grocery store, hearing their plans for a relaxing weekend, once Rene's business partners left.

"Kind of convenient, the poison being found in that man's house," Dr. Holwood observed.

"Too convenient," Xander said, nodding. "Especially that perfectly timed tip. Whoever framed Anne and tried to frame me wanted to give us a really good motive for beating Martinez senseless."

"I didn't," Anne insisted.

"I know that. You know that. But considering all the talk about how you beat up that mugger, and the lawsuit he's got against you, public opinion won't be in support of your story. In a twisted way, you're a hero to a lot of people, and they won't *want* to believe you when you say you didn't do it."

Anne bit her lip against shouting that she didn't want to be a hero.

"If it's just circumstantial, how can Anne really be a suspect?" Dr. Holwood asked.

"They found a book with her business card dropped in a corner of Martinez's study, along with my spare glasses—with my name and address in the case. Rather clumsy planting of evidence, if you ask me."

"My book? But I left it in your—"

"My car was broken into last night, before I went to visit Hannah. Luckily, I filed a police report about the glasses, so the police know it was a frame-up. At least, for me."

"I left my book in your car. I left a message on your answering machine to ask you to look for it. Will that help me at all?"

"My answering machine has the time and date stamp feature. But such things can be altered," Xander said, nodding.

"Will you stop thinking like a lawyer for once?" She tried to laugh and make it a joke, but Anne felt sick inside.

Who would beat up Martinez? The possibilities were vast. People he had verbally abused or run over or used nasty tricks against in the process of winning his cases and letting criminals walk the streets. But who would poison Hannah and Rene and frame Martinez for it? Someone who wanted to hurt him, obviously. But why would they also try to frame Xander and Anne for the attack?

"Somebody has a grudge against Arc, maybe," Anne murmured after a moment, trying to think her way through the tangles and dozens of new questions that rose every time she thought she had something straight in her head. "They're trying to hurt Arc through you and me."

"Or they're trying to hurt me, using you," Xander said. "Remember, you told Martinez that technically, I work for you. They smear you and Arc, they can put me out of business. We can make a case that the book was stolen and planted at the same time my glasses were, and by the same person. I have an alibi, despite what the anonymous tipster says. Rene's business partners were at the hospital, and they can vouch for me being there all night, until both girls were out of danger. Plus I have technology on my side—I was sending emails and texts and working with two of my part-timers, to get them ready to take over for me today, if I couldn't leave Hannah. How about you? Where were you between eight and ten last night?"

Stillness moved through her, but it had nothing to do with the mental and spiritual peace she had found after hours of prayer. She wondered if perhaps this was some kind of demonic timing, using her retreat time against her.

"I was in the park, either walking or sitting by the pond and thinking. Doing a lot of praying," she added, her voice dropping.

"Not alone?" Xander asked, hope making his face a pleading mask that turned to misery when she shook her head. "Come on, Anne! After what happened with Olson, why did you go back to the park alone?"

"I do my best praying and thinking when I'm totally by myself!"

"Hold on here, children," Doria said. She stepped over behind Anne's chair and rested both strong, small hands on her shoulders, squeezing gently. "You two are partners in this. You have a common enemy who is trying to do a whole lot more damage than just get you framed for attempted murder. If you don't work together, you'll never get out of this in one piece."

"Not murder. Martinez has a chance. When he wakes up, he can tell us who attacked him," Xander mumbled, looking away. His thoughts were clearly somewhere else.

"Uh oh." Anne felt that chill move through her. Other daughters of Quarry Hall had dreams or heard voices whispering in the wind – she had chills and sick feelings to warn her of trouble. "Martinez is supposed to die. What happens when people find out he's going to wake up eventually? If we're supposed to be framed for trying to kill him, what good will it do when he wakes up and tells them who really did it?"

"Good thinking." Xander dug in his pocket and pulled out his cell phone. "I have some friends in security at the hospital," he explained as he punched buttons. "Hopefully they'll be able to keep an eye on him until we can convince the police Martinez is in trouble."

"The problem is," Anne murmured, more to herself than the other three, "there are lots of people who will gladly believe we did it. And people who are like Martinez and won't believe us because they *would* do it. How do we prove we didn't? You can't prove a negative."

Chapter Twenty

Anne clasped her hands hard, resting her chin on her clenched fists and her elbows on the table. The sun had risen enough to shine in through the living room window at the right angle to bounce back up into her eyes, but softly, so she was blinded but with no ache. Like being surrounded by a sheltering cocoon of light. Anne's spinning thoughts veered over to her devotions that morning, admonishing her to be a light in the world.

How can I be a light here, Lord? If I'm accused and if people think I'm guilty, everything I say will just be hypocrisy to them. The real hypocrite out there is the one who set me up, but how do I find him? Lord, what am I going to do?

She ached deep inside, thinking about the peace she had attained last night, during her walking and then talking with the Holwoods, and praying. The peace and sense of standing on solid ground that she had awakened with this morning... had fled so quickly.

No, she instantly corrected herself. As Joan was fond of saying, quoting someone else, if a distance came between her and God, guess who moved?

Lord, please ...

That was all Anne could pray. She knew the Spirit would expand her prayer into what it should be. She had to simply trust that it would be more than enough—as always.

~~~~~

Anne wasn't officially charged, but she was a suspect. Police officers would be checking on her from time to time to get statements and to talk to the Holwoods and anyone else she had spent time with recently. Xander advised her to make sure she was with someone at all times, to avoid any more blank spots in her accountable activities. Anne bit her lip to keep from remarking that that particular caution seemed useless, since the horse had already escaped the barn and there was no good in closing the door now. Xander had other cases to take care of at the Justice Center that day. Anne's best course of action was to stay in Tabor, as close to her apartment as possible—or better yet, spend the day with Doria so she had a witness to where she was at all times—and try to think of what to do next. Then Xander left for work.

Hannah came to visit, just before lunch. She was pale and looked like she had lost at least ten pounds overnight. Anne almost didn't recognize her, dressed in wash-faded jeans and a Butler-Williams sweatshirt, with her silky hair pulled back in a severe ponytail. The young woman laughed when Anne could only stare at her, after opening the door.

"I'm not here to blame you," she said, muffling a snicker. "Xander said the safest place for both of us to be right now is together."

"Uh—Rene?" Anne blurted, when she couldn't get her brain on track right away.

"Vic and Baxter swooped in and carried her off to their gym. Vic has an apartment at the back of the gym, so Rene will be fine while she's recovering. If there's a threat against me, I don't want her anywhere around if the guy tries again."

"Well, I have witnesses that I'm pretty good with my fists, but who'd think to look for me here?" she offered. Her attempt at humor fell flat. "Look, Hannah—"

"Someone poisoned me and tried to frame Martinez for it. The man's a slime and works for slime, but he's too smart—and too arrogant, quite frankly—to try to kill someone just for the distraction angle."

"Hannah, they're trying to frame *me* for beating up on Martinez. Until he wakes up, I'm the only suspect. Even then, he might lie and tell them I did it, just to hurt Xander."

"No. He might try a lot of dirty tricks, but he won't lie to hurt anyone like that. He'd be more interested in finding the real criminal for revenge. Hey, can I come in?" She glanced over Anne's shoulder and her smile widened. "Hi, Mrs. H. Mind if I camp out here for a while?"

"Not at all, Hannah." Doria came up behind Anne and gently slid the doorknob out of her grasp, pushing the door open. "It's been a rough day. I'm glad to see you're doing better."

"Yeah, well, you spend four hours in the emergency room with Xander holding your hand, you'll feel better in a hurry." She winked at Anne as she came in.

"Hold it." Anne stared at the two as they settled down on the couch. "I can imagine Xander sending you here so I can beat up someone who tries to get at you, but—"

"I don't hate you." Hannah's smile faded. "That's what you were going to say, isn't it?"

"Not hate, exactly. But you're interested in Xander, and he's too busy and oblivious to realize it, and you were hurt that he was looking out for me."

"If I was thinking clearly, I would have realized that he was looking out for you because of the carjacking and as Joan's friend. Whatever I was thinking and feeling, it was wrong. I'm a Christian too, as little as I seem to practice it lately. I thought I was smarter than that."

"Guilty," Anne said, raising her hand, earning a chuckle from Hannah.

"You weren't going after Xander. You're checking us out—and that made me nervous. Xander's whole life is wrapped up in Common Grounds, helping people who normally wouldn't get help. That's who or what I should rightfully be jealous of, not you."

"Well, don't tell Alexander the Great, but I'm really here to assess the situation for adding to the staff and increasing the funding, and sending law students to learn from Xander."

"Really?" She started to stand up, face glowing. Anne thought Hannah would hug her in a moment.

"Stay put," Doria ordered. "You're still recovering. You keep forgetting, young lady, that you were at death's door — or at least you felt like it — not too long ago. Honestly, I don't know what to do with the two of you, out to save the world." She winked at Anne as she got to her feet. "Now that you're over that silly problem with Xander, I think it's a good time to make up for lost time and become good friends." With a nod for punctuation, she glided out of the room.

"She's right," Anne said. "To be honest, I was ready to dislike you, even before we met."

"Me?" Hannah looked caught between laughing and frowning. "Why?"

"Well, Joan says Xander is constantly talking about how wonderful you are."

"Really?" She fell back dramatically in the deep seat of the sofa. "It'd be nice if he said so to my face."

"Yeah, wouldn't it? Men," Anne said on a sigh. "Don't get your hopes up, though. All he ever talks about is how well the office runs now that you're working for him, and how he wouldn't be able to get along without you, and he's afraid somebody will try to lure you away with double the salary he can pay and how you'd make an incredible lawyer with your instincts. He says you're a treasure, if that's any help."

"Well... it's a start. Now if he could just realize I exist beyond the office, we'd be getting somewhere."

"Maybe he'd appreciate you more if you threatened to leave."

"No!" Hannah grinned, but Anne knew she hadn't mistaken the flash of panic at that suggestion. That told her a lot about the depths of Hannah's feelings for Xander.

The sounds of Doria working in the kitchen drew them in to join her, and the three of them sat at the big table, drinking tea and nibbling on cookies and talking. Anne mentioned Lisa Collins, and Hannah confirmed her assessment that Lisa and Todd should not get back together until he learned to be more sensitive and attentive to her.

"But at least he's brave enough to get her a ring," Hannah added. "He's standing up to what his father wants."

"I had a close encounter with him. Is he as cold as he seems?"

"Take my advice, and dress warmly when Mr. Montgomery is around." She grimaced. "That's not nice of me. I cannot stand the man. The funny thing is that I never really had any encounters with him until after I applied for the job with Xander. Then suddenly, he's concerned for my welfare, that I'll be tainted by the catastrophic failure that's sure to fall on Xander — his words — when his idealism is revealed for the sham it is and his castles in the air come falling down."

"Somehow, I find it very hard to believe that man could wax so poetic," Doria murmured. She raised one eyebrow and sipped demurely at her tea.

Anne caught a quiver in the corner of the woman's mouth before the teacup covered it. She couldn't stop a few snickers. That set off Hannah. Doria put down her cup with a little clatter and pressed the fingers of one hand over her lips. Her shoulders shook with silent laughter.

"We are not nice at all," Anne said.

"No, we aren't, but thank goodness God is a lot more forgiving than Saint Arthur Montgomery," Hannah said.

She blinked and stared at Anne's hand as she cupped the teacup in both hands. Her sudden alertness sent a prickle of warning across Anne's scalp.

"What's wrong?" She held still, when her first instinct was to tuck both her hands down in her lap where they were hidden from sight by the table.

"Where did you get that ring?" Hannah asked.

"This?" Anne held out her hand, resting it flat on the table. She lightly stroked the oval of stone with the tip of her index finger. "Daddy was into fossils and rock collecting. My folks were in Michigan and dug up this stone. He made it into a ring for Mom to remember the trip by."

"So you've always had it? It's not something new?" Hannah licked her lips and seemed to struggle to drag her gaze off the ring. "You wear it all the time, I bet."

"Of course. Why?" That prickle turned into a chill that slithered down her spine and tangled in her gut.

"You'd better keep that ring hidden. I read the police report — lawyer's privilege. I mean, Xander and I are both working to defend you."

"Thanks," she whispered, when she wanted to shout and demand an explanation.

"The doctor noted oval dents all over Martinez's face," Hannah said slowly, "like someone had something on their hand when they punched him."

"Then check out the condition of Anne's ring and measure it against the dents," Doria said in an exasperated tone. "From the little Xander said, Anne should have done damage to her hands and to her ring to do that

156

much damage to such a big, strong man. The fact that there is no damage — no bruising or cuts — counts in her favor."

Hannah and Anne stared at each other a moment, their mouths dropping open. Then they started laughing.

Half an hour later, they met Lieutenant Donovan at the Tabor Heights Library with an official police department evidence camera. In front of the head librarian, who was also a notary public, they took pictures of Anne's hands, next to a newspaper with the day's date. They used the library printer to print out the photos immediately. The librarian and Donovan signed a paper and initialed the photos, sealing all of them with his notary stamp, stating that Anne had indeed photographed her hands on that date and had proved to his satisfaction that she was who she claimed to be. They made three copies; one to seal in the safe at Xander's office, one to give to Dr. Holwood for safekeeping, and one that they mailed to Quarry Hall. The postmark would be evidence no one could dispute if the case actually came into court.

"You know, it's funny how things are working out," Hannah said, after they were back in their sanctuary of the Holwoods' house. They sat outside on the steps, enjoying the quiet of the sunny college town afternoon. "I was mostly frustrated. Xander appreciates me as a friend and co-worker, and we're doing good things. I should be happy with that, but I want him to notice me romantically, too. It never occurred to me that he was just too..." She shrugged, grinning.

"Too much a single-minded man to notice you as a woman?" Anne hazarded.

"Well, at least I know he really does care about me, as a person, not just as a very vital piece of office equipment. One time when I woke up, feeling like I had emptied out everything I had eaten for the last week, I swear he was crying. That has to count for something, right?"

"Absolutely. But how do you follow up on it without him feeling like you're hunting him down?"

"I don't know." Hannah pouted and gently slapped Anne's arm. "A fine friend you are, reminding me how hopeless it is."

"Even someone as oblivious as Xander will wake up eventually. Just consider how many people know how you feel about him."

"Oh, great." She tipped her head back against the porch pillar and slouched, groaning.

"Don't worry. No matter how many people harass him about the two of you, he won't notice. I even said something, but did it do any good? He'll pull his head out of the sand, look around, and go right back down where it's safe and dark and separated from everything."

"That's supposed to be encouraging?" Hannah managed a brave little smile.

"But he's a really smart guy, so I'm kind of confused how he could miss how you feel about him. I could ask Joan to have a talk with him. She knows how to kick him back into gear."

"That's almost as bad as me chasing him down myself. A man who has to be talked into saying he loves someone... does it ever really count?"

"Maybe not talked, but shamed into it?" Anne suggested. "You should have seen the look on his face when someone suggested we were rivals. That Simons guy suggested you were more likely to poison me, rather than me poison you."

"He really creeps me out. He starts out nice, and he's all jolly and supportive, and very vocal about all the good Xander is doing, but then you catch him watching you all the time and he's... what's wrong, Anne?" Hannah asked, when she sat up and everything in her gaze went fuzzy.

"Simons knew I got my truck back, but I *hadn't told* anyone. And he was looking for my backpack." Anne shivered at the chill of an unpleasant hunch that traveled across her body. "What if he was trying to plant poison in my backpack, to frame *me* for poisoning you?"

"But they framed Martinez..." Hannah's mouth dropped open too. "They're out to get you, aren't they? To hurt Xander and Common Grounds?"

"It's the only thing that makes sense. If it's Simons. We really have to unravel all that gossip we've been hearing at the Justice Center. What do you want to bet he's in the center of every single web?"

"He certainly liked talking about how you beat up on that mugger."

"Like he wanted everyone to know I had violent tendencies?" Anne nodded. "He's really got it in for Martinez... and he's upset at Xander for demanding everyone gets a chance to defend themselves. His idea of justice—"

"Is to take them out and line them up against the wall and bring in the firing squad," Hannah finished for her. "Where's my phone? I have to tell Xander all this so he can start asking questions. Oh, why didn't we see this before?"

"Because he was still putting together his plan."

"And we were acting like a couple of cats fighting over a bird," Hannah added.

"Xander's an awfully big bird."

"When it comes to relationships, I have the feeling he's a big chicken."

"No, he's just oblivious. Is he worth all the frustration and waiting?"

Hannah paused just long enough, frowning in thought that Anne didn't know whether to laugh or worry. Then her friend — and yes, it was a relief to realize she could consider Hannah her friend now — nodded and grinned.

"Well, I'll be praying for you. You're certainly going to need it. But like the dogs at Quarry Hall, once he's housebroken and he's decided you're the one for him..." Anne sighed dramatically. "It's going to be incredible." That got chuckles from Hannah.

They helped each other to their feet and went inside. First they called Xander and had to leave a message on his cell, because he was probably in conference and wasn't picking up. Then, they went out to Stoughton to get Argus from the vet. The big dog wasn't up to defending Anne, but he was on his feet again and his nose and ears were just as sensitive as ever. Besides, Anne considered him her guardian angel and good luck token. All her problems had started *after* he was taken away from her by the carjacker's bullet.

~~~~~

Xander came to the Holwoods' after work, with pizza. He brought enough for the three of them, plus the Holwoods and their foster children. Then he, Anne, and Hannah retreated to Nikki's big attic room for a strategy session.

The big surprise of the day was that Martinez's assistants and his client were willing to practice some deception to help Xander clear Anne and find the real assailant. The other members of the firm insisted Martinez really didn't hold anything against Xander, personally. Much of the glaring and sneering was theatrics, intimidation to rattle the opposing side in the case. Anne wondered if she had been guilty of generalizations, smearing Martinez with the same brush that painted his client as the enemy. Maybe that was why Martinez was so obnoxious and aggressive — people expected him to be just as slimy as the people who employed him. The man was good at what he did, and did whatever it took to defend his client, whether the man was guilty or innocent. Didn't Xander have the same attitude? Just because Xander made sure his people were *worth* defending before he took on the case didn't really make that big a difference between him and Martinez, on a professional level. As Xander said, everyone deserved to have their say in court and to be considered innocent until proven guilty.

With the help of the police investigating the attack in River Vale, a few friendly doctors at the hospital, and the gossip mill at the Justice Center, quite a few false stories circulated that day.

First, Hannah was deathly ill in the hospital and could possibly die of the poison found in Martinez's house. That meant she couldn't go home and couldn't be seen by her ordinary circle of acquaintances, in case the truth got back to the wrong people. No evening classes at Butler-Williams.

Next, no suspects had been formally identified. If Simons was the guilty party, it would drive him crazy to think his carefully laid but heavy-handed clues were being ignored. That would force him to act, just to get the police on track again. Xander had friends working on court orders to search Simons' home and get his telephone tapped. If he used the phones at the Justice Center, they would have a hard time proving it was him, specifically, making the calls.

Martinez was stable, and the doctors were hopeful he would regain consciousness soon. Unfortunately, no one on the medical staff could agree on what "soon" meant. The rumors planted by Xander and some helpful judges and lawyers said Martinez had already regained consciousness, and could be coherent enough to talk to the police in another day or so. If Hannah and Anne's theory was correct, Simons would have to finish the job to keep Martinez from clearing Anne.

"But if he doesn't do anything, and Martinez dies, what do I do?" Anne had to ask.

"Arc gets their money's worth out of me," Xander said, and crammed the last piece of cold sausage and onion pizza into his mouth, biting off a large portion with weary savagery and swallowing after only a few chews.

Chapter Twenty-One

The police searched Hannah and Rene's apartment, following the list of everything the roommates had done and eaten all weekend. Knowing the suspected poison was Lasix had helped narrow down the possibilities of where the powdered pills could have been slipped into their food. The flour cannister held remnants of Lasix powder. Anne fought nausea when she heard that news, remembering clearly how Hannah and Rene talked about their plan to make bread for the weekend. Fortunately, they hadn't made the bread until Sunday afternoon, after church, because the meeting with Rene's business partners, Vic and Baxter, had gone into the evening on Saturday. They ate the bread dripping with enough butter and honey to mask any odd taste, and only had two more slices each before they began to feel sick and didn't want to eat anything else. They had toast for breakfast the next morning, but only a few bites each before the symptoms flared up again. They had spent most of Monday drinking tea and sleeping, too disoriented to realize how bad off they were, or to be suspicious that they had the exact same symptoms. Vic arrived to check on Rene just moments after Xander had come to check on Hannah. Vic had insisted they had to go to the hospital.

"What's really frightening is that I mentioned a new bread recipe I wanted to try out when I stopped in the bailiff's room on Friday to talk to a couple of friends. Simons was there. If it was him who poisoned me," Hannah said with a shudder, "he knew I was planning on making bread for the weekend."

"That means he got to your house before you did on Friday, broke in and planted the poison, and got away without anyone noticing," Anne said. "Either that, or he was waiting, watching your place on Saturday, and broke in while you were out shopping."

"I have some friends investigating Simons' background. Let's hope he has locksmith training," Xander said.

"Why?" Hannah asked.

"Because I already had some friends in the Tabor PD check out your apartment, and they couldn't find any trace of forced entry. Since you rent from the Gordons, I had them look the place over too, and they didn't see anything off. They take good care of their houses, and they'd notice if something was damaged, even if the rest of us didn't. If Simons didn't break in by himself, picking the locks like a pro, that means we have to find some accomplices, too."

"Oh." Anne wished she hadn't had that fourth piece of pizza.

A scratching on the door made them all jump. Anne held her breath, expecting a stranger to burst in on them — or worse, the police come to arrest her despite the arrangements Xander had made to avoid her being formally charged. Then she heard Argus's familiar whine.

"Oh, you big idiot," she murmured, and scrambled to get to her feet and answer the door.

They had left Argus downstairs with the children, both because the Holwoods' foster children were already in love with the big dog and because Anne just didn't want him struggling up and down the stairs. She dropped to her knees and wrapped her arms carefully around her companion and fought tears. What would she do if she ever lost him? More than ever, she wished she could pack up her truck and simply leave Tabor, head home to Quarry Hall where she was safe from trouble and vendettas. Argus was likely to be spoiled by the children, but that didn't make up for what had happened to him. Even if she wasn't officially charged and no one had said anything, she knew better than to even contemplate leaving town until she was vindicated.

They rearranged the seating so Argus could lie next to Anne, pressed against her leg, her hand on his neck. Then Xander filled them in on what he had retrieved from the gossip mill of the Justice Center, both before and after he fed in their carefully prepared lies.

Everyone was talking about the attack on Martinez. Many believed he got what he had coming to him. Several rumors said his beating had come from dissatisfied clients. Anne feared that because the theory was so plausible, the police might ignore Simons as a suspect and look elsewhere.

Several people repeated a particularly tasteless joke on the lines that they shouldn't make Martinez linger and suffer — if he was going to die, they should help him along with the same poison used on Hannah. On the off chance someone wasn't joking about that, Xander had asked his friend at the hospital to reinforce the security guards and limit the nursing staff who attended him, to make sure no one really did try to poison Martinez.

The doorbell rang. Argus didn't even raise his head at the sound. Anne hoped it was because he sensed no danger coming to the door, not because he was exhausted. She heard men talking while Xander related some of the rumors he had been hearing, twisted versions of rumors he and some helpful attorneys had begun to flush the real attacker out into the open.

Her heart skipped a few beats when she heard heavy footsteps coming up the stairs. Anne flashed back to that everlasting night when she had hidden in the closet of her home. She had broken free while the Ogre killed her parents, but couldn't get out of the house, terrified he would catch her. She had heard footsteps and nearly strangled on screams that wouldn't come out of her throat. The approaching people were policemen, investigating at the request of the lady across the street. She watched all her neighbors, knew their routines down pat, and worried because Anne's family wasn't acting normally.

"Anne?" Xander asked, reaching out a hand to her.

"Hmm?" She jerked. Sometimes in her dreams, the policemen turned into more ogres.

Someone knocked on the door. Argus raised his head but made no sound. All three looked at each other for a moment.

"Anne?" a man said, his voice slightly muffled through the door. "It's Mike Nichols. We need to talk."

She scrambled to her feet and stumbled across the attic room to the door. Her first reaction on seeing the police officer was relief – he wasn't in uniform. Then Anne wondered why he was there at all.

"It's about the entrapment case?" she blurted.

"Well, sort of. We have this little prayer group that meets on Tuesdays after we get off shift. Some guys from Padua, Hyburg, Stoughton, and Cleveland police. Karl Hiller asked for prayer because of some trouble for Common Grounds." Mike nodded when Xander sat up straight. "He started telling us all the details and I just about dropped my teeth when I heard your name mentioned, Anne."

"I didn't do it." She tried to grin but shivered deep inside. "I swear."

"I know you didn't."

"But I don't have an alibi for where I was when Martinez was getting beaten to a pulp."

"Yeah you do." He grinned and jabbed his chest with his thumb. "Me."

"But you can't –" Anne lost her breath and her mouth dropped open as the possibilities flooded over her. "You were on patrol and you saw me in the park?"

"Me and Nathan Lewis, one of the park rangers. I saw you drive down into the park and came back a few times to check on you. Figured you might need some help if Olson decided to come after you with heavier artillery. Then when I went off duty, I asked Nathan to check in on you. He has it in his log that he saw you sitting by the water. Wrote down the license of your truck. Wrote down the time you left."

Anne hid her face in her hands and cried. Hannah scrambled up and sat next to her, an arm around her shoulders.

~~~~~

The last thing Anne wanted to do was go Downtown with Xander the next day, but she knew she had to do it to knock Simons – and if not Simons, the real attacker – off balance. As long as people weren't aware of the facts, as long as she hadn't been officially named a suspect, the real criminal in the case would be on pins and needles, wondering when the authorities would follow up on the manufactured clues. If she was walking freely, the guilty party would be pushed to do something else just to tighten the noose around her neck.

If it really was Simons. If he had a grudge against Xander. If Martinez truly was his target, or just a convenient tool. If Arc was the target of some larger power and Simons was just a tool. If she was totally wrong in her suspicions.

Who could tell?

Anne did a lot of praying, from the time Xander left and Hannah settled in to stay the night in Nikki's room, the short walk across the street with Argus for company, settling her companion in her apartment, and many times when she woke up during the night. Argus liked her apartment and didn't react to anything, so she knew she was safe there. It was almost amusing to realize she did wake up every few hours through the night, because she thought she would be able to sleep like a baby with Argus curled up on several rugs next to her bed. He wasn't up to climbing up onto the bed to sleep next to her. She also prayed through her morning routine, aloud, only stopping to eat and read her devotions.

When Xander came to the apartment to pick her up, she walked Argus across the street to spend the day with Hannah and Doria. There was always the chance someone knew enough to guess where Hannah would be hiding once she left the hospital. Anne left her truck locked up in the Holwoods' garage, just in case someone decided to plant some evidence in it. Mike Nichols and Todd James searched her truck with another officer present as witness, to verify there was nothing in the truck that didn't belong there. They videotaped it and signed a deposition, in case some other authority decided to do a search later, on another anonymous tip, and actually found something. She hated all the precautions, but knew they were necessary.

The ride Downtown was silent as well, both she and Xander praying. There was nothing else to say, really. All their talking and speculating and planning had been done last night. Today, they stepped into the lion's den. The problem was, as Xander pointed out, they had no idea what were rocks, what were booby traps, what were allies, and what were lions.

Xander got the call at nine that Martinez had taken a turn for the worse.

It wasn't just the fact that he was still unconscious, which was bad enough in itself — the longer he took waking up, the more damage there would be, the slower his ultimate recovery. His fever had returned, blood poisons were rising, and other integral blood counts were off balance, when just the evening before he had been heading toward recovery.

One of the nurses on the floor was a friend of the Holwoods, a member of Tabor Christian, and belonged to Doria's prayer chain group. Doria had called her with the latest details that morning, to keep Anne and Martinez in prayer and to ask friends at the hospital to keep an eye on things. The nurse responded to what she could only describe as a hunch and mentioned Hannah's poisoning to the doctor in charge. They immediately did blood tests and verified Martinez had been poisoned.

That meant someone was able to slip past the guards already established for Martinez and poison him, either an injection or something in the IV drip. Who could move around a hospital without being detected? Someone in a uniform, who looked like they belonged, either a doctor, nurse, or security officer.

"A bailiff's uniform looks an awful lot like a police officer's uniform, doesn't it?" Anne murmured, after Xander gave her the news. She glanced down the length of the hall, where a knot of bailiffs were talking, chuckling over something. From the glances being cast their direction, Anne had the awful certainty they were non-fans of Martinez.

"Careful," he said. "Don't go hanging all your hopes on a certain someone being guilty."

"But it's so neat and tidy." She tried to smile. Her face felt frozen stiff.

"Too neat and tidy. What if it's someone trying to make us think it's him, just so we waste time chasing him and evidence?"

Anne scowled at him. Judge Hardworth's bailiff stepped out into the hall and beckoned for them to come in, so she couldn't respond further.

Xander and Anne went to the hospital after his final meeting of the afternoon. It was only three, so there was little traffic to fight. Anne slouched in the front seat and closed her eyes and prayed. She couldn't decide if she was more concerned about herself, or Martinez's life. She couldn't decide if she was ashamed at her selfishness, or not.

Would Martinez be just nasty enough to say that she did attack him, forgoing justice for the sake of revenge?

At the hospital, Xander led her down the hallways and up stairs with the assurance of someone who had been in and out of that particular facility often. Martinez wasn't in ICU, but the next best thing. According to the latest phone call, the hospital administration was considering moving him to ICU to keep better track of him. The unit had the added advantage of no doors, all the patients in curtained cubicles around the central nurses' station, meaning no one could get to the man without witnesses. At the moment, they were able to walk onto the floor and down the hall to Martinez's room without being challenged—until they rounded the corner and saw the police officer standing by the door, and another one sitting in a chair next to the lounge a few doors down. The one in the chair saw them and waved to Xander. He got up, gesturing for them to follow him into the lounge.

"What's the news?" Xander asked, before Anne could finish stepping into the room after him.

"There was a gap about seven this morning, no more than half an hour—it's inevitable when you're putting together a guard detail at the last minute," the officer said with a shrug. His gaze flicked over Anne's features, then back to Xander, visibly asking questions. Xander responded with a short nod. "Even when it's privately funded."

"Privately?" Anne said. "Xander—"

"Joan called me yesterday," Xander said, trying to smile. "She said whatever it took, money was the last thing we should think about."

"Anyway," the officer continued, "the nurse on duty said she'd keep an eye on things, but the guy down at the other end of the hall was ringing for more medication and she stepped away to take care of him. She saw a uniform hurry by as she was going in, and thought it was the next guy up, coming on watch. She didn't think about it when she didn't see him for another ten, fifteen minutes. Until they narrowed down the time the patient was poisoned. There are traces of poison on the outside of the IV bag."

All it took was a few minutes—of relaxed vigilance or just good timing. That made all the difference in the world.

Anne didn't pay much attention after that, though she was able to nod and shake hands when Xander introduced her to various friends on the staff who had agreed to help protect Martinez. Some people weren't assigned to the floor, but they either asked friends to look in on the man or pulled strings to get information or passed the word along with prayer requests. Anne was amazed at the vast network of favors and friends Xander was able to call in. He had a reputation that made people willing to help when he asked, and a personality and character that gained him friends—or enemies.

Anne didn't know what she felt, contemplating her situation. She was basically a tool to either destroy Xander's reputation and his effectiveness, or harm the Arc Foundation. The lawsuit from Bruiser Olson was the least of her worries right now. She wished it were the largest problem in her life.

Could any good come from this? How was God using this?

~~~~~

"The man has the iron constitution of a horse," Xander said the next morning. He winked at Anne as she came around the corner in the hallway and found him with a knot of bailiffs and attorneys. "I'm not the kind of guy who prays for trouble on his enemies, but I would have appreciated a few more days of peace and quiet while I worked on other, more important cases."

That remark earned a few chuckles from some people, attorneys and bailiffs alike. Anne tried to edge her way around the group, to avoid notice. She was tired of this game Xander played with Martinez's safety and her life and his reputation, and it was only Thursday. She noticed Simons standing at the edge of the group. His eyes burned with intensity as he listened to someone commenting on Martinez's determination to win, no matter what, but he didn't laugh with the rest when the woman turned it into a humorous remark. Simons caught her movement and something changed in his face when he saw her. Anne didn't know if it was her imagination, but she thought she saw anger in the big bailiff's square face. Did his skin get a little redder? Did his mouth flatten?

When the authorities allowed Martinez to be moved last night, Xander and his allies had agreed the story would be Martinez was awake, in and out of consciousness, unable to talk but able to communicate by nodding and shaking his head. The story, to be dragged out of them piecemeal by the gossips and curious, was that the police had named a suspect and Martinez had shaken his head no.

The true guilty party had to move soon, if he wanted to cover his tracks before Martinez could start to talk and tell the police who really attacked him.

Anne felt like she had targets painted on her forehead and her back.

"Now I know how Joseph felt," she had muttered, during their drive Downtown two hours earlier. "No matter what he did, someone was always out to get him. Sure he made mistakes, but did he deserve everything that happened?"

"God worked it out for the good of everyone," Xander had said.

"Yeah, but if an angel had told him that there was a higher purpose during it all, do you think Joseph would have believed?"

~~~~~

Anne's head hurt by the time she and Xander came back from lunch. It had been a struggle finding a place where they could sit and talk in privacy, without being constantly interrupted with inquiries about Hannah's health, Martinez's recovery, and any progress on who really had attacked him. They needed to be alone to talk. Sophie had come up with a massive file on Simons, which she sent via email to both Xander and Anne to access on their phones. The bailiff certainly seemed to be their man, just from circumstantial evidence alone.

But then, circumstantial evidence pointed the finger at Anne and Xander, too.

Simons had military training. He lied about his age to get into the Navy and almost made the SEALs. He won awards in hand-to-hand combat—and was dismissed for stirring up vendettas against superior officers who committed crimes and yet were given light sentences by the military tribunals that investigated them. He was suspected of taking a vigilante stance in some instances, but there was no proof, only the testimony of people who heard him talk and knew what he could and would do.

He had FBI training and was an expert in various poisons and concocting weapons out of everyday objects. He had been dismissed for arguing with instructors over ethics. According to his files, he was a part-time martial arts instructor — and several schools refused to employ him or wouldn't let him near anyone under the age of fifteen. No one would say exactly why. Anne suspected it wasn't because Simons was a closet pedophile, but because of the dogma he tried to instill in the children.

He had various and sundry training while in the Navy and FBI, including locksmithing and dismantling bombs. Anyone who could dismantle a bomb could build one. Anne seriously hoped she wouldn't have to face that particular challenge before this was over.

"Looks like he's our guy," was all Xander would say after they read the files together. Then he turned the subject to what he and Anne and Hannah would do for dinner that evening.

Xander abandoned her shortly after returning to the Justice Center from lunch. He merely said he had some things to check on. Anne didn't like the brooding look in his eyes.

Simons caught up with her while she was trying to clear her head enough to pray in a quiet corner in the hall outside the meeting room.

"I hear you did it," Simons said, holding out a hand to shake hers.

"Did what?" She honestly didn't know what he meant for two heartbeats. Anne looked at his hand and wondered if it was hard or mushy, sweaty or dry, cold or hot. Even if she didn't believe he had tried to frame her, she wouldn't have shaken his hand.

"Cleaned Martinez off the face of the earth," he said, lowering his voice and leaning in closer. He made Anne wish she were still standing. The man seemed huge, towering over her chair like he did.

"Me?"

Chapter Twenty-Two

Anne tried to laugh, but she glanced down at his hand, resting on the arm of the chair, and saw the oval ruby in a ring like a class ring, on his right hand. He wore it on his index finger. For more impact on punching someone? She thought it was larger than the oval stone in her ring. No one had come back to her yet on the measurements of the oval dents on Martinez's face. Would they match Simons' ring?

"Martinez is very much alive and conscious. Who would start a nasty rumor like that?" she added, managing a breathy little chuckle.

"You mean that he's dead, or that you're a hero?" He chuckled, leaning closer. It was all Anne could do to keep from leaning back. She expected his breath to smell of rotted meat or wounds gone bad, but it smelled of peppermints. That little detail seemed hugely grievous.

"I didn't do it."

"I heard the police got an anonymous tip putting you at the scene. Heard they found Martinez was making up dirty pictures of you."

Anne mentally kicked herself for not following up on that information from the crime scene. They had no idea if Martinez really did make dirty pictures of people, or if that evidence had been planted, too. For all she knew, someone had thought to check into that, but it galled her that she hadn't been the one to think of it.

"Dirty pictures of me? How would he even get pictures of me? I've never seen him with a camera." She shook her head and reached into her purse to pull out her book to read, hoping he would take the hint and go away.

Anne froze, her fingers clasping the book. It wasn't the same book the police had found at the scene, which had to be kept for evidence and comparing some fingerprints that weren't hers. But would Simons know that? Could she use that to goad him into acting?

"Darn." She slowly withdrew her hand. "I keep forgetting I lost my book somewhere. I never go anywhere without something to read."

"Lost your book?" His eyes glimmered with some hidden joke. Anne knew she had her man. "Where'd you lose it?"

"If I knew that, it wouldn't be lost, now would it?"

"What kind of book? I like fantasy, myself."

"Really?" Anne bit back a remark that Simons didn't seem like the man who could separate fact from twisted, brutal fantasy, much less have a stable enough footing in the real world to enjoy fantasy.

What if he said that because the book he stole was a fantasy?

"Yeah. I just started this new one—wish I had brought it. I'd loan it to you for the day, since you're bored." Smiling a little wider, Simons took his hands off the arm of the chair and stepped back. "You ever heard of the Undying series? It's about these people who find out they can't die, they just live on forever and ever, and they get divided up into two armies. One group wants to help the ordinary mortals and the other group wants to rule the world. I thought it sounded good."

"That's amazing." She hoped her voice didn't sound as weak to him as it did to her. That was close to the blurb on the back of the stolen book. "That's the book I lost."

"Really? Hey, I'll bring it in tomorrow and loan it to you. No—I got a better idea. How about I take you out for dinner and we talk books, okay?"

"Talk books?"

"You like Chinese? There's this great place just over the border from Tabor. Right off the highway. It's right on your way back home. A buffet. All you can eat. Of course, a skinny kid like you probably wouldn't care, but a big guy like me tries to get his money's worth!" He chuckled. "How about it? We can relax, talk books, get a break from all this."

"It sounds good," she answered slowly. Anne felt that shiver inside. A warning, or prompting her to follow up on this chance? Maybe there was a totally different break he had in mind. "Xander doesn't really like to read unless it's all legal stuff, and all he knows to talk about is court cases. What Hannah sees in him, I have no idea. Let me think about it, okay?"

"Sounds great." He winked at her as he walked off. Anne gripped the arms of her chair and fought not to slide out of it, waiting until his footsteps vanished around the corner.

"We got him," Xander whispered from behind her.

Anne almost shrieked. She held perfectly still, positive that Simons would come back around the corner, see them talking, and realize Xander had heard everything. If he had been perfectly innocent in his intentions, that wouldn't matter. But what if he was up to something?

"How does he know where I'm staying?" She kept her voice down. "I didn't tell him."

"The same way he found out everything else about you. That's another hole to plug. The thing is—" Xander stepped around her and settled down in the chair next to her. "—I know that Chinese buffet he was talking about. It's right across Sackley from the hospital."

Anne tried to smile. "Darn—I love Chinese, but I've just lost my appetite."

~~~~~

"We never did finish what we were talking about before, did we?"

Simons said, as he pulled out of the parking garage across the street from the Justice Center.

"Hmm? Talking about what?" Anne settled back in the leather seat of the sleek roadster and wondered just how much money bailiffs really made. Or did Simons have investments on the side? Someone so dogmatic about justice wouldn't be involved in illegal activities, would he? Or was he one of those people who demanded the letter of the law from everyone but themselves?

Stop analyzing everything!

"About you being a suspect."

"Me? Nope." She tried to smile, and glanced up at the street sign as the sleek silver car turned a corner. "Xander usually doesn't go this way."

"Thought we'd take the scenic route." Simons smiled.

He looked like a bald Paul Bunyan, in a red plaid shirt and khaki pants instead of his uniform. Anne almost asked him why he had changed, when they met in the lobby ten minutes ago. After all, if he was the one who snuck in to poison Martinez, he had worn his uniform then, to blend in at the hospital. Why no uniform now?

"Oh. Okay."

She shifted a little, feeling the bulletproof vest scratching under her arms and at her waist. Xander had borrowed it from a Cleveland cop — he seemed to know just the right people everywhere. It was guaranteed to stop bullets up to armor-piercing rounds, but knowing that little detail wasn't any comfort. What were the chances that Simons was carrying a gun using ammunition that powerful? Then again, he could be carrying it in his trunk, and would pull it out to use on her when they got to some isolated spot where she was totally lost. A bulletproof vest wouldn't do her much good if the gun was pointed at the back of her head, would it?

"I heard you were fingered for beating up on Martinez," Simons pressed, giving her another of those sideways glances and secretive smiles.

"They asked me a few questions, but they believed me when I said I was out walking in the park. The Holwoods can vouch for me."

"Sure, but unless they actually saw you in the park during the time Martinez was beaten to a bloody wreck..." He shook his head, almost managing a believable expression of sympathy. "The guy lives in the ritzy section of River Vale, right? Wouldn't take much to get from where you're staying to his place, beat him up, get back to the park, and still get a walk in. You never lied, did you?"

His low, rumbling chuckle made Anne feel like a tiger had just tried to purr like a kitten. She hated cats.

She wished Argus were here.

"Could we stop by the Holwoods', first?" she said, giving him a crooked smile she prayed looked sheepish and not strained. "I haven't seen Argus all day. The kids said they'd take care of him, and all he's going to do is sleep in the sun, but I really miss him."

"German Shepherds are smart. Big dog like that is probably a good bodyguard, huh?" Simons nodded, studying the traffic ahead of them as they merged onto I-71.

"The best." She added another item to the list of personal details Simons shouldn't have known about her. That she had a dog, yes. Argus's breed and size, no.

"Too bad he's in such bad shape. The best thing is to take off across country and never look back. They'd never catch you. But you can't just vanish with a sick dog, can you?"

"Why would I want to take off? I'm innocent."

"Yeah, well, appearances can be deceiving. Too bad you don't have a real watertight alibi, huh?" Simons grinned again and shrugged.

What would he do if she told him about the police officer and park ranger who had verified seeing her and her truck? Would he give up whatever plan he had? To cover his tracks, would he go after Mike and Ranger Lewis? Could he get into the computers and records at the Tabor Police Department and the Metroparks administration, to erase their reports?

Simons seemed like a nice enough guy once he got rid of that uniform and didn't hover over her. Maybe he was depending on that perception to lure her into a false sense of calm, and then attack. Or maybe he was going to try to sweet talk her into supporting his agenda.

Anne wished this whole problem was over and done with.

Had Xander found someone to keep up with them? He knew better than to try to tail them through traffic. Simons was sure to notice and recognize him. Anne knew she could handle herself if Simons tried anything, and he was more likely to body slam her rather than shoot her. But right now, that wasn't much comfort. Xander seemed more certain of her skills and chances for getting out of this unharmed than she had felt, when they put together their plan just a few hours ago. He seemed to think she could escape everything, untouched.

So why had Xander borrowed the sticky-hot, stiff, bulletproof vest for her?

Maybe he remembered that even when an angel watched over Sophie and Joan last year, a bullet put Sophie in a wheelchair.

You think too much. Anne wished Argus were there, to meet Simons and pass judgment on the man. She never had trouble when she listened to his instincts.

Simons talked about the book Anne had been reading, that had been stolen from Xander's car. She was startled to realize Simons actually had read some of the book. Had he run out during his break, bought a copy at the mall, and read some of it, just to trick her? Or was he reading the book for real, because he really did like such stories? She found it rather irritating that the man she suspected of so many dastardly actions had something in common with her.

But then, he wanted Martinez to stop helping crooks evade justice, just like she did. The only real difference between them was their choice of methods and the lines they stopped at in the pursuit of justice.

That was a sobering thought.

Simons carried the weight of the conversation, which suited Anne just fine. She tried to relax in the lush leather seat, and paid attention to her surroundings. It was some comfort that she did recognize the route Simons took. If he tried something and she had to jump out of the car, she could find her way back to familiar territory. She hoped.

"You know, I'm really curious," Simons said as they reached the bottom of the off-ramp and a red light. "Everybody's been saying Martinez is awake, just not ready to talk. Want to stop in and see if he's fingered anybody yet?"

"They wouldn't tell us," slid out of her mouth without her having to think. It was a natural enough reaction to the suggestion — wasn't it?

"Eh, I know a few folks at the hospital. What do you say? I bet you'd have a better appetite, knowing you're off the hook."

"And what if he decides to be a snot, and lies?" Anne returned. "That's assuming your friends can get us in to see him, anyway."

Please, Lord, let him be lying about having friends. Especially friends who would tell him Martinez was moved last night.

"Oh, my friends can manage a lot of things." He chuckled. "Want to try it?"

"Sure. Why not?" Anne hoped Xander's friend was following closely.

Why had she agreed to this?

Simons could very well know she was part of a trap. Wouldn't someone smart enough to frame her and Xander suspect her sudden cooperation? For all she knew, Simons had allies waiting, ready for him to lure her and her friends in to blow them all away.

They parked around the back of the hospital, in an area Anne suspected was for employees only. For all she knew, Simons was a part-time security guard at the hospital under another identity. It would be easy for him to get to criminals who were escaping justice by being ill. How hard would it be for him to foul up life-support equipment or hide medicine at a crucial time, turn off monitors, put a heavy pillow over someone's face? There were a thousand little ways to kill someone who was bad enough off to be in the hospital.

Why had he brought her here? Surely the charade couldn't go on for much longer, if he was planning on killing her. And where were Xander's friends?

Lord, I know I was stupid and over-confident. Please take care of me. I'm not ready to come home. Anne followed Simons' lead and got out of the car. *I don't know if You think I'm ready to come home, but I sure hope not!*

Simons had a key card for the security door at the back entrance. That spoke of a part-time job, friends inside, or powerful allies.

There was no one in the back hallways of the hospital, among the stockrooms of linens and mattresses, plastic-wrapped medical supplies, cleaning solution in huge bottles, extra parts for beds and carts. It was far into the dinner hour. Everyone on duty was probably just starting their evening shifts and busy helping patients with their dinners. Simons had picked a good time to come in. No one to see him; no one to lie to about what he was doing where he didn't belong.

They took a service elevator up, went through three doors, made enough turns in hallways that grew wider and better lit, and they stepped out a service door into a hallway lined with patient rooms. She mentally oriented herself—she had come here from a different angle yesterday. They were only one door down from Martinez's room. No wonder the nurse on duty hadn't really noticed Simons when he came in to poison Martinez.

Please, Lord ...

That was all she could pray. Anne trusted the Holy Spirit to fill in the words she couldn't frame even in her mind.

The smell of the room, when Simons opened the door, made Anne gag. The air was thick with antiseptics and plastics, the closed-in smell of a man shedding poisons as his system fought to heal. It was worse than a gym locker full of dirty clothes, locked up for a week in a humid, scorching summer.

Anne tried to step backward. Simons caught her off balance and gave her just enough of a nudge to get her through the door. She stumbled forwards two steps and reached out a hand to keep from staggering into the bed.

"Smells pretty bad in here, doesn't it?" Simons asked in a lowered voice. He shut the door and turned the light on.

The curtain was pulled halfway around the bed. There was more equipment around Martinez's bed than Anne had seen last night. She guessed they hadn't been able to move him to another room as planned, after all. The lawyer was just a shadowy figure amid all the tubes and the oxygen tent and the wires of the monitors. He looked shrunken, somehow. Definitely paler. Anne shivered, feeling sorry for him. No matter how obnoxious someone was, no one deserved to die like this.

At the back of her mind, she knew she should be worried about the condition of Martinez's soul, but Anne had bigger worries right now. Martinez was in no condition to listen to a sermon, anyway.

"Hi, Martinez," Simons said.

The doorknob rattled. Anne waited for the click that meant it was locked, but none came. She almost smiled at the flicker of frustration on the bailiff's face.

"Here." Simons pulled a plastic bag from his pants pocket and held it out to Anne. She saw what looked like a medicine bottle and a syringe.

"What's that?" She backed up a step, almost running into the end of the bed. Martinez's breathing suddenly grew louder, more forced.

"You're a smart girl. You figure it out."

He tossed the bag. Despite herself, Anne reached out to catch it. *Fingerprints*, a warning voice shouted inside her head, and she pulled her hands back barely in time, letting the bag drop to the floor with a loud clatter-thud. In the moment she was distracted, Simons pulled a gun from inside his shirt. There was much to be said for baggy flannel shirts, she decided. Anne wished Argus were here. He would have attacked Simons before the man could have pulled the gun.

"I'll bet a smart girl like you knows how to use those," Simons continued. He smiled in an almost genial way and gestured with the gun for her to pick up the bag. "Don't worry about air bubbles. Martinez is in no condition to care, and your little present will go to work a whole lot faster than an air bubble could."

"But—why?" Anne tucked her hands behind her back. Where were Xander's friends? Why hadn't a nurse shown up yet? Weren't they supposed to be watching this room like hawks?

"Poison. Syringe. IV tube. Fingerprints. You figure it out." He waved the gun at her as his grin faded.

"I just want to know why you're doing all this."

"No delaying tactics, little girl. It works in the movies, but this is real life. You think if you keep me talking long enough, somebody will come running to your rescue?" Simons took one giant step and snatched at her shoulder, spinning her around to face the bed. The barrel of the gun jammed into the base of her neck. "Pick it up," he growled, pushing her down.

Fat lot of good this bulletproof vest is going to do me.

"Down, Anne!" a man shouted.

She was already to her knees, rolling to avoid Simons' grasping hand, before she realized the shout came from the man in the bed. Anne twisted around, trying to see, as Martinez erupted from the tangle of wires and tubes, leaped at Simons, and turned into Todd James.

The door slammed open and three officers burst into the room, tackling Simons. Anne skittered backward in a crabwalk and pressed herself into the corner, watching, holding her breath.

Simons roared, breaking free of the four sets of grappling arms. His face was a twisted, red mask, focused on Anne. One arm swung around, bringing the gun to bear. All she had read of his military training and marksmanship flashed through her mind as the open mouth of the gun filled her vision and white light exploded straight at her.

Anne tried to stand, tried to leap aside, but she had imprisoned herself in the corner. A force like a speeding semi truck hit her in the chest. Her back and then her head slammed against the two walls and she saw stars. She couldn't breathe as she slid down again, her legs turned to rubber.

She heard Simons' roar shatter into cursing as the four officers brought him down again.

Then she heard her heart racing. She was still alive.

Her chest shrieked pain as she took a breath. She smelled blood, but she wasn't going to die. At least, not from a bullet. Right now, trying to remember how to breathe took all her attention.

Chapter Twenty-Three

The cut at the back of Anne's head required two stitches. She bit her lip to keep from grumbling when the doctor insisted on X-rays and shaving that tiny portion of her scalp to make sure everything was all right and avoid infection. The rest of her hair would cover the bald spot, but the indignity of it all rankled.

She told herself to be grateful for the massive bruises on her chest and back. The vest had done its job, keeping the bullet from tearing her open.

The evening and night passed in a haze of telling her story over and over again. Anne was grateful for the painkillers a nurse gave her, even if they did make her sleepy. She could repeat herself multiple times without starting to scream, and the passage of time wasn't in a straight progression but seemed to loop around and spin through her mind. She was surprised when Xander finally came to get her and she looked at a clock and realized it was nearly 1am.

"Want to get something to eat?" Xander asked as they walked to the hospital parking garage.

"No." Anne forced a smile. It was an effort just to think. "Thanks. I just want to go home."

~~~~~

Simons truly did respect Xander, his moral stance, his dedication to justice, but he could never understand or accept Xander's insistence that everyone deserved a fair trial and equal defense. To Simons' simplified way of seeing, if a man was caught with a gun in his hand or he had a reputation for similar actions, then he was guilty and deserved to be punished. He was simply short-circuiting Xander's methods and trying to show the idealistic young lawyer that justice could still be served, but quickly, without wasting time, effort, expense, and sympathy on the known criminals. He also intended to punish Xander a little, by harming him through a friend who supported him and made his stance possible.

Anne wondered what Simons would have done about Bruiser Olson if he had had the time. She suspected, just from the little bit she heard of Simons' ravings on the audio records when they processed him, the bailiff would have gone after Olson with a gun.

When she packed up her truck and loaded Argus in for the long-delayed drive home two days later, the entrapment charges were falling apart. Girls who had hesitated to press charges in the past were coming forward now, testifying to how the man acted, establishing a pattern. Men were stepping forward from all the different locations he haunted as his hunting grounds, testifying to what they had witnessed of his manner toward women. Olson was a predator, and foolish enough to brag to people willing to kick him when he was down. The man's history and reputation and people's opinions of him would come up at trial, according to Hannah, and a jury would throw him out on his ear. The fact that Anne was so new to Tabor and Olson had left work early that night made it hard to prove entrapment specifically aimed at him.

Best of all, in Anne's point of view, Martinez regained consciousness just a short while after they moved him to a new hospital room, to set up the trap for Simons. He emphatically denied Anne or Xander had attacked him and identified Simons with a long string of curses on either side of his name. He called in his assistants and dictated a lawsuit against Simons from his hospital bed, which included slander, libel, assault and battery, breaking and entering, and illegally accessing Martinez's home computer. Simons had created the filthy pictures of Anne, just to make the lawyer look bad and give her more seeming motive for the attack.

Martinez had thanked Anne and Xander with actual graciousness for their efforts on his behalf. When he had asked what her problem had been with Winslow, Anne took a chance on being able to reach his heart, and explained how the other man had defended the Ogre in his murder, rape and molestation trial.

"I don't think I could do it," he said. "When someone calls me a liar, I don't forgive. Especially when it's proven that I'm right and they don't bother to apologize. Especially after what happened to you." The big lawyer had been silent a moment, contemplating the cup of tea the nurse had brought into his hospital room. "I know I probably seem like scum to you, the type of work I've chosen to do, but I will never stand up for someone who hurts kids. Not like that. Not when the kids don't have a chance to defend themselves. Not when they don't even understand what's happening them. It isn't right."

Anne had bitten her tongue to keep from asking him how he could distinguish between the crimes his clients committed that he seemed to excuse, and the ones he didn't. Everything tied together, in her way of thinking. Selling drugs. Selling alcohol to minors. Prostitution. Pornography. It all trickled down through the layers of society so that eventually, no child was really safe. But she kept her silence. Better to let Martinez think about it a while and come to his own conclusions. She suspected his conscience wasn't nearly as seared and hard as he made others think it was.

For now, though, she was on the road again, heading home to Quarry Hall and the kennels where Argus would heal completely. Her name was cleared. Arc could not be harmed. Xander's dream had weathered a brutal attack and came out even better in public opinion. She could almost laugh now, looking back at her fears and questions and anxieties and stumbling. Almost. It was another lesson behind her, another learning experience and a few more scars to make her stronger. Maybe a few deeper, older scars had been scoured away by her trials and troubles. Anne hoped so.

"Hey, Argus, how you feeling?" she murmured to her drowsy companion as she drove up the onramp of I-71 to head south. "Want me to tell you a bedtime story?"

Anne laughed when the dog flicked one ear at her and closed his eyes a little more. In another few moments, those dark slits would vanish into the creamy fur of his face.

"Okay. Once upon a time, there was an enchanted princess. No one would believe she was a princess, because she was covered in scars. You couldn't even see her face for the scars. She knew nothing but pain, day and night. And bad dreams when she tried to sleep. But there was a marvelous enchanter who came to her one night, when she hurt so badly she couldn't sleep, and all she could do was cry. He promised the princess that if she went out into the world and worked to ease the pain of others, one by one her scars and pain would disappear. The princess didn't think that was very fair—it wasn't as if she deserved what had happened to her, after all. She was innocent.

"But when she thought about it a little more, she decided the other people probably didn't deserve their pain either. They needed someone to care about them and ease their hurt, just as much as she did. So she went out into the world and she helped everyone she met, no matter how big or how small or how very stupid their pains and sorrows seemed to her. And after a while, she was so busy, she forgot to even look at her scars to see how many she had left. She forgot to stop and think about how much pain she had. Her scars and pain didn't fade as quickly as she wanted, but she was too busy to notice. She was too happy helping others find joy. And someday, when all her scars and pains and sorrows are gone, she'll still stay on the road, because it would hurt to stop. The end."

Argus licked her hand. Anne chuckled and stroked his head and pushed down a little harder on the gas pedal. She was going home.

THE END

THANK YOU!

Thank you for reading this book from Mt. Zion Ridge Press.

If you enjoyed the experience, learned something, gained a new perspective, or made new friends through story, could you do us a favor and write a review on Goodreads or wherever you bought the book?

Thanks! We and our authors appreciate it.

We invite you to visit our website, MtZionRidgePress.com, and explore other titles in fiction and non-fiction. We always have something coming up that's new and off the beaten path.

And please check out our podcast, **Books on the Ridge,** where we chat with our authors and give them a chance to share what was in their hearts while they wrote their book, as well as fun anecdotes and glimpses into their lives and experiences and the writing process. And we always discuss a very important topic: *Tea!*

You can listen to the podcast on our website or find it at most of the usual places where podcasts are available online. Please subscribe so you don't miss a single episode!

Thanks for reading. We hope to see you again soon!

About the Author

On the road to publication, Michelle fell into fandom in college and has 40+ stories in various SF and fantasy universes. She has a bunch of useless degrees in theater, English, film/communication, and writing. Even worse, she has over 100 books and novellas with multiple small presses, in science fiction and fantasy, YA, suspense, women's fiction, and sub-genres of romance.

Her official launch into publishing came with winning first place in the Writers of the Future contest in 1990. She was a finalist in the EPIC Awards competition multiple times, winning with *Lorien* in 2006 and *The Meruk Episodes, I-V*, in 2010, and was a finalist in the Realm Awards competition, in conjunction with the Realm Makers convention.

Her training includes the Institute for Children's Literature; proofreading at an advertising agency; and working at a community newspaper. She is a tea snob and freelance edits for a living (MichelleLevigne@gmail.com for info/rates), but only enough to give her time to write. Her newest crime against the literary world is to be co-managing editor at Mt. Zion Ridge Press and launching the publishing co-op, Ye Olde Dragon Books. Be afraid ... be very afraid.

And please check out her newest venture: Ye Olde Dragon's Library, the storytelling podcast. Interspersed between the chapters will be interviews with authors of fantastical fiction. Listen to the podcast on your favorite podcast app or listen on the website: www.YeOldeDragonBooks.com, and click on the Ye Olde Dragon's Library link.

www.Mlevigne.com
www.MichelleLevigne.blogspot.com
www.YeOldeDragonBooks.com
www.MtZionRidgePress.com

NEWSLETTER:
Want to learn about upcoming books, book launch parties, inside information, and cover reveals? Go to Michelle's website or blog to sign

181

up.

Thanks for reading! If you enjoyed this book, would you help Michelle by posting a review on Goodreads? Are you a member of Book Bub? If so, please follow Michelle on Book Bub, and you'll get alerts when new books are coming out.

As a way of saying thanks, Michelle invites you to the Goodies page on her website. It will change regularly, offering you a free short story, a sample audiobook chapter, sneak peeks at new cover art, inside information on discounts and new release dates, etc. Please go to: Mlevigne.com/good-stuff.html

Also by Michelle L. Levigne
Guardians of the Time Stream: 4-book Steampunk series
The Match Girls: Humorous inspirational romance series starting with **A Match (Not) Made in Heaven**
Sarai's Journey: A 2-book biblical fiction series
Tabor Heights: 18-book inspirational small town romance series.
Quarry Hall: 11-book women's fiction/suspense series
For Sale: Wedding Dress. *Never Used*: inspirational romance
Crooked Creek: Fun Fables About Critters and Kids: Children's short stories.
Do Yourself a Favor: Tips and Quips on the Writing Life. A book of writing advice.
To Eternity (and beyond): *Writing Spec Fic Good for Your Soul.* A book defending speculative fiction.
Killing His Alter-Ego: contemporary romance/suspense, taking place in fandom.
The Commonwealth Universe: SF series, 25 books and growing
The Hunt: 5-book YA fantasy series
Faxinor: Fantasy series, 4 books and growing
Wildvine: Fantasy series, 14 books when all released
Neighborlee: Humorous fantasy series
Zygradon: 5-book Arthurian fantasy series
AFV Defender: SF adventure series
Young Defenders: Middle Grade SF series, spin-off of *AFV Defender*
Magic to Spare: Fantasy series
Book & Mug Mysteries: cozy mystery series
Quest for the Crescent Moon: fantasy series starting in 2023
Steward's World: fantasy series reboot and expansion
The Enchanted Castle Archives: fantasy series